THE THICKETY
Well of Witches

ALSO BY J. A. WHITE

The Thickety: A Path Begins

The Thickety: The Whispering Trees

THE THICKETY
Well of Witches

J. A. WHITE

Illustrations by
ANDREA OFFERMANN

KATHERINE TEGEN BOOKS
An Imprint of HarperCollins Publishers

Katherine Tegen Books
is an imprint of HarperCollins Publishers.

The Thickety: Well of Witches
Text copyright © 2016 by J. A. White
Illustrations copyright © 2016 by Andrea Offermann
www.harpercollinschildrens.com

ISBN 978-0-06-225732-1

Typography by Amy Ryan
16 17 18 19 20   CG/RRDH   10 9 8 7 6 5 4 3 2 1
❖
First Edition

For my mother, who gave me the gift of reading,

and for my father, who helped me unwrap it

PROLOGUE

The afternoon had been sunny and full of promise when Bethany set out, but since then night had claimed the land and draped the dusty road in darkness. Just beyond the Windmill Graveyard the ocean crashed against high cliff walls, spitting geysers of dark water into the air. Bethany pulled her cloak tight around her shoulders.

I should have waited till morning before leaving. Mrs. Redding would have felt obligated to set a bed for me, had I asked. No doubt that would have been the more intelligent choice— what her mother would have called the *grown-up choice.*

But after Bethany had handed over that week's delivery of glorbs and collected payment, Mrs. Redding had begged pardon to attend to an unfinished chore and never returned. Bethany knew that Mrs. Redding was not being intentionally rude; she had simply forgotten that Bethany remained on her property. Things like this happened to Bethany all the time. Her mother claimed it was because Bethany was shy, but that wasn't it at all. She *loved* to talk to people; the trouble was keeping their interest. Bethany was serious by nature, and the jokes and effortless banter that came so easily to her peers eluded her. She wasn't particularly pretty, or athletic, or quick-witted; nor was she ugly, clumsy, or doltish. In fact, the only thing notable about Bethany was how spectacularly average she was in every sense of the word, fading into the background of most gatherings like a ghost.

There's nothing special about me, she thought.

The road curved away from shore between two rows of low-growing trees. Bethany thought about swirling a lantern but decided against it. The stars were illumination enough.

Someone was coming.

Though its source was yet obscured by darkness, from farther down the road Bethany heard the sound of squeaking wheels. A few moments later a covered wagon came into view, drawn by a single horse. From the wagon's roof swayed a single lantern that did little to reveal the identity of the driver.

Bethany tensed, slipping her hand downward until her fingertips grazed the dagger concealed beneath her cloak. Though more common farther inland, brigands were not unheard of this close to shore. She quickly unhooked the pouch filled with Mrs. Redding's copper and slid the majority of its contents inside her boot.

If they intend to rob me, I'll claim I have only a few coins.

As the wagon drew closer, however, Bethany decided she was just being skittish. Though the driver's down-turned face remained hidden beneath a hood, Bethany recognized a woman's soft form. Hands covered by pristine white gloves held the horses' reins.

Probably just a traveling merchant, Bethany thought, *come from peddling her wares in Tear's Landing or Hendon. Harmless.*

Bethany slid her hand away from the dagger and waved.

"Evening," she said.

"And not soon enough," the woman replied. "You would think I'd have had my share of darkness by now, but I still prefer it to the sun. I always have."

The driver's words were strange, but Bethany hardly heard them. Her attention was absorbed by the old-fashioned wagon that had squeaked to a halt in front of her, details hidden until this point now illuminated in the soft glow of lantern light. The wagon's mud-splattered wheels were bone white, and a row of bows arched from one side of its bed to the other like the ribs of some deep ocean beast. Instead of white canvas a strange translucent material stretched between these bows, providing Bethany with a glimpse of the wagon's shadowy cargo. She leaned forward to get a better look, cupping a hand over her eyes to shade them from the glare of the lantern. . . .

"Would you like to know what's inside?" a voice whispered in her ear.

Bethany turned in surprise. Without making a sound the hooded driver of the wagon had somehow slipped next to her. The woman's face remained hidden, but Bethany thought she glimpsed the hint of a smile.

"I'm sorry," Bethany said. Her voice was faint and hoarse. "I shouldn't have looked without your permission."

"One should never apologize for curiosity," the woman said, and pushed back her hood.

Bethany had never seen such a beautiful woman. She looked to be in her midtwenties, with porcelain skin and delicate features. Straight blond hair grazed her shoulders, framing large eyes that were not just one shade of green but a collage of slight variations. Barely perceptible lines separated each hue, like a stained-glass window that had been cracked into pieces and then reassembled.

"Now tell me," the woman said, "why is a child wandering alone on such a cold, dark night?"

Bethany's mind had suddenly grown dull and sluggish.

"I don't know," she said.

Not broken glass, Bethany thought, unable to look away from those crystalline eyes. *Webs. It looks like spiderwebs have been stretched across her eyeballs.*

"Were you looking for me?" the woman asked.

Bethany shook her head.

"Are you sure about that? *I* was looking for *you*. Maybe not you, specifically, but someone with your special gifts." The woman ran the back of her hand along Bethany's cheek. "You are the first, Bethany. I saw you all the way from the night sky. You *shine*."

Despite the strangeness of the woman's words, Bethany felt a slight thrill at being thought so worthy of attention.

"How do you know my name?" she asked.

"How do you *not* know mine? No matter. It's Rygoth." The woman straightened her gloves. "Soon all will know it."

A splinter of fear needled Bethany's spine. This was not the workaday fear of rats and dark passageways and stormy, sleepless nights with her father still out at sea, but rather the gasp-inducing terror conjured by her grandmother as she told little Bethany the old stories, the ones her parents claimed were nonsense, of a time when witches and monsters roamed the World.

Bethany pressed her back against the wagon, trying to get as far from Rygoth's eyes as possible, and the strange material shifted inward.

It's warm, Bethany thought, feeling its sticky heat against her back. *Why is it warm?*

"I'm late," she said, finally managing to peel away from those variegated eyes. "My parents will be worried."

"Will they?" Rygoth asked, and in her tone Bethany heard a second question: *Have they even noticed you're gone?* "I wouldn't dream of stopping you, love. Mommy and Daddy shall have their daughter back, safe and sound. *More* than safe and sound."

The beautiful woman spoke with soft, measured tones

that held within them far more threat than any brigand. Keeping her eyes on Rygoth's feet and her hand near her dagger, Bethany slowly backed away toward the front of the wagon. *Once I pass the horses I'll make a run for it along the open road. . . .*

"Have you ever noticed how infrequently your name is spoken?" the woman asked.

Bethany wanted to stop listening. She wanted to run. But her feet remained rooted to the ground, unwilling to follow directions.

"Think about it. How often do your neighbors, those who have known you from birth, even, identify you only by your relationship to others? Ansen's sister? Martha's daughter?" Rygoth leaned forward, as though imparting a secret. "It's because they can never quite remember your name. It's always on the tip of their tongue—it really is—but . . . sad. To be so tragically forgettable."

Warm tears flowed down Bethany's cheeks. She wanted nothing more than to get away from this woman and her truth-poisoned words, but though she screamed for her body to move, it was like a wall had been built in her mind, blocking the message.

"I can't move," Bethany said. Her heart beat madly. "What have you done to me?"

"I didn't want it to be like this," Rygoth said, "but you need to hear the truth. You're *special*, Bethany. You don't have to be Caleb Jenkins's dough-faced daughter anymore, the unseen girl behind the counter. Let me help you, and everyone will learn how extraordinary you really are."

"I just want to go home!"

"Shh, Bethany. Listen."

From inside the wagon came a chorus of hushed whispers. At first the words were indistinguishable from one another, but as Bethany listened she was able to make out distinct names. *Annabeth. Lenowy. Karin.* Bethany felt her body turn and face the wagon. She wondered if it was Rygoth forcing her to move or if she was doing it on her own. She wasn't sure anymore.

Rachel. Cordelia. Emily.

Rygoth watched her with a considerate expression, her eyes as beautiful and unforgiving as an unbroken landscape of snow.

"Do you hear that?" Bethany asked.

"I hear everything," Rygoth replied, and waved her hand. The strange material covering the wagon folded back, revealing hundreds of leather-bound books. Given the bumpy dirt road, such cargo should have been scattered all over the wagon bed, but though they had not been secured in any visible fashion the books remained in precise, even stacks.

That's where the names are coming from, Bethany thought. *The books. They're calling to their owners.* It shouldn't have made any sense—books couldn't *talk*—but she knew she was right.

One of the books whispered her name.

It wasn't the name her parents had given her but Bethany's *true* name, a combination of sounds that depicted her inner self as accurately as a mirror's image reflected her outward appearance. *The dull drone of insects filling lonely summer afternoons that stretched into forever. The scrubbing of a brush as she tried to straighten her hair into the same style as the other girls. The teasing giggle of conversations she would never be a part of.*

These sounds and others coalesced into a single word: her true name.

The names of the other girls faded away; there was only this new sound, *her* sound, drawing her forth. Bethany searched madly for its source, knocking entire piles of books down until she found it: a light gray tome with a black star, easy to miss, stitched into its lower spine. Bethany held the book to her chest, the leather smooth and oddly damp. Her heart pounded with a strange combination of exhilaration and fear, as though she were about to leap off some great precipice.

"This one's mine," Bethany whispered.

She turned to Rygoth, ready to offer all her copper, all her *anything*, in exchange for the book, but the beautiful peddler, apparently uninterested in payment, had already returned to her seat.

"I must go," she said. "There are so many others out there. I can feel their potential, waiting to be unleashed. Yours is not the only spellbook I aim to bestow tonight."

"Spellbook?" Bethany asked, turning the book in her hands. "But I'm not a witch. Witches aren't even *real!*"

The wagon pulled away and bolted down the road, rumbling hard enough to shake the trees. Bethany expected its wheels to crack into bits or slip off their axles but instead the wagon lowered itself, like a beast ready to pounce, and then sprang high into the air, where it swelled outward and sprouted long wings. The shape, now a wagon no longer but a monster large enough to blot out the stars, sailed through the night with a small figure perched upon its back.

As the shape vanished, a dark cloud lifted from Bethany's mind and she noticed the grimoire in her hands. She tossed it away as though it had sprouted nails and razor-sharp teeth.

I have to go home and tell the Mistrals what I have seen, she thought. *The old stories were right. Witches are real! But I'm not a creature of darkness like her, no matter what she said. I won't touch the book again. I'll just leave it here and come back with . . .*

Only when Bethany looked down the grimoire was somehow open in her two hands, the pages not paper as she had expected but impossibly thin mirrors stitched into the binding. *What kind of book is this?* Bethany wondered. She stared at her reflection, the short hair that never grew out the right way, her drab brown eyes. It was the type of face you would forget the moment after seeing it.

I wish people would notice me, she thought.

As though in answer, strange words that Bethany had never seen before etched themselves across the mirror-page, fragmenting her reflection into a monstrous distortion.

BOOK ONE

THE UNGHOSTS

"Gaining power will teach you about other people. Losing it will teach you about yourself."

— **Minoth Dravania**

23rd Sablethorn Lecture

ONE

The village of De'Noran was no more.

Where wooden buildings had once stood were now only charred debris. Even the grass was blackened and dead. Kara walked farther down the main road, remembering how loud it had been at midday with the bustle of commerce in full force. The rattle of wagon wheels. The soft buzzing of barter and gossip. The delighted screams of children playing in the square.

All was silent.

They should have been on their way to the World right

now, but Kara, upon seeing the changed village from the deck of their ship, had insisted on docking. Several men had followed the children ashore, quickly spreading through the abandoned farms to forage for supplies.

"Are you sure it was a good idea to stop here?" Taff asked. "If anyone sees us . . ."

He didn't have to finish this thought; the dark events of that day were deeply branded in her mind. It had started out so well. Grace Stone had been defeated, and the villagers had gathered together to formally announce their new leader: William Westfall, Kara and Taff's father. It should have been the happiest day of their lives—but Grace wasn't done with them yet. She had used her Last Spell to possess Father with the spirit of Timoth Clen, the most merciless witch hunter of all, and he had ordered the villagers to kill them. The two Westfalls had escaped only by fleeing into the Thickety.

"What if they're still here, hiding?" Taff asked, looking around the remnants of the village. "Watching us? We barely escaped the first time, and now——"

"Don't worry," Kara said. "No one's here."

"What about Father?"

"He's gone too."

Taff swallowed deeply.

"Are they dead?" he asked.

Kara shook her head. "Just gone."

Taff did not look convinced. He stared across the flattened village, his brow furrowed with concern.

"I hope nothing bad happened to them," he said.

Kara couldn't help smiling, amazed as always by her brother's ability to forgive others no matter how badly they had wronged him. He had been equally quick to absolve Mary Kettle after she had betrayed them, and in the end it had been his compassion that won her to their side.

"They might have moved to a different part of the island," suggested Taff. "They could have been fleeing something. Thickety monsters, maybe. I know they don't usually cross the Fringe, but when Sordyr lost his power maybe things changed."

Kara stopped at the place where the general store had once stood, now nothing but charred earth and barely identifiable lumps that used to be shelves and jars. She picked up a half-melted spoon and absently gazed at her upside-down reflection, remembering the day when Grace had tricked her into giving up her seeds. At the time, such childish cruelty had been the biggest problem in her life. She wished that were still the case.

"No animal could have done this," Kara said. "It's too organized. If it had been a beast from the Thickety there would be debris everywhere. Wood, glass . . ."

"People pieces."

"Taff!"

"What?" he asked. "You were thinking it too." He lowered his voice to a whisper. "Could it have been Rygoth?"

"No. Rygoth only does things for a reason, and this gains her nothing. I'm sure she's in the World right now, distributing her grimoires and gathering new witches to her side. After two thousand years stuck on this island this is the last place she'd be, now that she's finally free."

All thanks to me, her foolish little pawn.

Kara kicked a blackened piece of rubble that might have once been a clay pitcher and watched it skip across the ashes of the store.

"Ms. Westfall," said a man behind her. "There's something you should see."

The voice belonged to Anders Clement, a tall, wiry man with dark skin and a dusting of white in his hair. Before leaving Kala Malta, the villagers had appointed him captain of the ship that would transport a third of their number to the World. As a leader he had proven competent enough, but though he was friendly and gregarious to other members of the crew he remained strangely aloof toward Kara.

"What is it, Clement?" Kara asked.

"*Captain* Clement," he snapped.

Clearly he was still upset with her. Clement hadn't wanted to dock at the island in the first place, and it was only when Kara had demanded they do so that he reluctantly agreed. She wasn't sure what had hurt his ego more—taking orders from a child or from a girl—but Kara was certain she had caused him to lose face in front of his entire crew. Luckily she had listened to Mary's advice and concealed the fact that she no longer had any magical powers. If Clement knew the truth she doubted he would have listened to her at all.

"My apologies," Kara said. "What is it, *Captain* Clement?"

"There's something you should see." He nodded toward Taff. "Might be best if the boy stays here. Too scary for little ones."

Taff stared at him in disbelief.

"Seriously?" he asked. "Do you have any idea what kinds of things I've seen? I could give nightmares nightmares!"

"Suit yourself," said Captain Clement.

They followed the tall man deeper into the village, passing sooty rectangles that used to be buildings but were now little more than scorched wood and memories. *That's where the tannery used to be*, Kara thought. *And that long stretch is the barracks where the graycloaks lived. Over there was Baker Corbett's place—you can still see the stones from the oven.* A surprising feeling of nostalgia swept over her. She had never been happy here, but it *had* been home—and now it was gone.

They crested a hill and the center of the village—where the Fold had once gathered for Worship—stretched out before them. Sitting Stones had been painstakingly arranged in a series of concentric rings so all of the congregation would have a clear view of the Fenroot tree at the circle's center. This tree was the most important symbol of the Fold, and despite the destruction that had ravaged the rest of the village it remained whole and undamaged.

From its limbs hung hundreds of animal skeletons.

They swung back and forth in the wind, with little rhyme or reason to their arrangement. Some had been hung so high that they were just a glimmer of white in the late-afternoon sun; others were low enough to scrape across the ground. Mostly it was smaller livestock—goats, chickens, sheep—though on the opposite side of the Fenroot tree the unwieldy skeleton of a cow hung suspended by five ropes. Kara took some small comfort knowing that the animals had not been hung alive. The Children of the Fold, practical in all matters, would not waste good food; the animals had surely been butchered first, the meat salted and packed away for later consumption.

"Do you understand the meaning behind this"—Captain Clement paused for a moment, searching for the right word—"display?"

"Can something like this truly have a meaning?" Kara asked.

"Surely you must have some idea. These are *your* people."

Kara shook her head. "Not anymore."

"Look," Taff said softly, pointing to a shape just now turning in the wind to face them. Unlike the other skeletons, this one wore a black school dress with a white collar, giving it the appearance of a scarecrow. In the place where a human head should have resided sat a ram's skull with long horns curved inward. Raven-black hair, possibly from a horse's mane, draped over the empty eye sockets of the skull and down the back of the dress. Though the scarecrow lacked hands, a large black book had been affixed by copper wire to the left sleeve of the dress.

"Who's that supposed to be?" asked Captain Clement.

Kara remembered the Shadow Festival, a row of similar scarecrows lining Widow Miller's cornfield. *I'm one of them now, a figure to frighten children.* "I know what happened to the villagers," she said. "They burned down their homes because they knew they were never coming back. They could have just left everything the way it was, but the great Timoth Clen would have wanted a grand gesture, some sort of ceremony. He probably called it the Great Cleansing or something like that. He knew I'd be back here. Somehow he knew. The animals are part of the message. I love animals, you see. He knows that because . . . the scarecrow. It's me. All of this is for me."

"What are you prattling on about, girl?" Captain Clement asked.

"He wants me to know that he's taken his flock to the World, but he hasn't forgotten. He'll be looking for me. And when he finds me—"

Taff ducked beneath Kara's arm and nuzzled close, wrapping his arms around her.

"Who?" asked Captain Clement. "When *who* finds you?"

But Kara was done talking, and so it was Taff who answered.

"The man wearing our father's face," he said.

TWO

That night, Kara dreamed of the cornfield.

It began as it always had. Father—her *real* father, evicted from his body and trapped in this endless dream realm—stood in the center of the barren soil and felt for the pouch of seeds in his pocket. Only instead of planting them right away, as he had in dreams past, Father poured the black seeds into the palm of his hand and poked at them with a single finger. His befuddled expression held a hint of frustration. New wrinkles had appeared near the corners of his eyes.

He's starting to remember, Kara thought. *Grace's spell can only hold him in this place for so long before he realizes it's not real and begins to lose his mind. Once that happens, I won't be able to get him back again.*

Suddenly, Father's eyes narrowed in rage. He squeezed the seeds tight in his powerful fist. Kara couldn't hear him scream—for whatever reason, there was no sound in this dream—but she saw the tightening cords of his neck as he unleashed a silent shriek of frustration. In his eyes swirling mists of madness gathered like an approaching storm.

Kara awoke.

Time is running out, she thought. *If I don't save him now, I'll lose him forever.*

Knowing there would be no more sleep that night, Kara reached for the object beneath her bed and slid it into her satchel. She exited the room quietly, not wanting to wake Taff, and made her way across the silent deck of the ship. Above her, the stars twinkled like glowflies.

Kara still expected to see the black canopy of the Thickety whenever she looked up, and the presence of those scattered stars provided as much relief as beauty.

"I've escaped," she said, as though speaking the words aloud might imbue them with enough power to calm her frazzled nerves. "I'm safe." Except she wasn't, of course, not even close. Rygoth would surely kill her the next time they met, unless the thing inhabiting her father's body found her first, in which case she would be executed as an example to all witches. And then there was the World itself. The Children of the Fold had been forbidden to discuss it, so Kara had no idea what to expect.

What if it's even more dangerous than the Thickety?

She moved quickly, slipping from shadow to shadow in order to avoid the occasional sailor. The ship, which Captain Clement had christened the *Wayfinder*, was crudely constructed and devoid of ornamentation. Two decks below Kara dozens of men, working in nine-hour shifts, dragged long oars through the water. Taff thought that making men labor in such a fashion was barbaric, and tried to prove that he could build a ship with sails through the use of a perfectly successful model, but no one had been willing to take a seven-year-old's ideas about nautical engineering seriously.

With a quick glance in either direction to make sure none of the night crew was looking her way, Kara descended the ladder to the cargo hold.

A small lantern hung on a peg beside her, but Kara decided that the beams of moonlight shining through the ceiling boards would be enough to guide her way. The creaking and groaning of the *Wayfinder*, a worrisome backdrop their entire journey, was even louder down here. Ducking her head, Kara made her way past barrel after barrel of provisions secured carefully to wooden posts: water and ale, seed and salted beef, eggs packed in straw, and a purple grain that was the Thickety's version of rice. Livestock milled in simple wooden pens, their nervous cries reverberating against the low ceiling. These were creatures of land, and the rocking motion of the ship upset them.

"I understand," Kara said, hardly enamored of ocean travel herself. "But don't worry. We'll be on land soon enough."

The animals pressed themselves against the walls of their pens to greet her. Kara reached a hand between the wooden boards, and a white-gray goat nuzzled her fingers. She smiled. Though Kara was no longer a witch, she had not lost her way with animals, and after what Timoth Clen had left for her on the Fenroot tree she felt the need for their warmth, their *aliveness*. After tickling the feathers of a playful hen, she strode over to the larger pens at the end of the ship, where the horses were kept. Shadowdancer whinnied impatiently, insulted that Kara had chosen to visit those less important animals first. The chestnut-brown mare leaned over the tall gate and nudged her head against Kara's shoulder.

"How are you feeling today?" Kara asked. She slipped

an apple into Shadowdancer's mouth. "Shh. Don't tell Captain Clement I'm wasting people food on a horse. He'd be *soooooo* mad."

Shadowdancer still looked sickly and thin, having not yet completely recovered from her time as one of the Blighted, and her mane, when Kara pressed her face into it, smelled faintly of dead flowers. The mare's deep brown eyes, however, were once again her own, stubborn and mischievous and full of life.

Checking quickly in all directions to make sure that she was truly alone, Kara slipped into Shadowdancer's stall and ducked behind its walls. *I'm not doing anything wrong. How could I be?* Nevertheless, a feeling of guilt washed over her, to the point where even Shadowdancer's innocuous glance felt judgmental.

She withdrew the white grimoire from the satchel and spread it across her lap.

This isn't yours, Kara thought, her guilt intensifying. *You stole it from Safi and then left her behind in Kala Malta.*

That brave little witch helped you recover the elixir from inside Niersook, fought by your side—and you betrayed her. Kara reminded herself that she had only taken the grimoire to save Safi from its dark influence, but that was little consolation. If her intentions had been truly noble, then why hadn't she thrown the spellbook overboard yet?

Kara stared at the first page, carefully running her fingers over the smooth surface, and then flipped through the early portion of the book. If she had been able to cast spells, these first few pages—already used by Safi— would have rippled like black water.

They looked completely blank to her.

"Nothing," Kara told the mare. "I might as well be a person who never used a grimoire in her life. I might as well be a *boy!*"

Shadowdancer responded with a short snort. At first Kara thought the mare was mocking her, but then she noticed a mouse, white with a question-mark tail, skittering across the hay in the corner of the stall. Shadowdancer hadn't been trying to convey her opinion; she was simply annoyed that another animal had infiltrated her stall.

Kara held her palm flat along the hay and the mouse climbed onto her hand. "Hello there," she said, enjoying the tickling sensation of its tiny paws against her skin. *I'm not just a common witch*, she reminded herself. *I'm a* wexari. *I don't need a stupid grimoire to cast a spell.* She reached out with her thoughts, trying to build a mind-bridge to the mouse, the same technique she had used to control dozens of fearsome monsters in the Thickety.

The mouse stared at her, unimpressed.

Fine, Kara thought, *but maybe Niersook's venom only took away my* wexari *powers. Maybe I can still catch animals in the grimoire, just like I did when I first discovered I was a witch.* Placing the tiny rodent carefully on the floor, Kara opened to a page well beyond the ones that Safi had used.

She concentrated on the mouse.

"Hop onto my hand."

If it worked, the mouse's form would appear in the

grimoire, a sketch drawn in tiny words.

The page remained blank.

What did you think would happen? Kara thought as the mouse scampered back to the hay. *Your powers aren't going to just randomly return like a lost voice after a cold. They're gone forever.*

What was she going to do?

There were such obstacles in Kara's future. She needed to break the curse on her father. Stop Rygoth. Protect Taff. These were absurdly difficult tasks *with* her powers, but without them? She had no chance.

Be honest, though. That's not the real reason you're down here.

Kara slammed the grimoire shut and threw her head into her hands.

She missed magic so much.

After years of being ostracized Kara had finally felt like she was part of something. The creatures of the Thickety had accepted her in a way the Children of the Fold never had. For the first time in her life, Kara had *belonged*. Now that door had been closed to her forever, and the world, for a few months so vibrantly sharp, had lost its color.

And whose fault is that? If I had used my powers better, none of this would have happened. Father would still be Father. Rygoth would still be imprisoned.

I don't deserve to be a witch.

On the other side of the cargo hold, something clattered to the ground.

Kara sprang to her feet and looked in the direction of the noise. The far side of the hold was dark and suffused with shadows.

"Hello?" she asked. "Is anyone there?"

There was no response, and after a few moments Kara exhaled deeply, deciding it was nothing. *The way Captain Clement pilots this ship, it's surprising more things don't fall over.*

She stroked Shadowdancer's mane, wishing she had brought another apple.

"Be well, my friend," she said. "Soon we'll be on land, and you can run free."

Slipping between penned animals and towers of cargo, Kara made her way back toward the moonlight. Shadows seemed to stretch their arms toward her as she passed.

Though dawn was still several hours away, Taff was already awake, which didn't surprise Kara; their internal clocks had not yet readjusted to night and day outside the Thickety, leading to some odd sleeping hours. He sat in the center of their small cabin, surrounded by several toys from Mary's sack. *Not Mary's—it's his sack now*, Kara thought, still uncomfortable with the idea of her brother toting around enchanted objects, especially when he treated them with such childlike carelessness. Strewn about the floor, among other oddities, were a straw doll that would shake its head if you told a fib, a cracked boomerang that always returned no matter where or how you threw it, and a stone die whose faces had been embossed with pictures representing the five senses—ear, nose, eye, mouth, hand—save the last face, which bore only a red circle. Its use had thus far eluded them.

She closed the cabin door behind her. Taff didn't look up. Since they had left Kala Malta he had been in a sullen, quiet mood.

What did you expect? Safi was his friend. His only friend. He misses her.

"You shouldn't leave these all over the floor," Kara said, nodding toward the magic toys. "They're dangerous."

Taff raised his eyebrows.

"Dangerous? Like walking around with an evil book that should have been thrown overboard days ago?"

Taff hadn't been pleased when Kara told him she stole Safi's grimoire, but though he felt there must have been a more honest way to protect his friend, he understood the well-meaning intent behind Kara's duplicity.

What he didn't understand was why she hadn't gotten rid of it yet.

"I can do it for you, if you want," he said. "Throwing things overboard is fun. I like the little splashes."

"I don't think we're in deep enough water yet," Kara said. "We don't want it to wash up onshore. Some other poor girl might find it."

Ignoring Taff's dubious look, Kara sat down on her cot and felt several sharp jabs from the metal jacks that had been carelessly tossed across the mattress.

"Seriously?" she asked, chucking the toys at her brother.

Taff shrugged. "I need to make a mess. That's how I think."

"Mary would have happily explained what each of these did before we left."

"How would that be any fun?" he asked, honestly puzzled. "Besides, even *she* doesn't know what some of these toys do." He indicated a pile to his left: several pinwheels, a single arrow with a glass sphere at its tip instead of a point, tumbling blocks strung together with tattered ribbons. "I need to figure out all their powers so

I can finally do something useful."

"What are you talking about?" Kara asked. "You've been nothing but useful."

"I've had some good ideas," Taff admitted. "Maybe even some *great* ideas. But you've done all the hard stuff. It's my turn to protect you now."

Because I can't protect myself.

She watched Taff pick up a box-shaped piece of wood no larger than a shoe, this boy who should have been playing with toys and not trying to deduce their magical properties, and was overwhelmed by a feeling of tenderness so intense it almost made her dizzy.

"Guess what this one does," Taff said.

He handed the box to Kara and she turned it in her hands. A red door had been cut into the wood. Kara unhooked a simple latch, revealing a tiny storage compartment.

"It's a hideaway," Kara said, smiling. "I had one of these when I was little. I used it as a treasure trove for

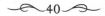

buttons and dried flowers. Father made it for me—a birthday present, if I remember true. I watched him build it. He was so quick with a saw, so precise. That's probably where you get your—"

She stopped, noticing the tears swelling in Taff's eyes.

"I'm sorry," Kara said. "I shouldn't talk about him."

"No," Taff replied, shaking his head. "We *should*. Otherwise it's like saying that he's gone or something, which he's not. He's just . . . lost. That's all. We're going to get him back, I know it." Wiping away his tears, he nodded toward the hideaway. "This one works a little differently than the one Father made you. I think it might be useful."

"No doubt," Kara said, handing him the box, "but now's not the time." She knelt down so they were eye to eye. "There's something you need to know."

She hadn't anticipated telling him tonight, but seeing Taff's undiminished love for his father made Kara realize that she had no right to keep the truth from him. If there was a chance, any chance at all, he needed to know.

"I wanted to be certain first," Kara said. "I couldn't bear the thought of giving you false hope. But I guess there's really no way to be sure, not with something like this."

She hesitated, reluctant to release the words into the world. After this, there would be no going back, like reporting the death of a loved one.

"I know how to save Father," Kara said.

With a shout of unbridled joy Taff leaped onto his cot, jumping up and down so high his head almost touched the ceiling. "Yes!" he exclaimed. "Yes! We're going to be a family again!" Kara watched this impromptu celebration with a mixture of happiness, for the sight of her brother's smiling face had never failed to warm her heart, and dread, for she knew what she had to tell him next.

Taff fell backward onto her lap, his legs dangling across the cot. Kara pushed his hair back so she could look into his eyes.

"There's no reason to celebrate," Kara said. "This isn't a matter of snapping your fingers and everything is okay again. It's going to be incredibly dangerous. And it might not even work."

Taff waved her concerns away.

"You saved our village from a powerful witch. You freed the people of Kala Malta from Sordyr. You restored the Thickety. I'm not worried. Whatever we have to do, we'll do it. Together."

Kara pushed Taff into a sitting position and turned on the floor to face him. She took a long, steady breath, unsure how to begin.

Just tell him everything at once. Like swallowing a thimbleful of medicine.

"We need to enter the Well of Witches."

Taff looked surprised, maybe even a little unsettled, but hardly terrified. Of course, he hadn't been there when Aunt Abby's grimoire opened up. He hadn't seen the witches reach through the portal and drag Grace into their world. He hadn't heard their voices: *One of us, one of us, one of us.*

Kara had seen it all. She was terrified enough for both of them.

"But the only way to get into Phadeen is by using the last page in a grimoire, right?" Taff asked. "That doesn't seem like a very good plan."

"There's another way, according to Sordyr. An entrance that only *wexari* know."

"He told you that before we left?"

Kara shook her head. "He wrote it down."

The former Forest Demon—now just a man—had penned Kara a lengthy letter to help answer some of her questions about Rygoth and the world. Taff hadn't read any of it. For all his intelligence, he had always struggled with reading. Sordyr's cramped, antiquated handwriting—coupled with the nonstop rocking of the ship—had not helped matters.

"What did he say?" Taff asked.

"Sordyr writes about a place called Sablethorn, which is where he was trained to be a *wexari*. It was a school, just like back on De'Noran, only instead of studying about letters and numbers they studied magic."

"That sounds *a lot* more interesting," mumbled Taff.

"The headmaster was a man named Minoth Dravania, and he was the greatest of all *wexari*. Sablethorn was a place of peace and knowledge."

Kara's gaze went distant as she imagined what it might have been like to be a *wexari* studying in Sablethorn, how different her life would have been had she grown up during that time.

"As the years passed," Kara continued, "Minoth became worried that his students were becoming too distracted by worldly affairs to gain mastery over their craft. So, using his great magic, he created a paradise just 'outside the world,' as Sordyr put it, where *wexari* could study undisturbed. There were gardens and mountains, waterfalls and rushing rivers. Sordyr said that there had never been a more beautiful place."

"What does that have to do with——"

"Minoth Dravania had a name for this paradise. He called it Phadeen."

Taff scrunched his face in confusion. Phadeen and the Well of Witches were supposed to be the same place. That's why the terms were used interchangeably.

"I don't get it," he said. "Is Phadeen the pretty place with the gardens or the scary place with the witches?"

"Both. Princess Evangeline's Last Spell corrupted the paradise built by Minoth and transformed it into the Well of Witches. But the entrance to the original Phadeen still remains in Sablethorn. Sordyr thinks we can use it to get inside. A lot safer than going through a grimoire, at least."

Taff picked up a toy arrow and spun it in his hands. Fluid as black as a grave beetle's carapace sloshed inside the sphere at its end, reminding Kara of the venom they had retrieved from Niersook.

"So if we find this Sablethorn school, we can get into

the place that used to be Phadeen but is now the Well of Witches."

"Exactly."

"But *why* are we going in the first place? What could possibly be there that could help Father? There's nothing but . . ."

He paused, comprehension dawning.

"Grace," he whispered.

Kara nodded.

"Only the witch who cast a Last Spell can reverse it," she said. "It has to be her."

"But she's dead."

"Not according to Sordyr. Only trapped."

"It doesn't matter. Even if we find her, she's not going to *help* us. She's *evil*."

"I didn't say it was a perfect plan, but it's Father's only chance. Grace isn't just going to volunteer to undo her spell. You're right about that. But we have something very important that we can exchange for her cooperation.

In fact, it's what she wants more than anything else in the world."

"What's that?"

"Her freedom," Kara said. She inhaled deeply before speaking again. "We're going to help Grace escape the Well of Witches. And in return she's going to give us our father back."

Before Taff could respond, something broadsided the ship with a thunderous crash. There was no warning, no time to prepare. Kara's shoulder slammed into the wooden frame of the cot. Her teeth clacked together painfully.

"What was—" Taff began, and the ship was struck again, harder this time. For a brief moment Kara felt a feeling of weightlessness, her entire body floating through the air, and then she crashed to the suddenly canted floor. The two Westfalls slid and rolled and slammed into the opposite wall. The floor stabilized and they rose to their feet, unharmed save for some nicks and bruises, bracing

themselves for the next strike. A sound that Kara at first took to be rushing water rose from the deck above them, except as the ringing in her head cleared she realized that it wasn't water at all.

It was screaming.

THREE

Taff tossed the rest of the magical toys into his sack while Kara grabbed her satchel. The two children made their way toward the upper deck through a tide of people rushing in the opposite direction. Most were silent, their energy focused on escaping as quickly as possible. "What is it?" Kara asked, and an old woman with a star-shaped birthmark just above her upper lip muttered, "Monster, monster . . ."

These are survivors of the Thickety. They've spent their entire lives surrounded by monsters. What could frighten them so?

She soon found out.

Those brave enough to remain on the upper deck had taken up spears and swords and were attempting to hold back a beast unlike anything Kara had ever seen. Even with the rest of its amorphous body hidden beneath the ocean waves, the creature towered over the ship. From a dozen appendages protruded polyps of every imaginable color and shape, some ridged and bulbous, like mushrooms, others short and spiky. It looked like an underwater mountain come to life, awoken from its immateriality by some sort of dark magic.

"Rygoth," Kara said.

The creature lifted one of its limbs high into the air, slow and languid, and brought it crashing down across the bow of the ship.

The deck pitched upward. Kara snatched Taff by the elbow and grabbed the nearest guardrail before she lost her footing. A burly man slid past them, scratching for purchase at the surface of the deck. Before he slipped overboard, gravity pulled the ship level again. Frigid water crashed over the railing, chilling Kara's ankles.

"How do we stop it?" Taff asked.

Kara's first instinct, honed from months of practice in the Thickety, was to build a mind-bridge with the creature. She was in the midst of considering possible ways to do so—*it must be lonely from all that time spent in the ocean depths, so perhaps a memory of companionship and warmth*—before quickly realizing that there was no point. Her magic was gone.

She had never felt more helpless in her life.

Another appendage crashed into the ship. Kara heard a terrible cracking sound from somewhere deep within the bowels of the ship, a mortal wound. The deck did not right itself perfectly this time but remained tilted upward at a slight angle.

"Hurry!" Kara exclaimed, grabbing her brother's hand.

They wove through grim-looking men and women

holding swords and spears that were as useless as tooth-picks against such a mammoth foe. Taff, having abandoned his wooden sword back in Kala Malta, withdrew the slingshot he now wore on his belt and fired at the beast as they ran. Kara heard an invisible stone clink off its body and bounce ineffectually into the ocean.

As they passed directly in front of the beast, a single, translucent hole opened in its chest, revealing a cornea of starry night. At first Kara thought it was an eye, but then the top and bottom moved in a terrible mockery of lips.

"Kara," said a familiar voice. "There you are."

Rygoth.

She was speaking through the monster somehow, her tone whisper-soft yet louder than a thousand screams.

"Do you like my latest creation?" she asked. "I call him Coralis. Perhaps I needn't have made something so grand, but I thought I owed you a memorable end, at least. And I do so enjoy using my powers now that I'm free." Her voice, which had been flitting and playful, dropped to a colder, more serious tone. "You shouldn't have followed me, *wexari*. I would have left you alone, had you stayed on the island."

"You stole my magic."

"Your magic was *wasted* on you," Rygoth said. "You were never strong enough to wield it."

Kara felt her lip began to tremble and hated herself for it.

"Oh," Rygoth said, "I've hit the mark, haven't I? You understand. You're not worthy of such power. You never were. And yet despite all that, *I permitted you to live*. And you disrespect that gift by attempting to interfere in my plans. My children informed me the moment you left the shore. All the animals of the sea and land are my eyes, girl. Did you really think you could pursue me unnoticed?"

"I'm going to—" Kara said, the tears coming freely now. "I won't let you—"

Rygoth's laugh rippled through Coralis's body. "Didn't anyone teach you not to make empty promises? Oh—I

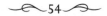

suppose not. Your mother, no doubt, died before she could impart any valuable lessons. And your father— well, he wants you dead as much as I do. Poor, powerless Kara. Since you refused to accept my gift of life, allow me to give you another gift instead."

Coralis swung an arm downward and Kara braced herself, excepting another devastating blow, but the limb stopped before it struck the ship and hovered little more than a stone's throw from Kara's head. From this distance she was able to see the shells and polyps that composed Coralis's body up close, their swirls and colors lacking only a different context to be beautiful.

A tentacle with serrated edges poked out from between the inner folds of Coralis's torso. *Here comes the attack,* Kara thought, but she was wrong again. The tentacle did not seem nearly long enough to reach them, and instead of striking the ship it slashed at the appendage hovering over her head, at the point where it met Coralis's body. The giant creature rocked back and forth in apparent pain but continued to strike itself until finally, with a burst of ermine fluid, the limb was cut free from its body and fell.

Kara dove out of the way as shards of wood exploded into the air.

The severed appendage stretched across the length of the deck. A salty smell pervaded the air, like the sea but older somehow, and rank. Kara and Taff approached cautiously, along with the remaining members of the crew. Kara saw Captain Clement glare in her direction, as though this had all been her fault from the very beginning.

Taff drew back the pocket of his slingshot.

The limb began to move.

It wasn't the movement of something alive, exactly, but the pulsating shudder of an object containing living things *inside it*. A spider sack full of hatching eggs. A corpse ballooning with maggots.

From within the shells, creatures emerged.

An older crewman who had gotten too close found

himself suddenly face-to-face with a crablike monster as large as a child. It had six claws in all, four on which it walked, spreading them open and closed for balance as needed, and two for pure violence. It attacked the crewman, snapping off his forearm as easily as cutting thread.

"Shunings!" Captain Clement exclaimed.

Kara had never seen a shuning up close, but she knew what they were; on rare occasions one of the deep-ocean dwellers, no doubt lost and disoriented, had made its way onto the shore of De'Noran. The moment it was sighted someone would ring the alarm, bringing dozens of well-armed graycloaks. Eventually, through the use of nets and spears, the single shuning would be killed, though it often took a few men with it.

Kara now saw at least a dozen of the creatures clicking their way from the folds of the severed limb.

Taff fired his slingshot at an approaching shuning, and one of its claws bent back at an impossible angle. It scuttled away in the opposite direction.

"I need to get up higher," Taff said. "I'll be able to pick them off."

"No!" Kara shouted, grabbing his arm.

"I can help! One of us has to do something."

The implication of his words fell heavily between them.

Because you can't help at all.

"Kara . . ."

"Be careful," she said, releasing his arm.

Higher ground will be safer anyway. I doubt these creatures can climb ladders.

Taff quickly vanished into the mill of moving figures attempting to fight off the vicious beasts. Kara saw a short-haired woman drive her spear through the unarmored joint of a shuning, pinning it to the deck. Before she could withdraw her weapon, however, a second shuning was upon her, and then a third, and the woman disappeared from view.

Someone grasped Kara's shoulders and spun her

around. She found herself inches away from Captain Clement's furious face.

"Help us, witch!" he screamed, shaking her. As he spoke, blood curled down the side of his face and into his mouth. "My people are dying! *Do something!*"

She felt movement against her leg and screamed as a shuning opened its claws, preparing to snap them together just below her knee. Captain Clement kicked the creature and it skidded across the deck. He raised his sword, ready to pursue it, but paused a moment to look back at Kara.

"Worthless," he muttered.

He's right. There's nothing I can do to help them.

Despite the sounds of violence surrounding her, the desperate scrambling of people fighting madly for their lives, a sudden weariness settled over Kara.

She fell to her knees.

Just a little rest. There's nothing I can do anyway.

"Kara," someone said.

It was a girl's voice. A voice she recognized.

"Safi?"

At first she thought she was imagining things, but turning to her left she saw that Safi was indeed standing next to her, the familiar dark skin and sharp green eyes, hair tangled and unkempt.

"How are you here?" Kara asked.

"Later," Safi said. She managed a small smile and pointed at Coralis. "I think we should worry about the giant monster first."

With long, fine fingers she snatched the grimoire from Kara's satchel and entered the fray, the book already open before her. A shuning charged in her direction, but Safi spoke a few words and the creature flew into the air and over the side of the ship as though caught in its own personal tornado. Safi spoke again and a second shuning spun upward and shattered against the mast of the ship. Shards of black shell clacked to the deck like hail.

Kara followed in Safi's wake as she continued her rampage, eliminating one creature after another. *She must have been hiding on this ship the entire time. That's the only thing that makes sense. But if she knew I stole her grimoire, why didn't she try to take it back before this?*

An explosion of brilliant fire lit the night sky.

The world sharpened and Coralis wobbled backward, its appendages flailing high in the air as it tried to regain its balance. A second explosion, this one even brighter than the first, struck it high upon its torso, and Coralis fell into the ocean. The ship rose on a massive wave. Kara was certain it would capsize this time for sure, but she heard Safi scream a long string of indecipherable words and the ship suddenly straightened, as though a giant hand had reached down from the sky and steadied it.

The remaining crew and passengers of the *Wayfinder* cheered in triumph.

At the center of them all stood Safi, the grimoire now closed in her hands. They clapped her on the back, threw their arms around her slender shoulders. Taff rushed over, the slingshot dangling from his hand, and hugged her tightly. There would be time for explanations later; right now he was just happy to see his lost friend.

Kara made her way to the edge of the ship, where the ocean stretched out in every direction beneath clouds as wispy as frayed cotton. The sun just now rising over the horizon streaked the darkness with early-morning hues. It was a gorgeous sight—a *magical* sight—but it did little to brighten Kara's spirits.

If it weren't for Safi, everyone on this ship would be dead right now. And it would be my fault. I'm the one Rygoth wants. I'm the reason she attacked us. And there was nothing I could do to stop her!

How can I defeat Rygoth? How can I save Father?

I'm nothing without magic.

Nothing.

FOUR

At a feast in her honor, Safi told Captain Clement that she had snuck aboard the *Wayfinder* in order to help Kara and Taff pursue Rygoth. "I knew they'd need me," Safi said, "but I also knew that my father would never let me go. It was the only way." The other adults at the table, still in awe over Safi's defeat of Coralis, readily accepted this story as fact. Kara didn't blame them. It sounded convincing enough and, as with all the best lies, it held a kernel of truth. When the children retired to their cabin that night, however, Kara sent Taff for water and extra

blankets and took a seat opposite the girl.

"You ready to tell me the whole truth?" Kara asked.

Safi, her hair now braided in twin pigtails, had scrubbed the grime from her skin and procured a green dress that was long in the arms but otherwise a good fit.

"The truth is that you stole my grimoire."

"You're right."

Kara waited for the anger. The accusations. Not so long ago, a woman named Constance Lamb had taken Kara's grimoire. She knew from experience how betrayed Safi must feel and expected no less than unbridled hatred.

Instead, Safi threw herself into Kara's arms.

"Thank you," she said, kissing Kara's cheek. "Thank you, thank you, thank you."

"You're not mad?"

"Of course not!" Safi exclaimed, taking her hands. "You *had* to steal it. That was the only way. If you had tried to talk to me about it first . . ."

"You wouldn't have listened."

Safi nodded.

"The grimoire was controlling me," she said, and then added quietly, "It made me do something I'm ashamed of."

"Tell me."

Safi stared at her lap, looking very much like the shy, awkward girl Kara had first met in Kala Malta. *It was a good idea to send Taff away*, she thought. Unlike Kara, he could never truly understand what it was like to be controlled by a grimoire, and for this reason Safi would be more likely to conceal the whole truth. She wouldn't want her best friend to think ill of her.

Even with Kara as her only audience, however, Safi needed to turn her back before beginning.

"Sorry," she said. "It's easier if I'm not looking at you."

"Take your time. You'll feel better afterward."

"Promise?"

"Promise."

Safi took a deep breath and began.

"After the battle with Rygoth, I thought I had lost

my grimoire forever, but several nights later I awoke to find myself standing in the Thickety with the book in my hands. I was scared, but excited, too, because I had really missed casting spells. You don't know what it's like to have all this power and then just suddenly not be able to—"

Safi stopped and glanced at Kara over one shoulder.

"Sorry," she said.

"Keep going."

"I cast a lot of spells that night. Just harmless little things, just to—just because I needed to, I guess. I promised myself I would tell you in the morning, only the morning came and I realized that you would take the grimoire from me if you knew the truth and I didn't want that. I wanted to go to the World with you and Taff. I wanted to help fight Rygoth, and for that I needed to practice. At least, that's what I told myself. Really I just wanted to cast more spells. That was all I cared about. I know that now. I hid the grimoire in the forest and every

night I found myself back there again. The spells became stranger. Not always what I wanted to cast. I turned a tree to cinders. I created black sucking whirlpools in the earth. I don't think I hurt any of the forest animals, but—but—"

"The grimoire wanted you to."

Safi nodded.

"And then one night my father saw what I was doing. He must have followed me. I'm actually surprised it took him so long to realize that I was leaving each night. Ever since what happened with Rygoth he's been even more overprotective than usual."

"He loves you," Kara said.

Safi nodded, tears in her eyes.

"When he saw what I was doing he tried to take the grimoire from my hands and . . . a spell appeared. I didn't think. I just cast it. Papa froze for a moment and left. The next morning he had no recollection of what had happened. I should have been thrilled! But every time Papa smiled at me or kissed my cheek I felt my heart sink. It was like I was lying to him every minute of the day, even when we weren't talking." Safi wiped tears from her cheeks. "But it was worse than that, because there was a small part of me that was *laughing* at him too. My father, who had never shown me anything but love and kindness, and when I looked at him all I could see was this fool who should never tell me what to do again."

"It was the grimoire putting those thoughts in your head."

"I know," Safi said, her eyes looking off into the distance. "I heard it sometimes. A voice whispering in my ear. That's when I knew I had to get away, that if I kept using the grimoire it would change me forever. So I snuck aboard the *Wayfinder* the night before it left. I knew I wouldn't be much help without my grimoire, but on the other hand I would be far away from its influence. I could be good again."

Cold dread settled in Kara's stomach.

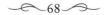

"You hid on the ship because you were trying to get *away* from the grimoire," Kara said. "And I brought it on board. I ruined everything."

"That's not true. Now I know that—"

"Why did you hide so long? Why didn't you just come to me from the very beginning?"

"I meant to. Only then I saw you with the grimoire and became very confused. I thought you had stolen it for your own use, which is ridiculous, since you—you know. Can't use it."

"But the grimoire convinced you otherwise."

"It wanted me to hurt you. I kept hearing it. The whispering in my ear. I didn't trust myself, what I would do, so I hid in the cargo hold and waited for things to get better, for me to be myself again. And then Coralis attacked and I knew I had to use the grimoire and help. I had no choice anymore."

"I'm so sorry," Kara said. "I didn't know. If I had just left the grimoire back on De'Noran . . ."

"We would all be dead! Why do you think I was thanking you?"

"I thought it was because you knew I was trying to help you."

Safi smiled. "That's nice too, but mostly because now I know what a fool I was to try to escape the grimoire in the first place. It would be completely selfish not to use my powers. Rygoth is gathering witches to her cause. I saw it."

In addition to being able to use a grimoire, Safi had another special gift: she sometimes saw glimpses of the future. She had foretold Kara's arrival in Kala Malta. She had witnessed the destruction Rygoth would bring to the World.

"What did you see?" Kara asked.

"A tall banner bearing a double-fanged spider. Rygoth marching at the head of a vast procession of witches, each holding a grimoire from Kala Malta. She hasn't gathered all of them yet, but once she does no one will be able to defeat her. We need to stop Rygoth now, and you can't do that on your own. You need me."

"So you're just going to keep casting spells? Haven't you learned anything? Don't you realize how dangerous that is?"

"Of course! That's why I'm so glad you're going to teach me how to control my grimoire."

Safi clapped her hands together and giggled.

"You can't be serious," said Kara.

"Who better?" asked Safi. "Before you learned how to use your *wexari* powers, you had total control over your grimoire."

"That's not true. I never got the best of the original grimoire I used, the one that belonged to my Aunt Abby. It was only when I used my mother's grimoire that I was sort of able to—"

"That's right! Even more reason for you to teach me. Your mother was able to control her grimoire for years."

Kara shook her head.

"I'm not my mother. I'm not even a witch anymore."

Before Safi could argue the point there came a soft tapping at the door. "Are you two finished talking about girl stuff in there?" Taff asked, and Kara couldn't help but smile when she opened the door and saw him standing there empty-handed. Her brilliant brother had known from the beginning that she didn't need water or blankets.

"You have to come up on deck," he said, yanking them forward. "People are singing and dancing! It's still pretty far away, but you can finally see land! It's *everywhere*. The World, Kara! *The World!*"

The sun had risen by the time they finally docked, shedding light upon a gargantuan landmass that stretched across the horizon like an anchored sky. *The Thickety was but a mere copse of trees compared to this*, Kara thought, feeling suddenly small and insignificant. She led Shadowdancer down the gangplank of the *Wayfinder* and paused before the shore.

I can't believe I'm really here.

All the children of De'Noran had wondered what the World might be like, and Kara had been no different—but actually *going* there had been a distant, impossible dream. Yet here she was. She took a first, hesitant step onto the beach, fearing her foot might pass through the sand like clouds. The sand was just sand, however, the trees just trees. Indeed, the gull-populated beach looked almost identical to De'Noran's. It was only as Kara regarded her surroundings more carefully that she began to notice the differences: winter-bare trees whose branches folded inward like umbrellas, strangely shaped seashells that cracked beneath her feet, a foreign smell in the air just a shade sweeter than pine needles.

The real difference, however, was the contours of the World itself, not flat like De'Noran but rising and falling in every direction as far as the eye could see. The Thickety had been terrifying, every shadow holding the promise of violent death, but the vastness of the World was unsettling in its own right. Kara was reminded of a time before her mother's death, when she had wandered away and found herself on a part of the island completely unfamiliar to her—the pure, childhood terror of getting lost.

This place is big enough to swallow us whole, she thought.

Taff ran past her, doing a cartwheel across the beach; if he shared any of Kara's fears it didn't show on his beaming face. "We're here," he said, picking up a handful of sand and watching it spill through his fingers. "We're really here!"

"It's hard to believe, isn't it?" Kara asked, mussing his hair.

She thought of her best friend back on De'Noran, a boy named Lucas who had been sold to the Children of the Fold when he was just a baby. He had lived life in virtual servitude as a Clearer, cutting and burning the growth of the Thickety before it overtook the village, but had always dreamed of traveling to the World and finding

his real family. After the death of Fen'de Stone, Lucas had seized the opportunity to do just that. This had been several months ago, and he had never been far from her thoughts. She found it comforting, knowing he was out there—that at least she had one friend in the World.

Perhaps our paths will cross. Stranger things have happened.

Burly, unshaven men dragged crates of supplies down the gangplank while Captain Clement shouted orders from below. Safi, who had risen late, approached them now, twin pigtails swinging from side to side. Inside her satchel the white grimoire pressed against her hip.

"I never even dreamed I would see other parts of the Thickety outside of Kala Malta," she exclaimed, "and now I'm in *the World*! It's so exciting! So where's this school we have to find? What was it called again? Sablethorn?"

"Shh," Kara said. *How did Taff talk me into telling her everything? She means well, but she has a loose tongue.* "Rygoth has spies everywhere. That's how she knew I was on the ship."

"Don't worry," replied Safi, slapping her satchel. "I cast a spell this morning that should take care of all that. Anyone tries to eavesdrop on our conversations, all they'll hear is gibberish."

"You cast a spell?" Kara asked.

Safi looked down at her feet like a schoolchild just caught copying answers off her neighbor's slate.

"Just a little one."

"No spells. Not unless I'm with you."

"But it was harmless."

"*This* time," said Kara. "Besides, you need to conserve your pages. You'll use them up faster than you think. Trust me."

Safi smiled.

"I thought you weren't going to teach me," she said playfully.

"I'm not," Kara said. "I'm just offering some helpful advice."

They gathered their belongings. Kara hung two large

sacks filled with pans and blankets and other supplies over Shadowdancer's back and helped the smaller children mount the mare. "That too much weight for you, girl?" she whispered in the horse's ear. Shadowdancer snorted, as though Kara had insulted her by even suggesting it.

They trotted away from the bustle of the disembarking passengers toward the trees at the edge of the sand. Some men and women watched them go with interest, but most were intent on their own concerns. The World was new to them as well.

"Hold up!" shouted a voice behind them.

Captain Clement, somewhat out of breath, had run the length of the beach to catch up with them. "I wanted to tell you something before you went trouncing off all unawares," he said. "There's a town west of here. Less than two days by foot. One of my men saw it through his spyglass before we docked."

"Are you going there as well?" Kara asked.

Captain Clement shook his head. "If the old maps are correct, there's a large city due north. Nine days' journey, maybe ten. Depends on how wagon-friendly the roads are. And how safe."

"But it will be a lot safer without me around, right? Because at least Rygoth will leave you alone."

"Exactly," Captain Clement said. "That's why we need to part paths." Kara wasn't sure she would ever like the man, but she appreciated his lack of pretense. "These people are my responsibility, Kara. My first duty is to them." Clement turned toward Safi. "I would be doing Breem a disservice if I did not ask you one more time—won't you please come with us? You are of Kala Malta, child. You belong with your people. Perhaps your father will join us soon. He must be out of his mind with worry."

This struck a chord with Safi, which Kara suspected had been Clement's intention. The girl missed Breem deeply and was plagued with guilt for abandoning him without so much as a good-bye.

"I left him a letter explaining everything," she said softly.

"He doesn't want words. He wants his daughter."

"My path lies with Kara and Taff. There are terrible things coming. I've *seen* them, and I must do what I can to stop them. Father will understand."

Clement scoffed. "You might know a lot about magic, but you know nothing about fathers. I could make you come, you know."

Safi's hand strayed to her satchel.

"You could try," she said, a dark expression clouding her face.

Captain Clement coughed into his hand and then strode back to his people, leaving the three children alone in the World.

They walked along the beach, Taff stuffing his pockets with shells at every conceivable moment, until they found a set of stone steps crudely chipped into the rocks. The climb was steep (particularly for Shadowdancer, who did not like the feeling of anything other than dirt beneath her hooves), and by the time they reached the top, Kara's legs burned. With hands on knees she took stock of their new location: a large road stretching out in either direction for as long as she could see.

"Let's find this Sablethorn," Kara said.

Taff reached into his sack, pulling out a porcelain rabbit riding a bicycle. There might have been an extra chip or two in its long ears but other than that it looked no different than the first time they had used it to guide their way through the Thickety.

"Mr. Rabbit!" Safi exclaimed. "I love this little guy."

"Mr. Rabbit?" Taff asked.

"Well, what do *you* call him?"

"Anything that's not 'Mr. Rabbit.'"

Taff placed the toy on the ground and scratched a line in the sand, so he would be able to calculate how far it traveled from its original distance, and then whispered

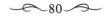

"Sablethorn" into the rabbit's ear. After a brief hesitation the bicycle began to shake rapidly, its metal components vibrating like the wings of a hummingbird. A spoke from its tire came undone from the hub and *pinged* into the air.

"What's happening?" Kara asked.

"I don't know," Taff said. "It looks like it's trying to move, only something's not letting it."

Kara bent forward for a closer look. Indeed, the rabbit seemed to be straining against an immovable force, like someone trying to push a boulder uphill. The bicycle inched forward and a thin crack split open the rabbit's right boot.

"Tell it to stop," Kara said. "Hurry!"

Taff was leaning down to whisper in the rabbit's ear when the entire toy shattered into porcelain dust and broken wire.

"No!" he exclaimed, falling to his knees. A tire rolled past him and he caught it between two fingers.

Safi placed her hand on Taff's shoulder. "What happened?"

"I'm not sure," he said, staring down at the little tire in his hands. He was near tears but fighting it. "If I had to guess, I'd say that someone doesn't want us to find Sablethorn."

After Taff had swept the remnants of the rabbit and its bicycle into his sack, they decided to head for the town Captain Clement had suggested. Kara supposed that was as good an idea as any, certainly much better than just randomly picking a direction and walking. Fen'de Stone had done an excellent job concealing precise details of the World from his Children, but if what little Kara had heard were true it would take years to cross from one end to the other. There were entire cities the size of the Thickety, as well as impassable mountains, rivers, and deserts.

Any destination—even one suggested by Captain Clement—was better than none at all.

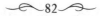

They followed the road west along the cliff, silty ground crunching beneath their feet. As they walked, Kara began to notice subtle differences between De'Noran and this mysterious new land. Flowers with heart-shaped petals, yellow birds with calls as low as foghorns. Nothing magical, nothing like the Thickety. Just *different*. Other sights weren't quite as easy to explain. A gully filled with brackish liquid smooth and shimmery to the touch. Hunks of oddly shaped metal corroding in the sun. And, strangest of all, a flexible tube dangling from a series of evenly spaced metal poles rising to a point just below the treetops. The translucent tube looked like it had water sloshing around inside of it, and ran parallel to the road for several hours before veering through the trees and out of sight.

Into one of the metal poles someone had etched the word *SWOOP*.

"What is *that*?" Safi asked. She was still new to riding a horse, and nearly slipped from Shadowdancer's back as she pointed toward the tube.

Taff's eyes blazed with curiosity. "I'm not sure. Maybe it transports water from one place to another?"

"Then why build it so high?" Safi asked.

"To keep the water away from animals?" Taff suggested. He turned to Kara. "What do you think?"

Kara gave him a playful nudge between the shoulder blades, spurring him onward.

"I think if we try to puzzle out all the mysteries of this place we'll never get anywhere," she said. "Let's keep moving."

At day's end they followed a path down to the beach and spread their blankets on the sand. Kara was exhausted, but as soon as she stopped moving a more pressing issue arose; despite her Kala Maltan cloak, lined with the warm fur of some unfortunate Thickety creature, she quickly began to shiver. The night's temperature, already frigid, danced on the edge of a precipice and might plunge to dangerous levels while they slept.

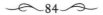

"We need to build a fire," Kara said.

Safi already had her grimoire open.

"Let me take care of that," she said, smiling at the spell revealed only to her.

"No," Kara said. She reached over and shut the grimoire. "Help me gather wood instead."

"But the spell is *right there*. All I have to do is say it!"

"Get some of those beach weeds too. They're dry enough to use for tinder."

With a look of profound disappointment, Safi slid her grimoire back inside its satchel.

While the girls built the fire Taff attempted to catch a crab lingering along the ocean's edge, but the invisible pellet from his slingshot ricocheted off its shell and the crab scuttled back into the ocean. Instead they dined on hardtack and boiled oats, along with a pot of bitter coffee. Kara, who no longer ate meat, gave Taff and Safi the last of the jerky.

When the meal was done, Kara scrubbed their utensils

clean in the ocean and lay on her blanket. She looked over at Taff, already asleep, his rapid snores complementing the lapping of ocean waves. *Pleasant dreams, brother.* Kara took out Sordyr's letter, intending to study it further before retiring for the night, and heard the soft shifting of sand as Safi knelt next to her.

"Why didn't you let me use magic to keep us warm?" Safi asked.

"There's no need to waste a page on something that can easily be done without magic. That's what the grimoire wants you to do. The more spells you cast, the faster you'll get to the Last Spell."

Safi pulled at her pigtails, a recent habit she had developed whenever she was thinking hard about something.

"And any witch who uses the last page goes to the Well of Witches," Safi said, remembering what Kara had told her in Kala Malta. "Where their souls will be drained to power other grimoires."

"Exactly."

"What do you think it's like?" she asked, staring into the fire.

Kara carefully put Sordyr's letter away and sat up, folding her legs beneath her. The ocean, infinite and black, rolled toward the horizon in undulating waves.

"I don't know," she said.

Kara hadn't spent much time trying to picture the Well of Witches as a physical location. The dark nature of the place was such that picturing it at all seemed to invite misfortune; she would no sooner ponder its inner workings than imagine the death of her brother.

I can't really be thinking of going there. Can I?

"Kara?" Safi asked, a look of concern crossing her face.

"You won't need to worry about what it's like," said Kara, "if you never cast your Last Spell. And to make sure that happens, you need to stop thinking about the grimoire as a helpful tool. It's not. It's your enemy."

"But it helped us on the ship."

"And also helped itself in the process. How many spells

did you cast in order to stop Coralis? How many pages closer to the Last Spell did it take you?"

Safi nodded carefully, mulling this over.

"It wants to be used."

"It *needs* to be used," Kara said. "Witches are its life-blood. All the spells, all the power—it's nothing but a giant trap. That's why you must never waste a spell. Each page is precious, and should only be used when all other options have been exhausted."

Safi grinned. "You're teaching me."

"No, I'm not. I'm just telling you about some things I learned."

"Also known as teaching."

Safi giggled, and Taff turned over in his sleep, mumbling some words of mild annoyance.

Kara smiled despite herself.

"Okay," Kara said. "We'll try *one* thing."

"A lesson?"

"If you want to call it that."

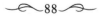

Safi clapped her hands together in anticipation.

"This isn't meant to be fun," Kara warned.

"Of course not."

Kara placed her elbows on her knees and rubbed her temples. She should not be the one teaching Safi how to use a grimoire. She was too young, and hardly an expert with the grimoire herself, and . . . not even a witch anymore! She wished Mary Kettle were here, or, better yet, Mother.

But they're not. It has to be you.

Kara took a few moments to think carefully before she spoke again, wanting to choose the right words.

"My mother used her grimoire for years and years without it ever turning her evil," Kara said with a certain degree of pride. "She was only a few spells from the end when she died, but I have a feeling she could have made those last the rest of her life. And she never hurt anyone. She was somehow able to overcome the grimoire's influence and live life the way she wanted."

"Was her grimoire different than others?" Safi asked. "Maybe some are good and——"

"That's what I thought at first too. But Mary Kettle says that all grimoires are evil by nature."

"Why?"

It was such a simple question that Kara was amazed she had never thought of it before. Why *were* all grimoires evil? The first grimoire had been a gift for an unhappy princess. Sordyr, its creator, had never intended to introduce such a dark force into the world.

So what happened?

"And why can't boys use them?" Safi asked. "I've always wondered about that one too." She picked up a shell and held it to her ear. "Not that I *mind*, of course. Girls are better."

"Taff can use Mary's toys. That's a type of magic."

"Sort of. The *real* magic is in the toys themselves, though. Taff can't cast a spell. No boy can."

"What about Sordyr?" Kara asked. "Before he lost his

powers his magic was as powerful as anyone's."

"Because he's a *wexari*. The rules are different for them. But even with all that power he *still* couldn't use a grimoire." With a single finger Safi scrawled the outline of a book in the sand. "Only girls. Why? There has to be a reason."

Kara agreed that it was curious, but there were more pressing matters to consider right now. *Safi is insistent upon using the grimoire. How can I keep her from hurting herself?*

"Let's get back to my mother for now," Kara said. "I've thought about this a lot, and I think she was able to control the grimoire by doing two things. The first was using it as infrequently as possible, and only when she had to. That's how she made it last so long. The second . . ." Kara paused, collecting her thoughts. "Remember how I said my mother disguised her grimoire?"

"By making it look like a regular school notebook. That was brilliant, by the way, casting a spell on her own grimoire like that."

Kara blushed as though the compliment had been intended for her.

"Yes—and it wasn't a spell the grimoire would have wanted her to cast. Its main goal is to be used—that's how it *survives*—so being camouflaged like that would have been the last thing it wanted. My mother must have *forced* it to cast such a spell. She bent the grimoire to her will, and I'm sure that wasn't the only time. I think doing that helped her keep its evil in check."

Safi grinned. "Like showing it who's in charge."

"Exactly. You think you could do that?"

"Make my grimoire look different?"

"Not necessarily," Kara said. "Though I suppose that could work." She tapped the open page of the grimoire. "Is the spell to keep us warm still there?"

Safi nodded, and Kara swallowed an unexpected pang of jealousy; to her, of course, the page looked completely blank.

"Change it," said Kara.

"To what?"

"Doesn't matter. Just exert your control over the grimoire. Make it do what *you* want it to do."

"But I thought you said not to waste spells."

"This isn't a waste. This is training."

Safi smiled.

"I've got a good idea."

Spreading her thin fingers over the open page, Safi closed her eyes. Her eyelids fluttered quickly, as though she were deeply asleep.

Ocean waves rolled over the surf. Fire sputtered and snapped.

"I don't think it's working," Safi said. "It doesn't want to let . . ."

"Try harder."

Safi's small chest pulsed inward and outward with deep, rapid breaths. She grunted softly from the base of her throat. At first Kara thought it was simply exertion, but then she realized that it was words—though not from

a language ever meant to be spoken.

Safi's eyes flew open.

"Did it work?" she asked.

Kara gave her a questioning look.

"Your powers!" exclaimed Safi. "I cast a spell to restore your powers! Did it work? *Something* happened."

A faint hope rose in Kara's chest.

Could it be that easy?

Kara didn't feel any different, but what did that mean? She hadn't tried any magic yet! She reached out with her thoughts, seeing if there were any animals in the area that might respond.

Nothing.

But it was the grimoire that cast the spell, Kara thought, trying not to let disappointment overwhelm her. *So maybe it can only return my ability to use a grimoire, not my* wexari *powers.*

Kara picked up Safi's grimoire and riffled through the pages, looking for the black whirlpools that would prove

she was seeing through the eyes of a witch again.

Blank, blank, blank.

"It didn't work," Kara said.

"Are you sure? Because I did *something*."

And then they both felt the increased ferocity of the campfire's blaze and saw its magical mauve hue.

"The fire," Safi said, frowning down at the book. "I cast the spell it wanted me to. I didn't even know." She grunted with frustration. "Let me try one more time. . . ."

"I think that's enough for tonight."

"Just one . . . It'll work this time. . . . I can feel it. . . ."

"Safi," Kara said.

She started to take the grimoire from Safi's hands but the girl pulled it away. "It's *mine!*" she screamed.

Silence stretched between them.

"I'm sorry," Safi said, throwing the grimoire on the sand. "I just . . . lost myself for a moment."

"I know," Kara said. "It's to be expected. It happened to me as well. It was only at the very end that I learned how to control its power."

Safi looked up, the raging campfire reflected in her terrified green eyes.

"But what if I'm not like you?" she asked. "What if I'm not strong enough?"

"You're going to have to be," Kara said, smiling slightly. "You're the only witch we've got."

FIVE

Their journey the following day was uneventful, but after the sun fell past its midday apex a large field opened before them. Rows of tall metal towers stretched across the horizon, each with a perfect circle of ten metal blades extending from its center.

Taff gasped in amazement and slid off Shadowdancer.

"What are *those?*" Safi asked. "Are they magic?"

"No!" Taff exclaimed. "They're windmills!"

"Are you sure?" asked Kara. They had a single windmill on De'Noran, squat and wooden and nothing like

the behemoths standing before her now.

"Definitely," Taff said. "Whoever built them used sheets of flattened metal instead of sails but it's the same idea." His body trembled with excitement, and Kara realized that these wonders constructed by human hands enthralled him in a way that magic never could. "I wonder what they're using them for," he said.

"I don't think they're being used at all anymore," replied Safi. "Look how *old* they are."

Blinded by her initial wonder, Kara had overlooked the copper patches covering each windmill like a rash. A strong breeze swirled through the field but most blades remained motionless, rusted to their hubs. Those that did turn emitted a horrible grinding noise.

"Sorry, Taff," Kara said, tugging at his ear.

She had assumed that her brother would be disappointed, but instead his eyes opened even wider than before.

"Are you kidding?" he asked. "If this is their old stuff, I

can't wait to see what their new stuff looks like!"

Safi playfully poked Taff in the ribs, which she knew was his most ticklish point. It should have been an innocent enough moment, but Kara saw the way Safi's hand strayed to her satchel afterward, just to make sure the grimoire was still there. An unconscious reflex, like brushing her hair away from her eyes.

"You want me to carry that for a while?" Kara asked. "It looks heavy."

Safi's smile faltered for only a moment.

"I've got it."

They continued west, the windmills looming to either side of them now, each footfall landing in a bladed shadow. Safi remained astride Shadowdancer, but Taff skipped along the road, his eyes flickering everywhere, not wanting to miss a single thing. Kara was glad to see her brother in such high spirits, but it was hard for her to share his enthusiasm. The rusty windmills were so foreign-looking that walking past them felt more like a dream than reality. She had seen unexplainable things in the Thickety, of course, but that had been different; in a land governed by magic, the unexplainable was expected.

But this was reality. This was supposed to be *familiar*.

I have no idea what to expect, Kara thought. The enormity of leaving De'Noran for the first time had been lost in more pressing concerns. Now, as though floodgates had opened, a stream of questions rushed through her mind: *Will the people here look like us? Will we speak the same language? Do they have schools? What do they eat? Do they hate witches?*

The extent of Kara's ignorance pressed down on her like dirt on a coffin lid.

Will anybody here be willing to help us?

They were close to reaching their destination, but Kara had never felt more lost.

It was dusk when they arrived at the town, its name carved into a placard that hung from a simple post by the side of the road. Though the letters were not quite as formally shaped as the ones Kara had been taught by Master Blackwood, she was able to read them just fine.

"Nye's Landing," she said.

The town cradled a kidney-shaped stretch of beach where large fishing boats bobbed up and down in peaceful repose. Ocean mist stretched its fingers between stilt houses sitting just beyond the clutch of high tide. From a cliff overlooking the beach, the beams of a lighthouse guided any stragglers home.

"Where are all the people?" Safi asked.

"It's a fishing village," Kara said. "They rise before dawn and go to bed early."

"*This* early?"

"I'm sure there'll be someone who can help us."

They crossed the beach and entered the main part of the town. It was much larger than Kara had anticipated, a mist-hazed labyrinth of narrow cobblestone lanes and simple buildings.

But no people.

The clack of Shadowdancer's hooves mingled with the pleasant tinkling of wind chimes that hung from many houses. The residences were mostly dark, though faint light leaked from a few of them. Kara thought she saw a face at a window, gazing at them with curiosity, but it quickly dropped out of sight when she turned in its direction.

"What's that?" Taff asked, pointing to a blue light floating in the distance.

Following the beacon through the mist, they found the source of the light to be a tall pole with a spherical glass enclosure at its top. Inside the sphere, water swirled, giving off a luminous glow the color of the sky.

"It's pretty," said Safi.

A second light appeared in the distance, and the children journeyed deeper into the town to find it. Just as they discovered a sphere identical to the first one, a third light appeared. They set off after it. The lane narrowed, forcing them to walk in single file, and then expanded again, opening into a large quad that Kara assumed was the center of town.

There a man wearing a knit cap stood before one of the poles, as yet unlit. From the ground in front of him emerged a black pipe ending in a curved handle. It resembled a well pump, except there was a hole at its peak and no spout from which to draw water.

"What're you youngins doing out?" the man asked. "It's near dark!"

"We're travelers," Kara said, "looking for a place to spend the night. Is there an——" She searched her mind for the word, which she vaguely remembered being used in some of the later stories in the Path. *When Timoth Clen traveled alone, searching for the Last Creed. The places he stayed . . .*

"You looking for an inn?" the man asked.

Kara nodded.

"Right behind you," he said. "Didn't you see? There's a bed on the sign in case you can't read. Now get."

Bending down next to the pumping device, the man reached into his pocket and withdrew something that looked like a blue marble between his thumb and index finger. With a quick, practiced movement he dropped the tiny object into the hole at the top of the pipe and pumped the handle up and down. Within the glass sphere the water bubbled and swirled. The marble rose to its center and began to dissolve, spreading plumes of sky blue through the clear water.

"What are you doing?" Taff asked.

"My job, boy. Gotta swirl the town lights. You ask me, it's a waste of good glorbs since the light don't stop her from coming, but the Mistrals ordered it to be done, and I ain't one to argue with the Mistrals."

With the marble now totally dissolved, the water inside the sphere began to emanate a soft glow that brightened and dimmed in rhythm with the man's pumping. Kara could hear a low drone that wasn't there before.

"How'd you do that?" Taff asked in amazement. "What

did you put inside? Is that what made the water glow?"

The man shook his head in disbelief, as though Taff had just asked him whether or not he should use his feet to walk. "Like I said, the inn's right there. Be patient with Mrs. Galt. She's a good woman, but she's suffered a loss, like most of us. Go now, get inside before they come."

"Who?" Safi asked.

"The unghosts," the man said, and walked off into the mist.

Several minutes later, after Kara had finally dragged a reluctant Taff away from the glorb-light ("But I don't know how it *works* yet!"), they opened the door of the inn and entered a room that was warm but in complete disarray. Unwashed plates sat on yellowing wicker tables. Grime matted the floor. Flies encircled a glob of congealed food.

Behind a long counter stood a woman. Her eyes,

half-concealed behind a wild tangle of blond hair, were swollen and rimmed with red. She gave no indication that she had noticed their arrival; all her attention was focused on a spot past them.

"Hello?" Kara asked.

The woman did not reply. Kara turned around, curious to see what could dominate her attention to the point that she did not notice three guests enter her inn.

There was only a window, cloudy with condensation.

"Mrs. Galt?" Taff tried, waving his hand in front of her eyes.

The woman jumped.

"Yes? Who are you?"

"We were hoping to get lodging for the night," Kara said.

"Right," Mrs. Galt said. She noticed, as though for the first time, the state of the room, and flushed with embarrassment. "I'm sorry about all this. Usually things are in a much better state, but . . ." Her eyes passed from one child to the next and she placed two hands on the counter. "Where are your parents?" she asked.

"They're a day behind us," Kara said, maintaining eye contact in order to make the lie more believable. "In a wagon." And then, realizing that this woman would never believe Safi was a relation, added, "Our parents and Safi's parents—this here is Safi—are traveling together. We broke a wheel, though, and the grown-ups decided it would be safer if we children traveled ahead. This way we could sleep in a town and not camp out, the weather being cold and such."

From the corner of her eye, Kara saw Taff fight back a smile. He loved it when his sister was mischievous.

"I wish you had come earlier," Mrs. Galt said, her voice shaky but kind. "I would have sent you back to your parents. This is no place for children, especially at night. Are you hungry? I'm sure I can scrounge up some salted fish and milk."

"I'm afraid we have no coin, ma'am," Kara said. "For

the food or the lodging. But we're not expecting to stay for free. I have items I can trade, or I can certainly help clean—"

Mrs. Galt waved her words away.

"Nonsense. I wouldn't think of charging you. Your safety is the most important thing. The most . . . important . . ."

Mrs. Galt's eyes, filled with a fierce and terrible longing, had strayed once again to the empty window.

"Ma'am?" Kara asked. "Are you all right?"

"I have to go," Mrs. Galt said, backing away. "Take the first door at the top of the stairs. Everything is ready for you. I'll bring you dinner soon."

She ran out of the room.

"What was *that* all about?" Taff whispered.

"I don't know," Kara said, examining the window. She noticed that the condensation had cleared in one small area, as though an unseen figure had breathed upon the glass. When she peered through the window, however, the misty street was empty.

Their room was barely large enough to contain the two small beds fitted beneath a simple painting of the lighthouse, but it was far cleaner than the lobby, for which Kara was grateful. Mrs. Galt delivered their dinner with a soft knock and hustled away before they opened the door. While eating, the children made plans for the next day. First priority was to find someone who knew the quickest way to Sablethorn.

"What about these unghosts the man mentioned?" Safi asked. "And the strange way Mrs. Galt was acting. It seems like these people might need our help."

She saw the way Safi's hands twitched as she said this, itching for a reason to use the grimoire.

"We have our own problems to solve," said Kara. "Too many, in fact."

"But aren't you *curious*?"

"Our father has only a little time left before we lose him forever. We can't allow ourselves to get distracted."

Which effectively ended all discussion, of course. Kara didn't like the heartless sound of her own words—especially in light of Mrs. Galt's kindness—but someone had to say them.

Taff and Safi each claimed a bed while Kara spread a blanket across the floor, angling her body as close to the window as possible and unfolding Sordyr's letter. It was difficult to make out the words by moonlight but that was all right; by this point she almost knew them by heart.

"You're always looking at that thing," Safi said. "Haven't you read it already?"

"Some parts I'm still piecing together. Sordyr's handwriting is terrible. And the ink is smudged in places."

"Maybe he was out of practice," said Safi. "He'd been a Forest Demon with branch hands for ages. It probably feels strange to have fingers again."

Taff giggled.

"What?" Safi asked.

"We have the best conversations."

"There're a lot of words here I don't understand," Kara said. "Perhaps I never learned them, or maybe they're old words that we don't use anymore. So I always feel like I figure out something new every time I read it."

"Like what?" Taff asked.

"You need to go to sleep. Both of you."

"I'm not tired," Safi said.

"Me either," said Taff. "Tell us a story!"

Kara smiled to herself, remembering the countless nights she had tucked Taff into bed, the ritual haggling over how many stories she would tell. It was a comfort to know that some things never changed.

"Let's see," Kara said, flipping through the pages of the letter. Small, cramped cursive covered every fragment of white space, front and back. "He writes about what happened before he made the grimoire for Evangeline. Back when Sablethorn was still a school and Phadeen hadn't yet been corrupted and changed into the Well of Witches. Magic had been good, and pure, and valued."

Kara paused, still finding the existence of such a world difficult to believe; it felt like a dream to her. "Rygoth and Sordyr were Sablethorn's most promising students, under the direct tutelage of Minoth Dravania himself, the headmaster."

"Are you telling me that Sordyr and Rygoth were *friends*?" Taff asked.

"Actually, I think they were a little more than that."

"Huh?"

"Eww," said Safi.

"Minoth sounds like he was a great teacher. He loved to bring students to Phadeen and create puzzles that they could solve only through the use of magic. Sordyr really looked up to him. But Rygoth didn't feel the same. She thought Minoth didn't trust her."

"Can't imagine why," said Taff.

"Things grew worse and worse between them. Rygoth kept breaking the rules, trying more dangerous spells— forbidden magic—with Sordyr covering for her. It all came to a head when she refused to participate in something called the Sundering."

"What's that?" Taff asked.

"A trial that every student in Sablethorn was required to pass in order to become a full *wexari*."

Safi sat up in bed. "You mean like a test of their powers? To make sure they were good enough?"

"I don't know. Sordyr doesn't go into specifics. He sometimes forgets to explain terms and phrases that must have seemed so common to him. But he made a sketch of the"—Kara riffled through the pages of the letter until she found what she was looking for—"*queth'nondra*. It's where the final part of the Sundering took place."

She showed them a charcoal drawing of a long, wavy tunnel leading up to a small dome covered with hexagonal tiles.

"It looks like a turtle," Taff said.

"The *queth'nondra* was Sablethorn's most important building," Kara said. "A time-honored tradition of—"

"You're right!" Safi said. "A turtle with a really long tail. It's so cute!"

Kara folded the page away.

"Inside the *queth'nondra*," she said, "which does *not* look like a turtle, prospective *wexari* were given the final task of the Sundering—which didn't really matter to Rygoth, since she refused to do any of it."

"Why?" Safi asked. "Rygoth may be evil, but she's an amazing witch. She should have been able to pass any test easily."

"Sordyr doesn't say, but apparently refusing to take it was such a big deal that Rygoth was forced to leave Sablethorn altogether. She begged Sordyr to come with her, but he refused. He couldn't just betray Minoth and give up his dream of becoming a *wexari*. It broke his heart to abandon her, though."

"Why?" asked Taff. "Rygoth's so *bad*!"

"Maybe she wasn't really bad, not yet," said Kara. "Or maybe it didn't matter to Sordyr. He cared for her."

Taff shook his head in a manner that indicated he would never understand grown-ups.

"What happened next?" asked Safi.

"Years passed. As soon as Sordyr graduated from Sablethorn he searched the World for Rygoth, finally finding her at a place called Dolrose Castle. She had become the king's adviser there. Sordyr hoped they could be friends again, but Rygoth wouldn't even let him through the castle gates. He still refused to give up, though, and when the king held a competition for a toy that could make his daughter, Evangeline, happy, Sordyr saw it as an opportunity to impress Rygoth and win her back."

"So he made the first grimoire," said Safi.

Kara smiled. "It's kind of romantic, in a way."

Taff stared at her in disbelief. "Except that the grimoire was evil and caused the deaths of everyone in the castle."

"I meant the part leading up to it, silly. Sordyr really loved her. He never gave up." Noting Taff's confused expression, Kara added, "You'll understand when you're older. Right now—bed. Both of you. No discussion."

Within minutes both children were sound asleep. Kara's own eyes were beginning to close when she heard a door squeak. Rising quietly so she didn't wake the others, Kara pressed her face against the partially open window and saw Mrs. Galt leaving the inn. She held a wooden boat in her hands.

"Liam," Mrs. Galt whispered. "Liam. I saw you at the window. Where did you go? They said it's dangerous if I don't ignore you, but I can't do it anymore. Mommy's here, Liam!"

Mrs. Galt held the boat forward in two trembling hands.

"I brought your favorite toy, Liam! I haven't forgotten about you!"

Mrs. Galt jerked her head to the right, as though she had heard something, then hurried out of sight.

Kara pressed her forehead against the cold glass of the window.

She's just taking a walk, that's all. It's not your problem. No need to get involved.

She let us stay here for free. She fed us.

She's in danger.

With a sigh of resignation, Kara slipped on her cloak and made her way out the front door.

Mrs. Galt was nowhere to be seen, but Kara could hear her footfalls in the graveyard-silent night. The moon had ducked behind a fold of clouds. Only the blue glow of the glorb-lights provided any guidance.

Kara paused at an intersection, unsure of which turn to make, listening carefully for the *clack-clack-clack* of Mrs. Galt's boots. The mist had partially dissipated but she could still taste salt in the air.

"See me?" asked a girl's voice behind her.

Kara twisted in the direction of the unexpected sound. She saw only cobblestones beneath swirling threads of mist.

"Hello?" she asked.

"See me?"

The girl sounded close, practically right in front of Kara, but that was impossible. There was no one there.

"Where are you?" Kara asked, scanning the empty road.

"See me?"

"I don't. I'm sorry."

"Look," whispered the voice, plaintive and soft. She sounded no older than six. "All alone. Scared. See me."

Pushing her cloak behind her back, Kara knelt so that she was at the level of a small child and looked carefully into the mist. At first, there was nothing, but then Kara heard faint breathing just in front of her, felt the tingling of warm breath on her chin. She smelled wet sand and sunbaked skin.

Gradually, a shape evolved into visibility.

It was just a faint image at first, an idea of a girl hovering in and out of existence. With each reappearance, however, new details emerged: curly auburn hair festooned with shells and ribbons, a yellow dress splattered with mud, coffee-brown eyes.

"There you are," Kara said.

The girl smiled.

"See you!" she exclaimed, and grabbed Kara's wrist.

A searing pain that seemed to surpass her skin and drive itself into the very marrow of her bone sent Kara sprawling to the stones. She examined her wrist, expecting the skin to be scorched red, but instead there was only a swollen bruise shaped like four little fingers and a thumb.

"See me!" the girl exclaimed. "See me!"

Her image had begun to fade while Kara examined her wrist. When she looked up at the ghostly shape again, however, the girl grew more substantial and took a step in Kara's direction.

Kara quickly looked away.

"See me?"

She could feel the little girl standing next to her. Hear her breathing.

They told Mrs. Galt to ignore her son. That's why. If you don't pay attention to them . . .

"See me?" the girl asked again, with growing desperation.

. . . *they can't see you. Or harm you. The unghosts. You have to pretend . . .*

"I'm cold."

. . . *they're not there. Close your heart to them.*

"See me, see me, see me. . . ."

The little girl's voice was growing softer, fading away. Kara closed her eyes. She knew she had to ignore the voice, but it was difficult, for she sensed no malice from the girl. The unghost had not hurt Kara intentionally.

She had only wanted to be seen.

Finally, the voice stopped. Kara opened her eyes. The girl was gone.

Somewhere in the night, Mrs. Galt began to scream.

SIX

Kara scrambled through the street, slipping once on mist-dampened cobblestones but quickly regaining her balance. She turned a corner and Mrs. Galt lay before her, slumped against the side of a small stone building. A line of hand-shaped bruises ran up her arms and legs.

"Stop, Liam!" the woman exclaimed. "You have to stop! I know you don't mean it, but you're hurting me!"

Kara saw a small handprint appear on Mrs. Galt's chin, and then, right above it, the bruise-colored imprint of a kiss. Mrs. Galt didn't scream this time, but her lips trembled.

Kara ran to the woman's side and helped her to her feet.

"Let's get back to the inn," Kara said.

Supporting the woman's weight, she half dragged her down the road. Lights had begun to appear in nearby windows. Kara heard a bell toll in the distance and, farther off, the *clop-clop-clop* of approaching horses.

"I just wanted to bring him his boat. They love toys. The children. The *unghosts*. Helps them remember what it was like before. But it's me he *really* wants. His mother. He stands outside my window and begs for me to hold him and I can't say no anymore!"

Mrs. Galt looked over her shoulder.

"He's still there," she whispered. "He's *calling* me!"

"You mustn't acknowledge him."

"You're not a mother," she said. "You don't understand."

Pulling away from Kara, Mrs. Galt started back toward Liam. Her eyes were resolute, as though she had finally made a decision long debated in her mind.

"Mrs. Galt!" Kara exclaimed. "Don't!"

"It's all right, Liam," she said, her voice calm. "Don't cry. I'll come with you. Forever. Just like you want me to."

She opened her arms wide.

From an adjoining street the figure of a boy dashed through the mist. Something long and white flashed and Mrs. Galt crumpled to the ground. Kara ran to the woman's side. Her eyes were closed and there was a large welt swelling on the side of her head.

"She was offering herself to the unghosts," said the boy, his face blurred by mist. "I had to make her stop. There was no other way to save her."

That voice . . .

The mist cleared, finally allowing Kara and the boy a good look at each other.

The world seemed to stop.

"Lucas?"

Her best friend had grown taller, almost her height now. He wore a long bow behind his back and strange clothes: dark pants and a gray turtleneck beneath a black coat that fell to his knees, the clothes hanging loosely on him as though intended for a larger frame. Without Kara there to cut it, his hair had grown to his shoulders. It was different in another way, too, though it took her a moment to place it.

"The green is gone," Kara said. She stepped forward and touched the new brown strands with the tips of her fingers.

Lucas blushed.

"It's been a long time since I've been around a Fringe weed," he said. "The color went back to normal. Does it look strange?"

"No. It looks right."

Lucas shook his head in amazement.

"What are you *doing* here?" he asked. "Where are Taff and your father?"

Lucas's question snapped Kara back to the reality of her situation.

"There's much I have to tell you," she said.

Mrs. Galt moaned gently, and Kara realized that their reunion would have to wait until they were certain the woman was safe. Removing her cloak, Kara slid it beneath Mrs. Galt's head.

"I really hope I didn't hit her too hard," Lucas said.

Kara swept her fingers over the swollen knot of flesh at the woman's temple. "It doesn't feel so bad, but we should get her someplace warm and comfortable."

"No wonder," Lucas said, noticing something past Kara. "She brought him a *toy*. I'm surprised she only drew the one unghost. Toys attract them like flies."

Looking over her shoulder, Kara saw a transparent boy with curly brown hair rocking the wooden boat up and down as though it were at sea.

"That must be Liam," Kara said.

"Don't *look* at him! You'll only make him real again."

"*You* looked at him!"

"I *glanced* at him. In passing. You're practically gawking."

She saw that Lucas was smiling, and she smiled back, the rhythms of their friendship falling into place like the tumblers of an old lock.

I've missed him so much.

They were trying to figure out the safest way to transport Mrs. Galt back to the inn when a group of men surrounded them. Like Lucas, they wore dark clothes and long bows on their backs, though some of the men held spears as well.

"What happened here?" asked the only man riding a horse. He had close-cropped hair and was dressed in finer clothes than the others.

"Good evening, North," said Lucas. And then, seeing the man's disapproving expression, added, "Sir. Mrs. Galt paid heed to her son's unghost. Brought him forth with warm words and his favorite toy."

"Of course she did," North said, though not without sympathy. "We knew this was coming. This is hardest on the mothers. Was she attacked?"

"Not exactly. I was forced to render her unconscious. Sir."

"You *hit* her?" North asked, shaking his head. "This is why a boy your age should not have been allowed to join the town guard. You mean well—I'll give you that, at least—but you lack the experience to make cool-headed decisions. If it wasn't for that grandfather of yours—"

"How can you judge him?" Kara asked. "You weren't even there!"

"And who exactly are you, girl?"

Kara was about to answer when North's eyes sharpened and in one shockingly fast motion he notched an arrow to his bow. The other men followed suit, their line of sight directed at a point behind Kara.

She turned around.

Safi and Taff were standing in the middle of the road,

looking very confused by all the attention. Safi held the grimoire open in her hands.

"We heard someone scream," Taff said.

"What are you doing?" Kara asked the men. She backed away until she was standing in front of the other two children. "This is my brother and our friend. Lucas! Make them stop!"

"You know this girl?" North asked Lucas.

"Yes," he said. "If you'd just give me a chance to explain . . ."

Safi flipped a page of the grimoire, and a nervous murmur swept through the crowd.

"Drop the book, child," North said.

His eyes, and the eyes of all the other men, rested on Safi's grimoire.

They know what it is. They're scared of it.

"Why should I?" Safi asked, a challenge in her gaze. "I've done nothing wrong."

"Because a witch has been terrorizing our town," said

North, "and I'm in no mood to take chances."

"I'm not the one you're looking for."

"Prove it. Give me the book as a show of faith."

Safi's eyes darkened. She tightened her grip on the grimoire.

"You can't have it. It's mine."

The men raised their spears, prepared to charge. Archers moved themselves into a better position to fire.

Kara whispered, "You better do what he says."

"Why?" Safi asked. Her finger glided over the open page, tracing words Kara could not see. "I can handle this."

"I know. But at what price?"

The men drew closer like beasts waiting to pounce.

"Safi," Taff said. "Please give them the book."

"It's *mine*."

North's bowstring creaked as he pulled it back farther, readying himself to fire. The shaft of the bow was translucent and swirled with the same blue liquid that illuminated the town. It whooshed gently, waves against the shore.

"On three," North said. "One . . ."

Something changed in Safi's face. Her expression seemed to *sharpen,* as though her features had been honed on a whetting stone.

"I can make your arrows burst into flames before they ever reach me," she said in a cold voice barely her own. "You too, if I was so inclined."

Now that the spellbook's open it wants to be used. She's caught in its thrall. Kara looked out at the faces of the men, their expressions hardened and merciless. *Safi is going to get herself killed—or take a life herself. There'll be no saving her after that.*

"Give me the book," Kara said.

"I have this under control."

"That's what the grimoire wants you to believe."

"Just trust me. Can you do that?"

"Two," said North.

"I'm sorry," said Kara.

She snatched the grimoire from Safi's hands.

"Kara?"

The men were on her before Safi could say another word. The girl stared at Kara in disbelief, too surprised to be angry, too surprised to even react, while the men gagged her and tied her hands behind her back. She winced in pain as they knotted the cord too tightly.

"Hey!" Lucas said. "Don't hurt her!"

The grimoire was torn from Kara's grasp and handed to North, who secured it in his saddlebag.

"She's a witch!" shouted one of the men. "She's the one been turning our children into unghosts!"

"That's ridiculous!" Kara exclaimed. "We just got here today. Whatever's going on, Safi had nothing to do with it!"

"Who knows if this one's telling the truth?" added a second man, his voice a sandpapery rasp. "Could be they're in league together. Could be all three of them have been hiding among us for weeks. Makes a lot more sense than blaming one of our own."

"The girl didn't hurt anyone," said Lucas. "Just because she's a witch doesn't make her bad, and if she's friends with Kara, then—"

"Speak for yourself, boy," snapped the first man. "You ain't got no children to worry on. Myself—I'd sleep better knowing there weren't no witches at all in Nye's Landing."

The men hoisted Safi to her feet and attached a second rope to the one that bound her hands. Safi kept her head down the entire time, even when they pulled the rope tight and began to drag her behind them like a leashed animal.

"Where are they taking her?" Taff asked.

"They'll put her in a cell for now," Lucas said. "Don't worry. We'll explain everything, and once the Mistrals—"

His attention was distracted by rising voices in the

crowd, exclamations of "Witch!" and "Kill her!" and "Do it now!"

Kara knew these sounds well.

The crowd had flared into a mob, a rapidly spreading conflagration fueled by hatred and fear. This was an entity far more dangerous than any single person; it fed on consciences and empathy, permitted its members to do the unthinkable.

"Burn her!"

"Hang her!"

"No!" a woman shouted. "Drown her in the ocean! An offering! The old ways for an old evil."

The mob roared its assent.

Safi struggled against her binds but there was nothing she could do. The group moved as one toward the beach, holding her aloft like an offering to an ancient god.

Lucas turned to North. The man sat astride his horse, not liking what he was seeing but frozen with indecision.

"You have to stop them!" Lucas exclaimed. "Now!

This girl here is the one I told you about, the hero of De'Noran."

Something flickered to life in North's eyes.

"You're Kara Westfall?" he asked. "The one who bested an evil witch back in Lucas's village?"

Kara glanced at Lucas in surprise and then nodded hesitantly.

"She's the only one who can help us!" Lucas exclaimed. "Nye's Landing *needs* her—and we're about to murder her friend!"

North stroked his carefully shaved cheeks, considering this information. Finally, he gave a short nod and exclaimed, *"HALT!"* His booming voice brought the mob to an instant standstill. "I forbid you to harm this girl. She will be imprisoned and await the Mistrals' judgment."

"Is that wise?" a man asked. "She's the one who's been—"

North withdrew his long bow and fired an arrow into the man's foot. He fell to the cobblestones, whimpering in pain.

"Is there anyone else who would like to question my judgment?" North asked.

No one did.

"Take the witch to the Stonehouse," he said. "You two, Lucas, come with me. We'll set this matter before the rest of the Mistrals."

Soldiers pulled Safi past them. Among the larger men she looked incredibly small and fragile.

"I'll fix this," Kara told her. "I promise."

Safi didn't even look in her direction.

SEVEN

Lucas guided Kara and Taff toward a beacon of torch-light shimmering at the end of the beach. They were followed by a group of armed men who stayed close enough to make their presence felt.

"What's going to happen to Safi?" Kara asked. "What's the Stonehouse?"

"Just a jail," Lucas said. "She'll sit in a cell until we straighten all this out with the Mistrals, and then she'll be released."

"You sure?"

"These aren't the Children of the Fold. The people of Nye's Landing are much clearer-headed about these things."

"They didn't seem so clearheaded just now."

Lucas ran a hand through his hair. "You're right. Everyone's a little on edge. But these are good people. They'll see reason in the end."

Kara wanted to believe him, but seeing the mob eager to drag Safi to her death had resurrected painful memories.

Lucas doesn't understand how quickly notions of right and wrong can change when people are terrified.

"Who are these Mistrals, anyway?" Taff asked.

"Sort of like the Elders back on De'Noran," Lucas said. "A council of four. South, East, West, and North—who you've already met. Their titles harken back to an older time, when Nye's Landing used to harness wind for power."

"We saw the windmills on our way into town," Taff said.

"Most of the old ways have changed since then, but the Mistrals have remained. Three of them will give you fair counsel."

"And the fourth?" asked Kara.

Through the black leather of his glove, Lucas scratched at the stumps of his missing two fingers.

"Don't worry," he said. "Just tell the truth and you'll be fine."

A few minutes later the beach ended in a massive rock wall that jutted into the ocean. A ring of torches had been set into the sand.

Four figures wavered in the light.

The Mistrals sat on cragged boulders arranged like the points of a compass. Using stern-looking North as her starting point, Kara figured out who was who. East, younger than the rest and nearly bald, fixed her with a haughty expression. South, the only woman, wore many necklaces of shells and smiled warmly as they approached. Only West, the oldest by far, did not seem to notice their arrival, concerned as he was with twirling his long white hair around his left wrist.

Taking Kara's hand, Lucas made his way to the center of the circle.

"Good evening, Mistrals," he said, kneeling on one knee and clasping his hands above his head. Kara, unsure what to do, awkwardly followed his lead. "I humbly apologize for the unannounced arrival, but I believe I have a solution to our town's problem. Do you recall, when I first came here, what I said of De'Noran and all the dark things that happened there?"

"Witchcraft and magic," North said. "We thought you a fool at the time. Or crazy."

"This started long before Lucas's arrival," South said in a gravelly voice. "For how many years have we all laughed at the Children of the Fold? 'That crazy cult that actually *believes* the old legends,' we said, 'slavers who scoff at the World and think the forest that covers their island is inhabited by monsters.'" She sighed. "Perhaps if we had not been so closed-minded we could have been better prepared."

"It's not too late," said Lucas. "This girl here is Kara Westfall. She's the one who used her powers to save our entire village from an evil witch. And now she can save Nye's Landing."

All four Mistrals turned to look at Kara.

"What are you doing?" she whispered to Lucas. "I never said anything about saving anyone."

Lucas gave her a half smile.

"It's what you do," he said.

"You dare bring a *witch* before us?" asked East, rising to his feet. Purple veins bulged from his forehead.

"A *good* witch," said Lucas.

"There is no such thing!"

"How can you be so sure of yourself?" South asked. "This is new for all of us. Just because this girl can use magic doesn't make her evil." Her brow furrowed as a thought occurred to her. "You're not evil, girl? Are you?"

"No," Kara said. "Not evil."

She considered adding *And I'm not a witch anymore, either*, but wasn't sure if that would be the wisest decision. It might be best for Safi if these adults believed that Kara had the ability to help them, at least for now.

"How old are you?" asked North.

"Thirteen."

Kara had celebrated a birthday right before they left Kala Malta. She had forgotten entirely, but Taff remembered and surprised her with a hairpin he had whittled from a piece of wood.

"Tall for your age," said South.

"Tell me about these unghosts."

"Like you don't know already . . . ," started East.

"Oh, hush," said South. She turned toward Kara. "Children started disappearing a few months ago— straight from their homes. They'd just go to sleep, everything normal as can be, and the next morning their beds would be empty. We sent search parties out but found no trace of them." She sighed. "And then they started coming back. Only at night. They call out, ask for help, and . . . they're *children*, so it's just so hard to refuse them."

"But you must," said North. "We don't think they mean to do any harm, but their touch upon the living is . . . unnatural."

Kara held up her bruised wrist, showing that she understood.

"Why do you call them unghosts?" she asked.

"Because though these children may *act* like spirits," replied North, "we are certain they are simply under some kind of spell and will someday return to us. Ghosts, if they exist at all, cannot touch the living."

"The children are enchanted, that's all," South said, her voice wavering. "*Enchanted.* Not—not—"

Dead.

The Mistrals' logic was flawed at best, but Kara understood why they so readily accepted it. To think otherwise would be to sacrifice all hope.

"There was a witness," said North. "Harren Lake. Saw a small figure in a cloak holding a book just like your friend's. Except . . ." North paused, remembering something. "Your friend's book is white. Harren said the book he saw was dark. Black or gray, maybe."

In Kara's mind, pieces began to slide into place.

Someone in this town has a grimoire. They must have gotten it from Rygoth—it's too much of a coincidence to think otherwise. This is exactly what she planned. Bring the spellbooks to the World, get them into the hands of unwitting witches. Sow disorder and chaos. Kara remembered the Bindery in Kala Malta, the tall piles of grimoires stacked in stone storehouses. There had been hundreds of books, maybe even thousands—and the great beast Niersook had carted them all across the ocean. *How many grimoires has Rygoth already distributed by now? How many towns and villages are suffering from her malice?*

A painful knot tightened Kara's stomach.

I'm the one who set her free. This is all my fault.

"I'll help you," Kara told the Mistrals.

"We did not *ask* for your help, girl," snarled East. He addressed the other Mistrals, slashing his hands through the air to punctuate each point. "Need I remind you that it is magic that is our true enemy? After everything that has happened, why would we trust a *witch*? As far as I'm concerned, the best thing would be to put an arrow through her chest right now."

"Let us not be rash," said North. "She is only a child."

"There is *magic in the world*!" East shouted. "We can't just sit here and act like the same old rules still apply."

Kara thought that the oldest Mistral, given the soft snoring sounds coming from his direction, had fallen asleep, but now he spoke for the first time. West's voice was quiet, like crinkling paper.

"What rules, exactly, are you speaking of?" the old man asked. "The ones that forbid us from ordering the death of an innocent child?"

"She's *not* innocent," East replied, but even he was deferential to the old man. "Neither is her friend."

"They have harmed no one."

"She had a *spellbook*! A weapon."

"My grandson here has a bow. Shall we murder him too?"

Grandson? Does he mean Lucas?

"That's different. He's one of us."

"Ah," said West, templing his fingers beneath his chin. "Are we at that point already? 'Them and us'?" His eyes grew dark, and East shifted uneasily in his seat. "You must be very wise indeed to understand this situation so completely when I, doddering old fool that I am, find myself completely lost."

"May I speak?" Kara asked.

The four Mistrals turned in her direction.

"Perhaps we should not let you," West said. "After all, our youthful East, having not looked into your eyes and seen the kindness there, is no doubt afraid your words will bring lightning and calamity from the skies." The old man smiled, revealing one last tooth dangling from his upper gum. "But since I'm so much closer to the Final Wind I'm willing to risk it."

Kara spoke slowly, taking the time to meet each of the Mistrals' eyes in turn. She remembered her father doing the same thing when trying to mediate difficulties between other farmers, back in the days before Mother had been taken from him.

"There is a witch among you," Kara said. "What she is doing is wrong, and must be stopped, but it's not entirely her fault. She is being controlled by her grimoire."

East scoffed. "That's just an excuse. Protecting her own kind."

"You can't possibly understand."

"And I suppose you do?" questioned East.

"All too well."

East held Kara's gaze for just a moment and then looked away.

"So what do we do?" asked South.

"Let me find her," Kara said. "Perhaps she'll listen to me."

"This isn't a time for *talking*—" East began.

"She's the only one who can undo the spell on these children!" exclaimed Kara. "If you kill her, you're killing them as well!"

The other Mistrals considered this and then nodded, which only served to infuriate East more.

"I refuse to sit here a moment longer and listen to this . . . *child*!" East exclaimed. "I've already *sent* for help. An *expert* on these matters. He will be here any day."

"Far too long for the children taken to wait," South said. She offered Kara a bright smile. "The wind has brought this child here for a reason. She is the one who will help us. I can feel it."

"There are two things I would ask in return," Kara said.

"See!" East shouted. "She's after a reward. I knew it!"

"First, I'd like my friend Safi to be released."

"I find this reasonable," North said. "*After* you've helped us, however. Not before."

Kara grimaced. Safi's powers would have been very useful while searching for the witch. Then again, after what happened she wasn't sure if Safi would even be willing to help her anymore.

"My second request is transport to Sablethorn."

Three of the Mistrals exchanged bewildered looks, while West, deep in thought, stroked his long hair.

North cleared his throat and spoke. "As the Northern Mistral, it is my duty to compile the most current maps of the land. There is no such place."

"We've only recently discovered that magic is a real thing," said South. "Is it so strange to think there might be a place not on your precious maps?"

"Those maps are constructed by the finest cartographers in the world! Just because you don't understand—"

"I know of Sablethorn," West said quietly. "Though I

was only a boy when I heard the name, and even then it was the distant memory of one as ancient and wizened as I am now. Really no more than a folktale. I cannot guarantee that it's even real. But as long as you're willing to take that risk, I'm happy to provide you with transport to its supposed location."

It wasn't the guarantee that Kara had been hoping for, but in the end it didn't matter; her course had been set since she learned of Rygoth's involvement. *I freed her. That means what happened to those children is my fault. I have to set things right.*

"I'll find your witch," Kara said.

She requested to be taken to Safi immediately so she could let the girl know they hadn't forgotten about her, but East argued that any contact between the two witches should be forbidden. The other Mistrals, too tired to argue the point, had granted East this minor victory.

Kara and Taff were dismissed.

Lucas led them back along the beach, the guards lingering even farther behind this time. Kara told him all that had occurred. When she reached the part about their need to discover the hidden witch, his face brightened.

"A problem!" Taff exclaimed.

He split off from the older children, deep in thought, walking so close to the waves that water soaked the soles of his boots.

Lucas eyed him curiously.

"What's he doing?"

"Being brilliant," Kara said. "Is West really your grandfather?"

Lucas nodded.

"On my mother's side. Once he found out we were linked by blood he took me in immediately. Grandfather is a great man."

Kara started to ask another question but Lucas raised his hand.

"We've but a short walk back to the inn and mine's not the story that needs telling tonight."

150

Kara started to talk, slowly at first, but then faster and faster, like a boulder rolling downhill. She told him everything she could remember as she remembered it, sometimes in the right order, sometimes not. She told him how the villagers of De'Noran had nearly stoned them to death. She told him about the Draye'varg and notsuns and other horrors of the Thickety. She told him how she had mistaken Sordyr for her enemy and Rygoth for her friend.

She did not tell him about losing her powers, however. Lucas had spoken so highly of her to the Mistrals (*"the hero of De'Noran," he called me*) and she wasn't ready to face his disappointment when he learned she was just an ordinary girl now. Instead, Kara told him that she was currently unable to do magic because she didn't have a grimoire. It was a half truth at best, and his look of sympathy made her burn with guilt.

By the time they reached the door of the inn Kara was so exhausted that she could barely keep her eyes open. Taff slipped inside without saying good night, muttering something about "wanting to check his sack for answers."

"Sack?" Lucas asked.

"Magic toys," Kara said, stifling a yawn. "I forgot that part. The witch named Mary Kettle, the one whose age was broken . . ."

Smiling, Lucas pushed the inn's door open for her.

"Tell me tomorrow. There's nothing more embarrassing than falling asleep during your own story."

"Tomorrow," Kara said, backing through the door.

It had been a terrible day. She had been roped into a dangerous search for a witch she had no hope of finding. Safi sat in a dark cell, probably cursing Kara's name. Sablethorn, the place she had to reach if there was any hope of saving her father, might not even exist. And yet, as Kara's head touched her pillow, sleep already tugging her into oblivion, she felt oddly optimistic for what the morning might bring.

Tomorrow I'll see Lucas again.

Kara fell asleep smiling.

EIGHT

When Taff awoke the following morning he had come up with a plan. It was like this with him sometimes, his mind still working while his body slept.

"We'll use Isabelle," he said, crawling out of bed and removing the lie-detecting doll from his sack of toys.

"You named your doll?" Kara asked, still groggy.

"Well, I have to call her *something*. And there was a girl named Isabelle back in De'Noran who was always tattling on the boys."

"I remember."

"Seemed fitting."

The straw doll was small enough to fit in Taff's hand but amazingly detailed, with braided hair, a hoop skirt, and twin circles of black thread for eyes.

"Tell me what you're thinking."

"We ask all the girls in town if they're a witch."

"And?"

"I'll keep Isabelle in my pocket and feel for if she shakes her head or not. If anyone's lying, we'll know right away."

Kara chuckled. Like the best plans, it was absurdly simple. She was a little embarrassed that she hadn't thought of it herself.

"What?" Taff asked.

"Nothing," Kara said, leaping out of bed and tickling his toes. "So how are we going to do this? Go door to door?"

"Too long. What about bringing everyone to us? A town gathering, like Worship back in De'Noran."

"That could work. Let's ask Lucas how they do things

like that here." Kara rubbed sleep seeds from the corners of her eyes. "I'm not used to our plans being so straightforward. There are usually more complications than this."

"Do you want to add some?" Taff asked eagerly. "The complications are my favorite parts."

"Maybe we should just keep it simple for now. I don't want Safi locked up a single moment longer than she has to be."

"Do you think she's all right?"

She imagined Safi in the darkness of her cell, trembling with cold, thinking of how Kara had snatched away her grimoire.

I was supposed to be her teacher. Her friend. She trusted me.

"Did I do the right thing?" Kara asked.

Taff picked at some dirt beneath his fingernails. "You wanted to make sure that no one got hurt."

"You didn't answer my question."

"I just want my friend back," Taff said, finally meeting her eyes. "Part of me thinks you should have trusted her.

The other part of me is glad you stopped her before she did something she couldn't take back. I'm not sure there *was* a right decision."

"Maybe," said Kara. "But was there a wrong one?"

When Lucas arrived later that morning, Kara told him that they needed all the women and girls of Nye's Landing in one spot. He agreed to help them without even asking why. "Just go down to the beach and wait for my signal," he said. "I'll do the rest."

Kara nodded blankly, stunned by this demonstration of absolute trust.

I've forgotten what it's like to have a true friend.

After close to an hour a bell tolled three times in succession and the residents of Nye's Landing began to trickle onto the beach. Lucas and North, along with several other members of the town guard, sent the men away and organized the girls and women into a long line. The potential witches glared at Kara, their resentment as clear

as their breaths pluming in the cold air.

"Sorry it took so long," Lucas told her. "I had to get permission from the Mistrals to gather everyone on the beach. East didn't want to allow it, of course. He thinks you're up to something."

"He believes that all witches are evil. Nothing will change his mind."

"*You* will," Lucas said, touching her arm. "You're the proof that magic can be used for wonderful things. That witches can be good."

Except I'm not a witch anymore. I'm nothing special at all.

"We should start," Kara said. "Long line."

Lucas quickly removed his hand from her arm.

"I'll send them up one at a time," he said. "That work for you?"

Kara nodded.

Lucas waved the first woman forward, a dour-looking old lady with a mop of stringy hair.

"I have some things to say," she started, her hand on

one hip. "First of all, let me tell you what I think about this spectacle you've—"

"Are you a witch?" Kara asked.

The woman was so shocked by the unexpected question that she could only cough out her next words.

"I am most *certainly not*! How dare you even *imply* that a woman such as—"

Kara glanced at Taff, standing by her side, his hand in one pocket. He gave her a slight nod: *She's telling the truth.*

"Next!" Kara exclaimed.

Lucas ushered the still-complaining woman away and nodded the next one forward.

Kara and Taff settled into a rhythm after this—question, nod, question, nod—with Lucas in charge of keeping the line moving. Eventually Kara stopped looking to Taff for affirmation, knowing that if Isabelle sensed a lie he would find a way to let her know. As the afternoon wore down the line of people, which had at first seemed insurmountable, shrunk to a more manageable level.

None of them were witches.

The boats had started to dock for the day by the time Kara reached the last girl, a bespectacled waif with a spattering of freckles across the bridge of her nose.

"Are you a witch?" Kara asked, unsurprised when the girl answered, "Of course not!" and skipped away.

"Anything?" Kara asked Taff.

"Sorry."

"You sure Isabelle's working?"

"Let's test her."

Lucas, looking tired and grumpy, was heading in their direction.

"Hey," Taff said. "Do you think my sister's pretty?"

"What?" Lucas asked, completely caught off-guard. "No. I never thought about it. I . . . what?"

With a huge grin, Taff withdrew Isabelle from his pocket. The doll was vehemently shaking her head no.

"See?" Taff said. "She works just fine."

Kara felt her cheeks grow warm.

"Could we have missed anyone?" she asked Lucas, anxious to change the subject.

"No way. North had one of his men keeping pace with the town register, making sure everyone was accounted for. You just talked to every female in Nye's Landing."

Kara sat on the sand, the sun on the downward arc of its day but still holding strong. Rough-looking men dragged long trawling nets filled with blue clams onto the shore and spread their catch upon the sand.

"I've never seen clams like those before," Taff said.

"That's where glorbs come from," Lucas said. "They're not edible, so they used to be thrown back into the ocean before someone smart figured out how to use them properly. Now they're Nye's Landing's most valuable commodity. Grandfather says that's only until the scientists figure out something new, though. Then the glorbs will be forgotten like the windmills and oil pits and empty mines. They already say there's a man in Penta's Keep who can bottle lightning."

Taff, practically shaking with excitement from this sudden avalanche of information, waved his hands in front of Lucas's face.

"Slow down," he said. "One thing at a time." He pointed toward the clams. "That's where glorbs come from? The things that make the light?"

"I found it hard to believe at first too," Lucas said. "Seems like just another kind of magic. But it's not, really. Those clams will be sorted through, and—" Lucas paused. "Wait. That reminds me. There *is* someone you didn't talk to. But it couldn't possibly be her."

"Why not?" Kara asked.

Lucas smiled, but there was something forced about it, a smile you rehearsed in a mirror.

"Because she's *Bethany*. Come on. You'll understand when you meet her."

The shop sat on a large hill past the bell tower, the Windmill Graveyard like a forest of toothpicks in the distance. It was a ramshackle affair, the wooden boards chipped and peeling, with a cracked door that half hung off rusted hinges. Letters constructed from water-filled tubes glowing a soft blue read *JENKINS'S GLORBS*. Despite the shop's less than desirable appearance, however, a crowd of townspeople jostled for position outside its walls. Some were trying to squeeze into the shop itself, while others seemed content just to stare through the window.

"Popular place," Kara said. "Must sell good stuff."

"Jenkins?" Lucas asked. "Nah. Overpriced, poor quality. Can barely power a lantern. Mr. Jenkins does most of his business outside town. People from Graycloud and Brenchton, don't know any better. Most of his glorbs he grinds down, sells for Swoop fuel."

Taff looked anxious to ask a thousand questions, but Kara placed a hand over his mouth and asked hers first.

"Why all the people then?"

"They're here to see Bethany," Lucas said, as though

the answer were obvious. "She's about to close up, but I'll peek in first and tell her you need a private talk. Wish I could stay, but I have to give the Mistrals a full report about how things went today. I'm sure East is going to give me an earful."

Lucas pushed his way through the crowd, clearly thrilled at the prospect of seeing Bethany, and Kara felt an unfamiliar twinge of jealousy. *What is so great about this girl?* A few minutes later a hand changed the sign in the window from *OPEN* to *CLOSED* and customers reluctantly began to shuffle out the door.

Kara and Taff entered the store.

The interior was just as drab as the exterior, the air hot and sticky and smelling of fish. Shelves stacked with glass containers of glorbs, grouped by size, lined the walls. Behind the counter stood a frumpy girl with short brown hair, brown eyes, and oily skin splotched with red.

That's Bethany? Kara wondered. *What's so special about her? And why is Lucas so certain she's not a witch?*

Then a feeling of warmth filled Kara's chest and she *understood.*

Bethany could never hurt anyone! She's everyone's friend. A great conversationalist. Unusually wise for her age. The funniest girl in town.

"Hello," said Bethany. "Lucas told me you wanted to talk."

The words were simple, but her voice rendered them as beautiful as any song.

"I love your store," Kara said. "We don't have glorbs where we come from. But we have corn. It's an island!"

She stumbled over her words. *Stop babbling or she won't want to be your friend!* Kara was suddenly conscious of how stupid her clothes were. *Why can't I be wearing an apron like Bethany? It looks so good on her!*

"This is beautiful," Bethany said, leaning over the counter and inspecting the shell-shaped locket Kara always wore around her neck.

"It was our mother's," said Taff. "She died."

Bethany nodded with the perfect amount of sympathy, and for the first time Kara felt as though someone truly understood the depths of her loss.

"It's a terrible thing to lose someone you love," Bethany said.

"Like Mrs. Galt," said Taff. "She lost her son."

Bethany reacted with surprise and . . . something else, a downward flash of the eyes that looked, strangely enough, like *guilt*. Except it couldn't be, of course. What would Bethany ever have to feel guilty about?

She's just sad for Mrs. Galt. That's just like Bethany, always feeling the pain of others.

Bethany smiled, the moment past.

"Would you like to see something neat, little man?" she asked. "Since you don't have glorbs where you come from?"

Taff nodded, his eyes wide with admiration. Kara could see the stirrings of a little crush there, which didn't surprise her. Not one bit.

From behind the counter Bethany lifted a long, circular tube sloshing with water. It hung by fishing line from two wooden posts that elevated it off the counter's surface.

"Mason Wainwright made this for me as a gift," she said. He certainly hadn't been the only one; on the table behind Bethany were charcoal drawings and bouquets of dried flowers and presents still wrapped in colorful paper. "It's a model of the Swoop Line. You might have seen it on your travels. It runs all the way to Penta's Keep."

Kara remembered the long track, the word *SWOOP* etched into the metal pole.

"This works basically the same way," Bethany said. "I just have to add the train."

She slid what looked like a long, narrow wagon onto a bracket attached to the underside of the track. The train, as Bethany called it, had been pieced together from painted sheets of metal, red with gold trim.

"And then the glorb, of course."

Bethany unscrewed a small section in the top of the tube and from a nearby container withdrew a glorb. Pinched in her fingers, it looked squishy and fragile, like a tapioca pearl that had been soaking for hours. She dropped the glorb inside the tube and it began to dissolve quickly, fizzing the water blue and causing it to swirl around the interior of the tube like an entrapped whirlpool.

The train started to move. Slowly at first, and then more rapidly, a steady circuit following the pull of the water.

Taff clapped his hands.

"I'm glad you like it," Bethany said.

"It's wonderful! But how does it work?"

"I'm not sure, exactly. The glorb magnetizes the water. I know that much, at least, but you'd need a scientist or a librarian to explain it properly."

Taff leaned forward, his face lit by the blue glow of the water.

"Are you sure it's not magic?" he asked.

Bethany drew back.

"Of course it's not," she said, her voice unexpectedly sharp. "Why would you ask such a thing?"

"I'm sorry. It just seems so impossible! Please don't be mad! I couldn't *live* if you were mad at me!"

"Magic isn't real," she said, smiling once again. "Everyone knows that."

She allowed Taff to watch the train circle for a few more minutes and then told them she had to close up for the night. It was only as they left that Kara remembered they had never asked Bethany if she was a witch or not. That was all right, though. What was the point? Bethany could never hurt anyone.

They started back to the inn. Kara had no idea what they were going to do next. She was out of ideas.

"You're quiet," Kara told Taff.

"There's something wrong with Isabelle."

"What do you mean?"

He removed the doll from his pocket.

"When Bethany said, 'Magic isn't real,' I felt Isabelle shake her head to say no. As though Bethany was lying. As though Bethany knew that there really was magic in the world but wanted to keep it a secret." Taff looked up at Kara, the thought troubling him. "But Isabelle must have made a mistake, because Bethany would never lie to us, right? She's *Bethany*."

"Of course," Kara said.

And yet she couldn't stop thinking about Taff's words all the way back to the inn. She remembered her false years in Imogen's dream realm, how real they had seemed to her at the time and what it was like to be enchanted.

I'd never met the girl before and I wanted to be her best friend. I still do! It doesn't make sense. Not without magic.

Kara was about to share her theory with Taff when Lucas came galloping up on a small brown horse. He started talking before he even slid off the saddle.

"I'm sorry," he said. "I tried to talk to them. But East said you had your chance, and all you proved was that no one in Nye's Landing is guilty."

"Listen," Kara said. "I think we've figured it—"

"The people want someone to blame, and they have a confirmed witch in custody. East convinced the other two that it was best for the town to act. Grandfather was dead-set against it, but—the vote was three to one. Good enough."

"Good enough for what?"

"They've announced that Safi is the one responsible for the unghosts," he said, "and tomorrow they're going to execute her."

NINE

That night, while Lucas brought the guard on duty a mug of hot coffee as a respite from the bitter cold, Kara and Taff snuck into the Stonehouse.

Inside were three cells. The first two were empty.

"Safi?" Taff asked, pressing his face against the bars of the third one. "Are you there?"

The cell was small and dark, with a straw mattress shoved into one corner and a wooden bucket in another. Safi sat huddled against the back wall, a dark shape with her hands around her knees.

"We're going to get you out of here," Kara said. "Just a few more hours."

"We know who the real witch is," added Taff.

When Safi spoke her voice was cracked and dry.

"Did you bring my book?"

"No," Kara said.

"You stole it from me."

"You were going to hurt someone. I had no choice."

In the darkness, Kara saw Safi shake her head. "The grimoire was listening to me. I had it under control."

"You *thought* you had it under control. I know what that feels like. It's a trick."

"Those men threatened me! I didn't start it!"

Kara curled her fingers around the cold metal bars of the cell. "You can't use the grimoire to harm people. There's no going back after that."

From a dark recess of her mind rose the slow-witted face of Simon Loder, Grace's constant companion. Kara could not remember the specifics of how she had ended the giant's life; that particular memory had been sacrificed to build a mind-bridge back in the Thickety. The guilt and shame lingered, however, like a well-scrubbed room that still exuded the tang of blood.

"Later, even if you break the grimoire's hold over you, you may try to tell yourself that it wasn't your fault, that you were under the influence of a dark force. You may even start to believe it." Warm tears blurred Kara's vision. "But at the strangest times—when you're by the river washing clothes, or maybe those few quiet minutes after you wake up but before you slip out of bed—the truth will make a bitter visit, and you'll know that blaming the grimoire will never be enough, because there was a life that once existed in the world, a life that had parents and hobbies and thoughts of the future, and you are the one responsible for *erasing it forever*."

Safi said nothing for a long time. And then, slowly and shakily, she got to her feet and shuffled toward Kara. Only two nights had passed, but Safi looked like she had been ill for months: her cheeks were sunken pits, her eyes dark hollows. The moonlight cast silver bars across her face.

"I had a vision," she whispered.

"What did you see?" Kara asked.

"Nothing."

"Nothing?" Taff asked.

"Blackness. Oblivion. And then Rygoth. The moonlight follows her. She wills it to and it must listen, for she controls the light of the moons and the sun as surely as animals now. She's walking on what should be the ground but it doesn't sound like dirt, and it's only when she sits down that I can see the bones supporting her weight. Mounds of them. Mountains. She's carrying a grimoire."

"Rygoth doesn't need a—"

"This one's different. It's light red—almost pink— with flower patterns on it, like something for a little girl. The leather has been stitched together with black thread. The book was taken apart and now it is whole again. Rygoth smiles. There's no happiness in it. There's no evil. Just *satisfaction*. The kind of smile you give after you've fixed a creaking hinge or mopped all the floors in the house. A job-well-done kind of smile."

Kara felt Taff pressed against her side, his tiny heart beating fast.

"What else did you see?" Kara asked. "Where is she?"

"That's the thing," Safi said, her eyes wide with terror. "There is no *where* anymore. No *when*. There is only Rygoth. And the silence."

Safi returned to her spot against the back wall of the cell, closed her eyes, and wept.

Kara, Lucas, and Taff watched Bethany's house from the shadows of the building across the road. Ocean-bit air whistled through the narrow lanes of the town, numbing Kara's fingers.

"This is a waste of time," said Lucas.

At first he had completely rejected the idea that

Bethany could be a witch. She was *Bethany*. However, after Lucas was unable to come up with a good reason why he considered Bethany his best friend—could not, in fact, remember a single time they had done *anything* together—he admitted the possibility that something strange was going on.

"Whatever Bethany is doing to these children is giving her the power to enchant the entire town," said Kara. "We made Bethany nervous in the store today, asked her questions she's not used to. She's worried about being discovered. She'll want to take a new child tonight to strengthen her spell."

"I just can't imagine Bethany being evil," Lucas said.

"I don't think she's evil," Kara said. "I think she's lost. I'm going to talk to her. Try to explain what's going on. If that doesn't work we'll improvise."

It was why she wanted Lucas there with his bow. Kara hoped they could settle this peacefully, maybe even undo the curse on the children if possible. But she had learned to never underestimate the grimoire's hold on its victims.

They waited, their backs pressed against the cold stone of the building. Taff huddled against his sister, his eyes fluttering in an awkward half sleep. Kara raised her hands to her mouth and blew on them for warmth.

"Your turn," she said.

"For what?" Lucas asked.

"To tell your story. How did you come to Nye's Landing? How did you find out that West is your grandfather? Where's the rest of your family? Mother? Father? Siblings?"

"Just Grandfather," Lucas said. "But that's all right. That's more family than I ever had before. As for how I found him, that's a dull story good for passing time and little else."

"We have time," Kara said.

Slouching closer, she turned her ear to Lucas—allowing him to keep his voice low—but kept her eyes on Bethany's house.

"I traveled from town to town, working odd jobs to fill my belly the best I could and talking with as many people as would listen. Eventually I got lucky. It turns out that my mother and father were merchants slain while carting their wares from here to Graycloud. I was with them at the time—though I was just a baby, of course—and it was the vandals who sold me to the Children of the Fold, probably with my parents' blood still fresh on their hands." Lucas regarded his own hands, black gloved and two fingers short, as though they had been somehow responsible. "Grandfather had no idea I was still alive. He assumed that I had been killed along with his daughter and her husband." Lucas brightened. "You should have seen his face the day we met. I've never seen truer happiness."

"Now you know," Kara said. "Your parents didn't abandon you to a life of slavery. They really loved you."

Lucas breathed deeply of the night air.

"I would have rather they lived."

At that moment Bethany slipped out the front door, carefully closing it behind her so it didn't slam shut, and lifted the hood of her brown cloak over her head. She stared down at a light gray grimoire open in her hands, like a lost traveler consulting a map, and started down the road.

"It's leading her to the next child," Kara said, shaking Taff awake.

"What are we waiting for, then?" Lucas asked. "We need to stop her now before she hurts someone else."

"Not yet," Kara said. "She might be like me or Safi, struggling against the grimoire. Or she might be like Grace. I need to know before we confront her."

"Why?"

"Many reasons. But mostly so we know how dangerous she is."

It would have been easier to follow Bethany had it been misty, like Kara's first night in Nye's Landing, but the sky was crisp and clear. They kept as far back as possible, waiting until Bethany had turned the corner of a new road before dashing to catch up, hoping not to lose her. Kara heard unghosts following at her heels, begging for attention. Though it broke her heart, she ignored them. Bethany stopped several times to rest. The more spells, the heavier the grimoire, and even though she had used only a third of the book, the added weight was significant. After one of these breaks, Bethany reversed direction and headed toward them, her pace faster, more resolute. The children scrambled for cover, thinking that they had been discovered, but Bethany suddenly stopped midstride. She turned one way, then the other. Again. Finally, she dropped the grimoire to the ground, walked several steps away, returned for it—and continued along her original path.

"Now we know," Kara said. "If Bethany were truly heartless she wouldn't be so indecisive. The grimoire has her in its thrall."

"What does this change?" Lucas asked. "We still have to stop her."

"You're right," Kara said. "But if I can get through to her, there's still a chance to undo the spell on the unghosts."

When they looked up Bethany was gone.

They ran to the next road, and the one after that, not caring so much about whether or not Bethany heard them anymore, just trying to find the girl before she finished what she had set out to do. Finally, circling back for the second time, Taff caught sight of a narrow lane they had missed, leading between two rickety houses that looked as though they had been uninhabited for some time. Bethany was kneeling at the end of the lane next to a small boy wearing sleep clothes, his hair sticking up in a misshapen clump. The pages of her grimoire, Kara noticed, were thin mirrors, the boy entranced by one of them now, gazing at his reflection with a blank look on his face as Bethany muttered strange words beneath her breath.

The boy started to fade.

Lucas immediately fired an arrow into the grimoire. The book flew out of Bethany's hands and skittered along the lane before coming to a stop, cover down, the arrow sticking out of it like a tiny flagpole. Lucas fitted a new arrow to the nocking point of his bow, twisted a dial. The water inside the translucent shaft swirled blue and hummed with power.

"Bethany," Kara said, stepping forward. "You have to stop."

The girl backed toward the grimoire like a cornered animal. Taff used this opportunity to run over to the boy, who was slowly—too slowly—regaining his senses.

"Go!" Taff screamed. "Get out of here!"

The boy disappeared down the road.

"I needed him!" Bethany exclaimed, taking another step toward the grimoire. The imbedded arrow was sinking slowly into the mirror-page as though being swallowed.

Lucas steadied his bow.

"You wanted people to like you," Kara said. "I under-stand. Where I come from, I didn't have any friends. People hated me. Despised me."

Bethany looked up in surprise, as though someone had shouted her name across a crowded square. For a moment she seemed to forget the grimoire.

"At least they acknowledged your existence. Sometimes I wonder if my own family would even notice if I left Nye's Landing and just kept walking."

"We can't choose our families," Kara said.

"We can't choose our*selves*," Bethany said, slapping her hand against her chest. "That's the real problem. But things are different now. Everyone likes me!"

"Because you've forced them to through magic. Does that feel right?"

Bethany's face flushed with color. "How do you know all this?" she asked.

"Because I'm a witch too. I've used a grimoire. I know how good it can feel. How natural. The unghosts are the grimoire's fault, not yours. But if you don't undo what—"

"What's an unghost?" Bethany asked.

Kara studied the girl's expression and saw only honest confusion.

She doesn't know. The grimoire has kept that part of the enchantment hidden from her. This revelation filled Kara with hope, because it meant that the grimoire was afraid of what Bethany might do if she discovered the truth.

"You have to listen to me," Kara said. "Something bad happens to the children you cast spells on."

"What are you talking about? I just borrow a little bit of their . . . energy, I guess you'd call it. I don't *hurt* them. Don't be ridiculous."

"The grimoire is hiding the truth from you."

"Or you're a liar!" exclaimed Bethany. She rocked from foot to foot, eyeing the spellbook. "Maybe you want the grimoire for yourself, *witch.* This could all be a trick!"

Words won't convince her. She needs to see for herself.

"Let me show you something," Kara said. "After that,

you can take your grimoire. No one will stop you."

Kara held out a hand for Taff's sack of toys.

"Sorry," she said. "I need those."

Taff didn't look pleased about it but handed over the sack. Kara immediately spilled its contents across the cobblestones.

"Hey!" Taff exclaimed.

The unghosts, unable to resist such a smorgasbord of toys, came almost immediately. A wooden wagon rose into the air and a translucent boy with brown skin and soft eyes appeared. He rolled the wagon along his forearm and giggled, the sound softer and more distant than it should have been, as though the boy were playing at the end of a tunnel. Another girl held Isabelle in her lap and brushed her fingers through the doll's hair.

Bethany drew her hands to her mouth in horror.

"What happened to them?"

"You stole something from these children and took it for yourself," Kara said. "Maybe the thing that makes them special—that makes *all* children special. You took an essential part of who they are, and what's left is angry, and sad, and confused. They wander the streets, not understanding why everyone is ignoring them, why they no longer have a place in the world."

Kara picked up the grimoire. She saw Lucas exhale deeply and lower his bow.

Bethany's attention remained on the unghosts.

"Can you change them back?" she asked.

"No," Kara said. "Only you can do that."

She opened the grimoire, noting that she cast no reflection in its mirrored pages, and handed it to Bethany.

"What are you doing?" Lucas asked, raising his bow again. "Why did you give it *back* to her?"

"Because she's going to fix what she's done. Aren't you, Bethany?"

"I can't," she said, shaking her head. "I don't know how. And the grimoire won't let me."

"Look at them. Look at their faces."

The unghosts stared at Bethany expectantly.

Please, a little girl mouthed, her silence more plaintive than words could ever be, and the other children echoed her: *Please, please, please.*

"I'm so sorry," Bethany said. "I never meant to hurt any of you."

Bethany ran her finger along a mirrored page of the grimoire. For a moment her face darkened and she glared at Kara with a horrific snarl of hatred, but the real Bethany quickly resurfaced, her face tight with strain as she battled the grimoire's influence. "No," she said. "No! I don't care if I'll be all alone again. I won't hurt her . . . or anyone else . . . not anymore! I want things back the way they were!" The grimoire shook fiercely as though trying to escape. Bethany tightened her grip. "Reverse the spell. Return those children to their mothers and fathers. *I command you!*"

A series of muffled cracks shook the interior of the book. Bethany turned the grimoire over, holding it by its

spine, and shards of broken glass clinked to the cobble-stones.

"Where's my mom?" a boy asked.

It was Liam, Mrs. Galt's son. Kara remembered his curly hair, though of course he had been little more than a hint of a boy when she first saw him. Not anymore. Along with all the other children, he was perfectly, vibrantly alive. The former unghosts stood in a semicircle, confused but otherwise unharmed.

Bethany's face was drenched in sweat and she looked as though she could barely stand. Kara, who knew the toll that magic could take on the body, ran to her side.

"You should sit down," Kara said, taking her hands.

"Who *are* you?"

"A friend. A real one, this time."

Bethany smiled.

"I like that."

The town bell tolled three times.

"That's odd," Lucas said. He had been in the process of

sliding his bow back into its sheath but now drew it forth again. "Why are they gathering everybody on the beach?"

Kara heard a *thump* behind her, like something falling from a great distance. She spun around to find Bethany pinned to the ground by a black net while two figures on a nearby roof assessed their handiwork with satisfaction. The net had been weighted down with metal balls, the force of it knocking Bethany's head against the stones. She wasn't moving.

The narrow lane filled with men.

Graycloaks.

They marched past the children at a uniform clip, every fourth man bearing a torch, and encircled Bethany.

"What are *they* doing here?" Lucas asked.

"I don't know," said Kara.

On De'Noran, the graycloaks had been responsible for enforcing the strict rules of the Path, a duty they embraced with merciless fervor. Seeing them again set loose old fears, like a hot blade dragged along a poorly

stitched wound. *Keep your head down! Don't let them recognize you!* Kara stole glances but saw no one familiar, which was strange—she thought she knew everyone in her village.

Who are these people?

"We have her! Bring the cart!" one of the men shouted. He rode a horse and held a red ball-staff that seemed to denote authority of some kind. He reached down to pat Taff on the head, and then allowed his gaze to play along the growing crowd of townspeople who had awoken in the night to investigate the commotion.

"Don't worry, good folk. You're safe now. The Children of the Fold have arrived. You've nothing to fear—unless you're a witch, of course!"

The men stood aside as a horse dragging an iron cage on wheels clopped through the crowd, stopping in front of Bethany. Two graycloaks dragged the unconscious witch roughly across the cobblestones and threw her in the cage.

Several people in the crowd applauded.

A graycloak wearing long black gloves took Bethany's grimoire and placed it inside a metal box, which was immediately closed and latched.

The cart pulled away.

I'm sorry, Bethany. I couldn't save you after all.

The graycloaks, focused on more pressing concerns, hadn't paid any attention to Kara and Taff. Now that the witch was secured, however, that would change. She had to move quickly.

"I don't recognize any of them," Kara whispered to Lucas, "but they're still *graycloaks*. If they report to Father, and he finds out I'm here—he'll burn Nye's Landing to the ground to find me."

"And Safi!" Taff exclaimed. "We have to get her out of that cell before they find her!"

"Go," said Lucas. "I'll distract them if I can."

In the end, however, Lucas didn't have to do a single thing; the distraction came to them. The people of Nye's

Landing, en route to the beach, had made note of the restored children, and an avalanche of bodies crashed into the narrow lane: parents pushing against the crowd to gain entrance, young ones screaming for their mothers, the graycloaks trying to maintain order but ill-prepared for this unexpected chaos.

Taff's toys were kicked and scattered by heedless feet.

"Wait here!" Taff exclaimed, and before Kara could stop him he vanished into the crowd. While scanning the packed lane for her brother, Kara saw Mrs. Galt hugging Liam as though she would never let him go again. The sight of their smiling faces filled Kara's body with welcome warmth. Things hadn't gone as planned, but she had done this one thing right, at least. Still, she couldn't help but be annoyed by the number of people *thanking* the graycloaks, as if *they* had been the ones responsible for their children's return.

Taff scrambled out of the crowd with only one toy, the wooden hideaway he had shown Kara on the ship.

"I had to leave the rest of them," he said, near tears but fighting it. "Right now, this is the one we need."

There was no time to ask him why; they had to reach the Stonehouse before the graycloaks did. The building was located on the western border of Nye's Landing, and Kara knew only one way to get there: a path that cut through the weedy hill overlooking the beach.

From this vantage point, they had a clear view of the activity below them.

Tall stakes had been driven into the sand, their tops covered with oiled liniment and lit aflame. Beneath these torches the townspeople huddled like livestock, fenced in by a rectangle of graycloaks. Anyone who moved too close to the perimeter was shoved backward with a quick jab of a ball-staff.

A man sat on a massive black horse, looking down at the crowd. People were still talking, milling about, and he wasn't going to speak until he had their full and undivided attention. He waited patiently. One by one, the people of Nye's Landing stared up at him, some already with reverence in their eyes. He was a special man, after all, one who invited devotion.

"Good evening, lost ones," said the impostor wearing their father's face. "My name is Timoth Clen, and I have come to save you all."

BOOK TWO
SENTIUM

*"A wexari makes magic, but it is
not magic that makes a wexari."*

—Minoth Dravania
40th Sablethorn Lecture

TEN

Kara's mother had been orderly with her affections, offering a hug or kiss only after she had finished planting the bulb in her hands or hanging herbs to dry, but Father had always given a more immediate response. As soon as he saw Kara tottering across the fields he would stop whatever he was doing—planting his ax into a stump, laying the plow on the ground—and throw her high into the air, calling her "Moonbeam, my little moonbeam!" as little Kara titled her head back and threw her arms toward the sky. That was why, even though Kara knew that the man below her was only the shell of the loving father she had once known, her first reaction was to run into his arms. He was safety, home; all the things she longed for so terribly.

But then he spoke and the spell was broken. Her true father could never sound so cold.

"We have imprisoned your witch," Timoth Clen said, his voice carrying along the beach. He wore a pristine white cloak, and his face, revealed by torchlight, was clean-shaven and freshly scrubbed. "You are safe once again, as are all those who follow the Path."

Behind him an endless parade of soldiers continued to march into Nye's Landing, some on horseback but most on foot.

Look at all those graycloaks, Kara thought. *No wonder I didn't recognize any of them.* Surely there were still people from De'Noran somewhere among their number, but the ranks of Timoth Clen had multiplied.

He has an army now.

"Maybe we should go down there," Taff said. "Maybe if Father sees us he'll remember that he loves us and that will break the spell."

"That's not our father. It's just the thing that stole his body."

"Can't we just try? He's so close!"

"He's never been further away."

East pushed his way to the front of the suddenly mesmerized crowd. He looked up uneasily at the man on the horse.

"I am the one who sent for your help," he said, rubbing his bald pate with his knuckles. "I heard tell of how you saved Fraenklin from a vile young thing who changed dreams to nightmares, and the village of Denholm from a flying witch whose scream could shatter both glass and bones. Truth be told, I found such tales dubious at the time, but now—"

"You are a believer," Timoth Clen said. "This is good. Denholm and Fraenklin are hardly the only villages we've saved, though, and we hear reports of new witches awakening every day. Magic spreads through the World like a plague."

The grimoires, Kara thought. *This is Rygoth's doing.*

She heard squeaky wheels and directed her attention to the opposite end of the beach. Between two perfect lines of marching graycloaks came a procession of horse-drawn rolling cages identical to the one used to imprison Bethany. From this distance Kara couldn't make out the faces of the prisoners. She saw only shadowy figures, some lying down, motionless, others with their faces pressed against the bars.

Witches.

Chained to the outside of each cage, about a dozen in all, were a number of mangy animals, whimpering and whining as though the slightest movement caused them unbearable pain. They looked like old dogs that had been beaten down by the world.

Kara knew better.

Oh no.

"We appreciate your help," East continued, "and will pay you whatever your fee might be for your services."

"Our mission is a duty, not a vocation," Timoth Clen snapped. "We ask for no coin. However, if any of the men or women of your town would like to join our crusade, we always welcome those eager to follow the One True Way."

She saw a few people step forward. More than a few.

"I see," East continued. He straightened his back, trying to look as authoritative as possible, but stuttering words betrayed his fear. "Now tell me, where have you taken Bethany Jenkins? She will be tried for her crimes here, of course, being a resident of Nye's Landing."

Kara would have liked to believe that East truly cared about Bethany's fate, but she had left such naïveté back in De'Noran. The Mistral's ego had been hurt, nothing more, and he wanted to regain some measure of the power stolen from him.

"My Children and I are making a pilgrimage to the

bones of my first life, a sacred place far to the north," Timoth Clen said, "though we shall stop to do good works where needed. There are so many witches out there, so many cages to fill. When we reach our destination, they shall all be purified in a blaze of righteous fire, and the World will rejoice, for they will know that the Children of the Fold have returned to them at long last."

Timoth Clen leaned forward and pinned East with his gaze.

"The witch of Nye's Landing, the one you call *Bethany*, shall be coming with us. I don't like to waste good kindling. Do you have any objections to this?"

"Of course not!" East exclaimed, nodding his head hard enough to shake the loose flaps of his jowls. "She's yours to do with what you will."

"I'm glad to hear that, friend." Timoth Clen straightened himself on his steed and addressed his next comments to the crowd at large. "And I'm gratified that the Children of the Fold could be of service. But witches are a crafty lot, like any other type of vermin; you might catch one, but there are always others lurking in the darkness. You needn't worry, though. I wouldn't dream of leaving your little town without cleansing it completely."

He waved two fingers forward and the chained creatures were set free. They looked like mangy dogs at first, a laughable army of malnourished strays, but as they limped along the sand their bones began to pop and stretch, their forms growing larger in the darkness. Soon the creatures loped on powerful hind legs, their jaws elongated and overpacked with fangs.

Nightseekers, Kara thought.

She had seen her first one the night her mother died. Fen'de Stone had wanted to know if Kara—then just five years old—was a witch, and so he had set a single nightseeker on her to perform its test.

But why so many now? Kara thought. *Who does Timoth Clen think is a witch?*

The graycloaks parted, allowing the nightseekers

entrance into the crowd of entrapped townspeople, and then they closed their ranks again so no one could escape.

Kara let out a small gasp.

He's going to test everyone, she thought.

The first nightseeker pounced upon an older woman with long, flowing hair. A translucent needle emerged from the creature's paw, and the woman whimpered softly as it pierced her forearm. The nightseeker slid the needle up its nostril and snorted the blood at its tip, pausing only a moment before leaping off the woman in pursuit of worthier prey.

She's not a witch, Kara thought.

"That's why Father gathered these people together," Taff said. "So he could test them all at once. It's a witch hunt."

"Timoth Clen," said Kara. "Not Father."

The nightseekers worked quickly and efficiently, never testing the same person twice. Pounce, pierce, snort. Pounce, pierce, snort. Once cleared, women and

girls were permitted to leave the perimeter, as were all the men. Some did. Others stayed to fight. Kara saw a bearded man wrap his arms around a yellow-tailed night-seeker and attempt to drag it off the girl pinned beneath its massive frame. The creature snapped its jaws lightning fast and the man staggered backward, his hands pressed against his neck. In a different area of the crowd a young girl screamed, a nightseeker having identified her as a witch. Two graycloaks dragged her toward the rolling cells as Timoth Clen watched with a smug look of satisfaction.

"But that can't be right," Taff said. "You asked that girl if she was a witch, I remember! She said no. And Isabelle didn't shake her head."

"That's because she wasn't lying. She honestly didn't know she had the talent. She's nothing but an innocent girl—and that monster's going to burn her to death anyway."

"We have to get Safi," Taff said, tugging at Kara's hand.

They sprinted to the Stonehouse. Its guard was gone, and a terrifying thought suddenly occurred to Kara: *What if they've already put her in a cage? What will we do then?* They burst inside, the air damp and cold like that of a cavern, and crossed the dirt-packed floor, shouting Safi's name. Kara felt relief flood her as they came to the third cell and she saw the small, familiar shape pressed against the back wall. It looked like Safi hadn't moved since they last saw her.

"We're getting you out of here," Kara said. "Come on. We have to hurry."

She tried to open the cell door and realized an important difficulty she had overlooked.

It was locked.

"Oh no," Kara said. "I'm so stupid! No, no, no!"

"Excuse me," Taff said, retrieving the penknife from Kara's cloak.

"What are you doing?" Kara asked as he unfolded the blade. "Can you pick the lock with that? Do you even know how?"

"Hold this," said Taff, digging the tiny hideaway out of his pocket and handing it to Kara. He scraped the blade of the penknife against the cell, producing a thin sliver of metal that he pinched between two fingers.

"Open it," he said, nodding toward the hideaway.

Unhooking the latch, Kara opened the tiny red door. Taff carefully dropped the metal filing inside the plain wooden compartment.

"I think I have to do the rest," he said with an apologetic shrug. "Mary's toys only work for me."

Taff lifted the hideaway from Kara's hand. He latched the door shut and placed it to his forehead.

"Please work," he said. "Please work."

Taff slowly opened the door of the hideaway. As he did, the door to Safi's cell swung open as well.

Kara's mouth fell open.

"That's a really neat trick," she said.

Taff shrugged.

"It's not a trick. It's magic."

The three children exited the Stonehouse and followed a path north, away from the beach. By now, Kara hoped, the Children of the Fold had completed their hunt and moved on to the next village, but it was always possible that one of the townspeople, interested in joining the Fold and wanting to gain Timoth Clen's favor, had mentioned Kara and Safi. Just in case, it would be wise to find a hiding spot as soon as possible. Until she knew the graycloaks were gone for sure, Kara didn't like being out in the open.

"I thought you were going to leave me," Safi said.

"Never," Kara replied, keeping her voice low. "Besides, it was my fault you were in that cell. I should have trusted you, like you said."

"Maybe not. Maybe I would have hurt someone. I don't know anymore. I'm so confused."

Kara took the girl's hand.

"We'll figure it out. Together. But right now we need to—"

She heard the nightseekers before she saw them,

padded footsteps that were far too soft to be boots, the clink of claws on cobblestone. Stalking them from behind and getting closer.

"Run," Kara whispered, pushing the two children forward. And then, realizing that the time for whispering had passed, shouted, "Run! Run!"

Kara could see them now at the bottom of the hill, four nightseekers sprinting at full speed, anxious to catch the girls who had escaped their test. The children ran. Unhooking the slingshot from his belt, Taff fired while moving. An invisible pellet clicked off the cobblestones. A second shattered a window. His third shot found its home. There was a crack of bone, a howl of pain. The lead nightseeker stumbled, its injured leg no longer able to support its weight.

"Yes!" Taff exclaimed.

His elation was short-lived, however, as three new shapes appeared at the top of the hill, cutting off any avenue of escape.

They were surrounded.

Behind them the approaching nightseekers stretched to their full height on narrow hind legs. They moved slowly, savoring the hunt. The lead nightseeker, larger than the others and with a silver thatch of hair on its chest, kept its eyes on Kara, as though claiming her.

She tried the door of the nearest house, pounded on it fiercely. Safi and Taff did the same to other doors. No luck.

Think, think, think. . . .

The lead nightseeker slinked closer, a low growl in its throat. It scraped the translucent needle that had emerged from its paw along the cobblestones, the resultant scratching noise sending a shiver up Kara's spine. She remembered what it had been like when she was five years old, her entire village watching eagerly as the needle pierced her skin. *But I'm not a witch anymore. It's Safi who needs to be protected.* She shielded the girl with her body as the nightseeker, only a few yards away now, leaned back on its muscular haunches and prepared to leap.

And then the night was alive with rattling wheels as a black carriage drawn by a pair of rampaging horses swung violently into the lane, tilting for a moment on two wheels. Regaining its equilibrium, the carriage barreled over the surprised nightseekers, running down two and clipping the leader before coming to a screeching halt just in front of Kara. Lucas turned in the coachman's seat, the reins of Shadowdancer and a smaller horse clutched in his hands.

"Get in! Come on! Come on!"

Shadowdancer whinnied impatiently, seconding Lucas's words.

Kara opened the door and shoved Safi and Taff inside the carriage. She heard nightseekers just behind her, their violent panting. She doubted they would harm Safi—a prized addition to their master's cages—but they might be frustrated enough to hurt a girl with no magical powers at all.

Kara wondered what nightseekers ate.

And then she heard the hum of Lucas's bow, a gathering storm of energy. The boy stood on the coachman's seat, the shaft of the bow gripped between three fingers while he drew back the bowstring with his good hand. He fired, and with a commanding *whoosh!* the glorb-powered arrow passed through the neck of the first nightseeker and into the silver-thatched chest of the second. There was a stunned silence, and both creatures collapsed.

The final nightseeker, upon seeing the result of this strange weapon, immediately turned back to its innocuous, doglike form and slinked away.

Kara got into the carriage, which started to move before she even closed the door behind her. The compartment was clean and comfortable, with a bench on either side. She slid between Safi and Taff.

On the opposite bench sat West.

Drifts of white hair hung across his face like an untended garden. West wore no shoes, and his toenails were so long that they hooked downward like talons.

Still, Kara thought he looked younger than when they had first met, as though the dangers of the night had rejuvenated him.

"You three are an interesting bunch," he said. "And not just to me. Someone mentioned your names, and now this man pretending to be Timoth Clen is obsessed with finding you. I fear he shall tear our entire town apart in his search."

"I'm sorry," said Kara. "We never meant to cause any trouble. They'll be after you too, now."

West waved away the thought.

"What are they going to do? Kill me? They're welcome to the last morsels of my life; the sweetest ones have already been eaten." He nodded toward the front of the coach. "I'm more worried about my grandson there. After all this time, the thought of losing him again . . . He reminds me of myself when I was his age. Except I was much better-looking, of course."

The old man leaned across the empty space between

the benches and took Kara's hands. Thick veins pro-truded from his wrinkled skin, but his grip was still strong.

"I owe you the deepest of apologies, Kara Westfall. I asked you to help our town, and you have performed your end of the bargain admirably. In exchange for this, you requested two things. The first was the return of your friend, which I'm glad to see you've accomplished on your own. No thanks to me."

"It wasn't your fault."

"True as that may be, there's nothing an old man hates worse than an unfulfilled promise. If I was young, and had the years at my disposal to amend such a wrong, that would be one thing, but . . . enough of all that. I'm here mostly about my second promise. Sablethorn." He linked his long fingers together. "Why do you need to go there, if I may be so bold?"

Kara saw no reason to lie anymore.

"A witch cast a spell on our father and possessed him

with the spirit of Timoth Clen. We aim to undo the curse, and for that we need to reach Sablethorn. There's an entranceway there into the Well of Witches, back from when it was Phadeen."

West raised his bushy eyebrows with amusement.

"You children really do lead the most complicated lives. That reminds me. Look under the bench there."

Reaching down, Kara pulled out the sack of magical toys. Taff screamed with delight and yanked them from her hands.

"Lucas went back to get them," West said. "He thought they might prove useful."

"Thank you," Taff said, beaming. "I thought I'd never see them again."

"There's something else," the old man said.

For a second time, Kara slid her hands beneath the bench. She withdrew a smooth object, oddly wet to the touch.

The white grimoire.

Safi's body went rigid. It looked like it was taking all her willpower not to tear the spellbook from Kara's hands.

"Thank you," Kara said. "I'm sure you took no small risk to retrieve this." She turned to Safi. "I understand what you're feeling right now. The pull of it is overwhelming. Like a man starving for days suddenly finding himself before a massive feast."

"Yes," Safi said.

Kara placed a hand on the girl's cheek. "You're not alone," she said, and the words, perhaps the most magical of all, caused Safi to shudder with relief.

"I'm afraid that if I use it now I won't be able to stop," she said. Tearing her gaze from the grimoire, she looked at Kara with pleading eyes. "Could you hold on to it for a little while? Just until . . . until . . ."

"Until you're ready," Kara said, sliding the grimoire beneath the bench.

The wagon bucked up and down over an uneven

surface; they had left cobblestones behind and were back on dirt roads.

"Farewell, Nye's Landing," West said.

"Are you taking us to Sablethorn?" Kara asked.

"That brings us back to my original point," West said. "I'm afraid you've been misled. As I said when you stood before the Mistrals, Sablethorn is not real."

"But you people didn't even think magic was real!" Taff exclaimed.

West leaned back in his seat, considering this.

"Your point is well struck. Who can say for certain what is real and what is make-believe in this changing world? Books grant magical powers. Storybook beasts hunt witches. Why shouldn't Sablethorn exist as well?"

"Where would it be?" Kara asked. "If it did exist."

"Beneath the Forked Library in Penta's Keep. A long journey. Months by horseback."

Kara remembered her last dream of Father. He had seemed so close to realizing that he was trapped in an endless cycle. Once he did, his sanity would disintegrate until there would be no saving him at all.

"We don't have months," Kara said. "Maybe not even weeks."

West smiled.

"Then you'll just have to ride something a lot faster than a horse. Luckily, we're only a three-day carriage ride from Ilma Station. From there getting to Penta's Keep is easy, providing you can supply the fares—which I can. Months of travel shortened to a day." West leaned back and crossed his ankles. "Chins up, children. You're going to ride the Swoop!"

ELEVEN

They traveled through the night and deep into the next day before Kara insisted that they stop to rest the horses. She stroked Shadowdancer's flank and fed her wild carrots, the simple trust in the animal's eyes calming her. Kara was in a foul mood and knew it. They had passed through Denholm earlier that morning, one of the villages that Timoth Clen had "saved" from a witch, and she had seen boys and girls dressed in gray cloaks waving hastily made ball-staffs. At the edge of the town, a sculptor had been chiseling away at a statue of Timoth

Clen himself. No one spoke about the nightseekers, or the three girls who had been dragged away in iron cages, innocent except for a certain unused talent.

What is wrong with these people? Kara wondered, her face burning. *Don't they see what he really is?*

But they didn't, of course. All they saw was a savior.

When she felt more like herself, Kara helped the others set up camp for the night. Once they had a strong fire burning, West broke a branch from a tree and led them over to a large patch of dirt.

"Timoth Clen will be looking for you," he said. "Rygoth as well. When you get to Penta's Keep you'll need to blend in as best you can. There are certain things you need to know. We can't have you acting like three children who grew up in seclusion and are completely ignorant about Sentium and its history. The last thing you want to do is raise any eyebrows."

"What's Sentium?" asked Taff.

West stared at him in disbelief. "This is precisely what I mean."

"Sentium is what people call the World," said Lucas.

"The World has a *name*?" Kara asked.

"Sentium," Taff said, trying it on for size. "Sentium, Sentium . . ."

"It sounds strange at first," Lucas said. "You get used to it."

Holding the branch with two hands, West traced a rudimentary map in the dirt: a large, oddly shaped continent broken into four major sections. He pointed at the heart-shaped center where the regions intersected. "Let's start here, at your destination. Penta's Keep. Thousands of years ago, King Penta, tired of the wars that kept tearing Sentium apart, decided to abolish his small, squabbling kingdoms and split the continent into four parts. Instead of kings he installed his greatest scholars—we call them scientists, these days—to rule each realm. Each of these regions would dedicate itself wholly and completely to a specialty that complemented the other three regions, forcing them to rely on one another. It was King Penta's hope that this interdependence would end all wars."

"Did it work?" Taff asked.

West sighed. "King Penta was quite wise for a ruler, but no man has ever been wise enough to abolish war forever. There was peace for a time—a *long* time, by Sentium standards—but these days the realms are more worried about what happens inside their own borders than working together for the common good."

Though Taff's eyes were rapt with fascination, Safi looked casually interested at best, her eyes sunken from lack of sleep. Kara was exhausted as well. She had sat by the girl's side all last night, keeping vigil in case Safi gave in to temptation and tried to use the grimoire. *I wish she could get rid of the thing altogether, but I'll need her magic if I've any hope of finding Grace.* She looked over at Safi, her once luminous green eyes like the faded embers of a dying fire. *Am I doing what's best for her? Or what's best for me?*

If only I still had my own powers. . . .

Noticing that Kara's attention had wandered, West tapped her with his branch and she wondered, not for the first time, if he had been a schoolmaster in his younger days.

The old man pointed to the southern region of the map.

"This is our realm, Ilma, founded by Landris Ilma, one of the original four selected by King Penta. Our job is to create new power sources for the rest of Sentium. Coal, kanchen, firetops, wind—and now glorbs. Our methods, always improving, are essential for the other realms to function. West of us, across the Longing Currents"—the old man drew two new lines, sanctioning off an area that was larger than Ilma, though not by much—"is the realm of Lux, populated by master glassblowers who can bend light to their will. Glass farmers refine sunlight to perfection and grow the finest crops in Sentium, and Luxsmiths create glass swords light enough to be wielded by a child but strong enough to meet the strike of any steel. It is also rumored that they can create mirrors that show more than just your reflection."

"That sounds like magic," Kara said.

"As does much of science. If you hadn't seen it with your own eyes, would you have believed that a little orb could make water glow and an arrow fly faster? Nothing magical about it, though. In fact, according to recorded history, there has never been a single act of magic in Sentium."

"But that's totally wrong!" Kara exclaimed, crossing her arms. "You've read Sordyr's letter. There were *wexari* under direct command of the king! And Timoth Clen cleansed the world of witches—we know that's true! And what about Sablethorn? How can you claim there was no magic when there was an entire school for—"

West held up a single finger, and Kara instantly fell silent, a slight bloom of color darkening her cheeks.

Definitely a schoolmaster.

"I said *recorded* history. Correct me if I'm wrong, but did you not grow up studying a text that taught you all witches were evil? Just because it's written down does not make it true. But let me finish my initial lesson before my thoughts flutter into the night, and I promise we'll circle back to this. Agreed?"

Kara nodded, surprised to find a smile creeping across her face. It felt like school, and there was something oddly comforting about the routine.

West made some more quick lines. "In the northeast, past the Echo Mountains, is Auren. Their specialty is sound. Excellent hunters. Instead of trapping their prey with nets or steel claws they use special bells to replicate the cries of the animals' young and draw the parents out of hiding."

"That's cruel," said Kara.

"But effective. The very nature of Auren. Their children are blindfolded in their formative years and taught to hear an iron filing drop to the grass, determine the weight and gender of a foe from a single footstep—as well as which sword hand they favor—and distinguish between lies and truth from the tone of voice." West chuckled. "They have a motto in Auren: 'Eyes are the great deceivers.' There is some truth in that, I think."

West drew the last line, creating a small area in the northwest.

"And finally we have Kutt. The less said about them the better. They study ways to cure disease, heal wounds. Make medicine."

"That doesn't sound so bad," said Taff.

"It's *how* they've made their discoveries that's the problem. There's been talk. Experiments on living animals, even people. They're the ones who caused the Clinging Mist, too, though they deny it, of course. It's under control now, except for the Plague Barrier."

Kara's head began to throb. *Clinging Mist? Plague Barrier?* Instead of satisfying her curiosity, each answer seemed to produce more questions.

All of this can wait. Right now I need to remain focused on saving Father.

"How does Sablethorn fit into all this?" she asked.

"As I said, the schoolbooks teach us that magic never

existed." West paced back and forth, thinking as he spoke. His bare feet left light impressions in the dirt. "However, there are a handful of people who believe in an alternate version of history, and in light of recent events I think we have to consider their views more carefully. According to them, the great wars that caused King Penta to divide his kingdom into four parts were actually fought between man and witch. It was a hard-won victory, leaving countless dead, and afterward the king declared that any mention of magic be struck from the records completely. This meant that Sablethorn, for countless centuries a school for good *wexari*, had to be destroyed as well, though when the king tried to do so he found it impossible to shatter a single brick. Instead he built the Forked Library right over it." West shrugged. "As I said, none of this is proven. There is every possibility that Sablethorn never existed to begin with."

"It does," Kara said. "It has to."

For if it didn't, her father was already lost.

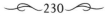

Two days passed. During the sunlit hours they made steady ground over rough roads. At night, West packed their heads with names and history and customs. Kara had trouble keeping everything straight, and Taff's attention—after the initial novelty had worn off—began to wander, but Safi had become a surprisingly apt pupil. For some reason these increasingly dry lessons had a healing effect on her. Kara was delighted to wake up after a brief nap in the carriage to find Taff and Safi playing a simple game of dice, the hint of a smile gracing Safi's face. She left them to it and made her way around the side of the slow-moving vehicle to the coachman's seat. Lucas, holding the horses' reins loosely in his lap, offered her his canteen.

"How's it going in there?" he asked as she took a seat beside him.

"Not bad," Kara said, and she meant it. There was a part of her that wished they could stay on this carriage forever, their own private world, but she knew that was impossible. The Well of Witches awaited them.

It was cold out here, especially with the wind whipping her face, but it was still an improvement over the stale air of the carriage compartment. The road ran between a half-frozen lake, above which the Swoop line dangled from massive stanchions, and a forest of tall, naked trees that might have been more impressive were it not for Kara's experience in the Thickety. In the far distance lazed a snowcapped mountain range.

She took a swig of icy water.

"Look at all that snow," Lucas said, smiling at her. "Back on De'Noran there was never enough of it to do anything fun. Remember that day we tried to go sledding with some old barrel lids and ended up covered in mud for our troubles?"

Kara nodded, though in truth she had no recollection of the day whatsoever. *I must have used that memory to build a mind-bridge in the Thickety. I never would have forgotten something like that.* Occasionally Kara would be faced with these gaps in her mind, moments that she missed as ardently as lost friends. She could have explained all this to Lucas, of course, but Kara was reluctant to admit that she had traded her memory of their day together for a spell. He might not understand.

"How long until our next stop?" Kara asked.

"We should be in Gildefroid any minute now," Lucas said. "It's a friendly little town for people on their way to Ilma Station. We'll be able to stock up before we board the Swoop."

Kara winced at his use of the word *we*.

He assumes that he's going with us. I should have spoken to him days ago.

From the beginning, they had known that West would not be coming with them to Penta's Keep—he felt that his age would only slow them down—but Lucas's plans had remained curiously unaddressed.

"Lucas . . . ," Kara started.

"Don't bother. I'm coming. I know it's dangerous. And you may think you're protecting me—"

"Actually, that's not it."

"—but now that you're not a witch anymore, you need someone to protect you. Let me help."

Kara stared at him in shock.

"I never told you I'd lost my powers. How long have you known?"

"Taff told me. The first night."

Taff!

"Not on purpose, mind you. He just likes to talk. Sometimes I wonder if he even knows he's doing it. Have you noticed that?"

"Yes," Kara said between clenched teeth. "I have."

"Why didn't you tell me?"

Kara dipped her head to her knees, trying to make herself as small as possible. When she spoke her voice was soft and timid.

"You were so proud of everything I did in De'Noran.

I liked hearing that. I didn't want to tell you that I wasn't special anymore."

Lucas turned in his seat and gazed at her intently.

"It's not magic that makes you special."

Kara's cheeks burned. His face was so close to hers. She needed words, something to fill the silence. . . .

"I want you to follow Timoth Clen."

"Huh?" asked Lucas, drawing back.

"That's why you can't come with us. I need you to follow the graycloaks. There's so many of them, and they can't move that quickly with all those iron cages. They should be easy to track, right?"

"I guess. I can go back to Nye's Landing and pick up the trail there. A single rider should be able to catch up in no time at all. But why in the world would you want—"

"Let me explain. When we find Sablethorn, we're going to enter the Well of Witches . . ."

"Which is insane."

"And come out with Grace . . ."

"Who's evil."

"So she can restore my father. But based on what I know about grimoires, I'm thinking that she won't be able to just undo the curse from anywhere. Grace will need to be near my father for the spell to work, so I'll want to get to him as quickly as possible—time is definitely a factor here. Not just for my father, but for Bethany and all the other girls. If we don't banish Timoth Clen from his body in time, he'll execute them all."

"You have no idea where he's taking them?"

"He said to the 'bones of his first life,' which I assume means the grave of Timoth Clen—the *real* Timoth Clen. Which would be incredibly helpful, if anyone knew where that was. The problem is, most people don't believe Timoth Clen ever existed at all. They think he was just a figure the Children of the Fold made up, along with magic and witches." Kara pushed back her hair with two hands. "Everyone thought our people were this crazy cult. And in some ways they were *right*."

The carriage rattled along the road. A school of golden-finned fish skipped above the surface of the lake, then once again vanished into its depths.

"This will never work," Lucas said. "Say I find Timoth Clen. How will you know where to find *me*?"

"That's the fun part." She reached into her cloak and pulled out two conch shells, handing him one. "You talk into this, and I'll be able to hear you on the other end and talk back."

"Magic," he said, turning the conch in his hands. "Is it safe?"

"Of course."

"And I'll be able to talk to you at any time? No matter how far apart we are?"

"I think so," she said. "We only tested them about a mile apart or so. And Taff has to be holding the other seashell, otherwise it won't work."

Lucas stared down at the conch.

"And this is really what you want?" he asked.

No! I want you to come with me! I don't want us to be apart again!

"Yes," Kara said, straining to keep the tears away. "This entire plan is crazy enough as it is, but it won't work at all without your help."

Lucas slid the conch into his cloak.

"All right."

"Thank you. Keep your distance, though. Timoth Clen can't know you're spying on—"

"Oh no."

The carriage had rounded a bend, revealing Gildefroid—or, at least, what was left of Gildefroid. Kara imagined that at one point the road before them had been lined with small shops and houses. They might have used glorb-lanterns to light the road, maybe not. She would never know. The buildings had all been reduced to heaps of wood and stone. Debris littered the street, forcing Lucas to slow the carriage to a pace no faster than walking.

"What happened here?" he asked. "It looks like a storm flattened the entire town, but that can't be—"

"Shh," Kara said. "I hear something."

A rhythmic sound drifted through the eerie silence. Kara, the daughter of a farmer, recognized it instantly: a shovel slicing through dirt. Lucas carefully navigated the carriage through the remnants of Gildefroid, the digging sound growing steadily closer, until they reached a large field just outside the town. It was a pretty place with a small pond at its center and plenty of trees to provide shade in summer. At one point it had probably been a gathering spot for town picnics and festivals.

It was now a graveyard.

Fresh mounds of dirt stretched out in haphazard rows. There were no headstones. Instead, simple wooden signs had been driven into the ground, each bearing a name painted with unsteady brushstrokes. A man stood three feet deep in a freshly dug hole and tossed shovelfuls of earth to the ground above him. His face was blackened

with dirt, his ungloved hands bloody and callused. Kara forced herself not to wince at the stench of him.

"Good afternoon," Lucas said.

"Afternoon, travelers," the man mumbled. He did not stop digging. "Ilma Station is close. Just keep following this road and you'll be there in less than a day."

"Thank you," said Kara. "That's helpful. But we don't need directions."

"What happened here?" asked Lucas.

"Look around you," the man said, digging even faster than before. "That's what happened. Telling the how of it won't bring them back."

"We have water," Kara said. "And food. Would you like some?"

The gravedigger paused in his work and considered his shaking hands. "Perhaps that would be wise," he said. After warning Safi and Taff to stay inside the carriage, Kara brought the gravedigger a fresh canteen of water and some hard biscuits and cheese. The man ate hesitantly at

first but then with increasing fervor, as though his body had suddenly remembered what it needed to survive.

When he was done, the gravedigger planted the shovel in the earth and rested on it unsteadily.

"I'll tell you what happened," he said. "But I don't expect you to believe me. *I* wouldn't believe me."

"Try me," said Kara. "At this point, there's not a lot that I *wouldn't* believe."

The gravedigger brushed his hair out of his face. Due to his stooped posture and drawling voice, Kara had originally pegged the man's age at around fifty, but she saw now that he had the unlined features of a much younger man.

Whatever happened was terrible enough to add decades to his appearance.

"There's a little girl who lives here—*used* to live here. Four years old. Summer's her name, and it's an apt one— she burns hot. Temper like you wouldn't believe, stomps her feet, throws toys, that whole bit. Her parents are good, solid folk, but what are you going to do? 'She'll

grow out of it,' they always said, and they might have been right, had things gone differently." The gravedigger scratched the side of his head with a mangled fingernail. "I imagine they were the first to die. I don't know what set Summer off, probably her parents telling her she had to eat what was on her plate or brush her teeth or some such matter. Usually she would just scream and cry and pound her fists like she was wont to do—'a Summer storm,' we called it—but this time it went a lot further than that. This time her temper brought entire buildings crashing to the ground."

"Sounds like magic," Lucas said.

The gravedigger spit into the dirt.

"Like I said," he snapped, "I didn't expect you to believe me."

"We believe you," said Kara, bending down to touch the man's shoulder. "All too well. How did you know it was her?"

"We didn't, at first," said the gravedigger. "We thought

it was just some freak storm. But then I saw Summer walking through the center of town. There was wood and glass and . . . people flying everywhere, but that little girl didn't seem to even notice. She was holding something in her hands, an——"

"——old book," Kara said.

"That's right," said the gravedigger, regarding Kara with newfound suspicion. He tightened his grip on the shovel. "How do you know that?"

"We passed through another village a few days back," Lucas said quickly. "They had witch troubles as well."

The gravedigger nodded, his suspicions seemingly mollified.

"Witches," he said. "I knew it."

"What happened to Summer?" Kara asked. "Did a man with iron cages come and take her away?"

"I don't know anything about that," said the grave-digger. "But I seen what *did* happen to her. I hid beneath some rubble and watched. I'm not proud of it, but I was scared, and——"

"There was nothing else you could have done," said Kara.

"Some women came on an old wagon. They were carrying books that looked just like Summer's. All except one of them. She wore these long white gloves, and she was the most beautiful woman I'd ever seen—but there was something wrong with her eyes. They were broken, like glass."

Kara rose to her feet.

"Her name is Rygoth," she said. "You're lucky to have escaped with your life."

The gravedigger nodded absently, as though the thought had already occurred to him. "She told Summer that she had 'passed her test' and was a real witch now. Then they all went off together, and that was that. I crawled out of my hiding place like a cowardly rat and starting laying my neighbors to rest." He lifted his shovel. "Which reminds me, I best get back to work. It's been three days already, and while I've tried to keep the bodies as fresh as possible there's only so much—"

"Why don't you come with us?" Kara asked. "We'll bring you to Ilma Station. You can start new. There's nothing left here."

The gravedigger shook his head. "Sorry, love. I am to finish what I started. After that I think I'll just sit and watch over them awhile. I couldn't save them, but I can give them that, at least. Someone to watch over them."

Kara spent a few more minutes trying to change the man's mind but quickly realized that it wasn't going to happen. As their wagon pulled away, Lucas leaned over and asked, "What did that mean? About Summer passing a test?"

"That's all this was to Rygoth," Kara said, looking out over the graves. "Those people died so she could see if one little girl would embrace the grimoire's evil or fight it, like Bethany. That's why Rygoth is distributing all these spellbooks. She wants to see what the girls do with them, so she can make sure she's gathering the right kind of witch."

"The ones who are like Grace," Lucas said. "The ones who like to hurt people."

Kara nodded.

Behind them, she heard the gravedigger renew his efforts. Night was falling fast, and there were still plenty of graves left to dig.

TWELVE

The next morning they arrived at Ilma Station. It was packed with people, some already waiting on the stairs leading up to the elevated platform. Taff, worried that there might not be enough seats, wanted to join the line immediately, but West assured him that there would be plenty of space. They purchased what supplies they could at an overpriced general store, including new clothes: a green woolen skirt and white sweater for Safi; for Taff, a white shirt, gray slacks, and a tie (which he despised); and, for Kara, a lavender dress made from

velvet. West thought these "city clothes," as he called them, would help them blend into the general population of Penta's Keep.

There were also bathing rooms, for which Kara was extremely grateful. Time vanished as she scrubbed the travel dust from her skin and washed her hair. When she finally came outside Taff greeted her with a look of exasperation.

"You took *forever*."

She caught Lucas looking in her direction, but when she met his eyes he looked quickly away, his face reddening.

He hates my dress. He's turning away so I don't see him laugh.

The Swoop pulled into the station.

It was quieter than Kara had thought it would be, arriving on the underside of the Swoop line with the *whoosh* of tunneled wind. Seven sections—West called them "cars"—had been joined together by metal rods. Each was painted a lighter red than Bethany's model but with the same gold trim, and though they were of slightly varying lengths, even the shortest car would have required a dozen horses to pull it along a road. Through the Swoop's many windows Kara spied faces pressed against glass; Safi and Taff, by some unbidden instinct, instantly began to wave.

"I guess this is good-bye," said West, enfolding each of the children in his spindly arms. "I look forward to meeting your father someday soon. Your *real* father."

"I would like that," said Kara.

He pinched her cheek, then ushered Safi and Taff onto the embarking line of passengers.

"What about Kara?" she heard Taff grumble, their voices already fading into the crowd.

"She'll be right behind you," said West.

"But why isn't she coming now?"

"Sheesh," Safi said. "You really don't understand *anything*, do you?"

Kara turned to face Lucas, who had been uncharacteristically quiet since Gildefroid. She felt as though he

had left part of himself behind in that wicked place, and it grieved her.

"Be careful," Kara said, hugging him tightly. "Don't forget, Timoth Clen has Father's memories as well. He'll recognize you from De'Noran. You must stay out of sight."

She drew back, Lucas's face surprisingly close to hers, and for a brief, stomach-fluttering moment Kara was certain he was going to kiss her.

Instead he said, "Don't do this. It's too dangerous."

"He's my father."

"Exactly. Is this what he would want? His children risking their lives to save him?"

"It's not just him. What about all the other girls? Timoth Clen is going to kill them!"

"I know," Lucas said, shaking his head as though his very words confused him. "I'm not saying that Timoth Clen is a good man. He's not. But he might be a *necessary* one. Rygoth is building an army of evil witches. And Timoth Clen, despite all his faults, is a witch hunter. He can stop her."

Above them, a whistle sounded. Any last passengers needed to board.

"I can't believe you're saying this," Kara said.

"You saw what happened to Gildefroid. What if Timoth Clen had gotten there in time? He could have saved those people!"

"How? By releasing his nightseekers and carting away a bunch of innocent girls just because they can use magic?"

"They're not all innocent, Kara. That's my point."

"So the bad ones and the good ones should all be treated the same? Is that what you think? Every witch should be imprisoned and killed?"

"Of course not!" Lucas clasped his head between his hands. "But there are no good choices here, and his way might save more lives than it hurts."

"It's *Rygoth* who has to be stopped!" Kara exclaimed. "And Timoth Clen is *not* the solution. If he's allowed to hurt innocent people his influence will spread. Soon it won't just be girls with the talent who are being punished. It will be any girl who's a little bit different than everyone else. The Fold will be reborn, and Sentium will become just another De'Noran."

"You don't know that. It could be that Timoth Clen is the only one who can stop the witches at all. You've lost your powers, Kara. There are no more *wexari*. Everyone who uses a grimoire turns evil. If you restore your father and take Timoth Clen away . . . who's left?"

The whistle sounded again.

"Find him," Kara said. "I'll need to know where he is when the time comes."

Lucas hesitated for a long moment before finally nodding.

"I'll do as I promised," he said, "but just ask yourself: What if you're making a mistake? What if getting your father back ends up hurting more people than it helps?"

The Swoop whistled, longer this time. Last call.

"Take care of Shadowdancer," Kara said.

She ran up the stairs. By the time she boarded the Swoop her cheeks were damp with tears.

Glorb-powered water propelled the Swoop along at unbelievable speed, the passing landscape a hectic blur of shapes and colors. Taff and Safi pressed their faces against the thick glass windows, gesturing with excitement each time a new wonder appeared. The interior of the Swoop was even more interesting. Passengers transplanted from all corners of Sentium sat on golden benches burnished bright. Some looked no different from the townspeople of Nye's Landing, but others were dressed unlike anyone Kara had ever seen. A tired-looking man stretched his arms in a glass jacket as flexible as linen. A group of four with stern expressions on their faces wore padded earmuffs, as though the loud noises of the car were too much for them to take. In the far corner of the car sat an isolated figure whose face was concealed beneath a black handkerchief. He—or she—drew air through a tube connected to a metal container.

After the colorless monotony of a childhood spent among the Children of the Fold, Kara should have been fascinated by this diverse new world.

She just stared at her lap.

Lucas is wrong. I'm doing the right thing.

She listened to the conversations around her (at least those in her language). Whispers and rumors about horrific tragedies that had befallen a handful of towns recently. Witchcraft! Evil! And a hero who led an army of gray-cloaked men . . .

Timoth Clen is not a hero!

Taff, drawn by the aromas of cinnamon and nutmeg, left to spend a few more of West's coins at the snack cart. Kara turned in her seat to face Safi. The girl looked older, but not in a good way. *Aged.* She had lost weight, and her wrists were as thin as toothpicks.

"How are you feeling?" Kara asked.

"Better," she said. "More like myself." Safi's eyes narrowed with concern. "How are you?"

"Confused."

"About what?"

"Everything! I want our father back, but maybe the world really *would* be better off with Timoth Clen in it. I need your help, but I don't want you to use the grimoire, not if it's going to hurt you. I want to believe that I can survive the Well of Witches, but I'm not a witch anymore. Am I a fool to even try?"

Safi dragged her fingers through her hair. She had taken the pigtails out back at Ilma Station and hadn't gotten used to wearing it straight yet.

"Let's see if I can help," she said, holding up a single finger. "First one's easy. Your father was a good man who loved you and Taff. Timoth Clen burns innocent girls alive. Plus, *it's your father's body.* Forget about what's right for the world. Do what's right for him."

Kara nodded, appreciating Safi's attempt to cheer her up, but she knew it wasn't that simple. Lucas's words echoed in her head: *What if getting your father back ends up hurting more people than it helps?*

Safi held up two fingers.

"Second, it doesn't matter if you want me to use the grimoire or not. I want to help. I'm using it. And you're right, it might hurt me. There's that risk. I've thought about it a lot, and I think maybe the only reason you could use it without being corrupted is because you're a *wexari*. You're special."

"That's not true. You resisted it. So did Bethany at the end."

"For a spell or two. But long-term, I think maybe the grimoire is bound to win."

"Don't say that."

"It's all right. I can do a lot of good before that happens."

Kara did not like the resigned expression on Safi's face, but before she could say anything Taff slid into the seat across from them. He handed each of the girls a warm cinnamon stick wrapped in waxed paper.

"I already ate mine," Taff said. "So if either one of you decides you're not hungry—"

Kara handed him her stick and he eagerly bit off the top.

"As for your third worry, about whether or not you're being a fool to enter the Well of Witches—" Safi smiled. "You don't need magic to be a hero, Kara. I believe in you. I'd follow you anywhere."

Taff, his mouth full of cinnamon goodness, mumbled his agreement.

Kara smiled shyly.

"Thank you," she said. "Both of you. For believing that."

Safi leaned forward and looked into her eyes.

"You're welcome. Now when are you going to start believing it yourself?"

Several hours later Kara decided that she was hungry after all. She sent Taff for more cinnamon sticks and three cups of mulled cider pressed from a tart fruit she did not recognize. Afterward, she fell into a deep sleep.

Father was waiting.

The land, as always, was freshly tilled and ready for seeding. In Kara's past dreams, Father had always scooped up a handful of dirt and let it run through his fingers before removing the pouch of seeds from his inside pocket. Not this time. Instead, Father collapsed to his knees, his body convulsing with what Kara at first took for tears but were actually soundless laughs.

Suddenly Father spun around as though an invisible hand had touched his shoulder. He looked relieved—happy, even—as he spoke soft words to the empty air, touching the contours of an unseen figure with his hand.

He's seeing things now, Kara thought. *Going mad, if he's not there already.*

She awoke.

"Finally!" Taff exclaimed, his hands on her shoulders. There were tears in his eyes. "You have to do something! Safi's not waking up!"

Kara rose to her feet, the desperation in her brother's voice waking her instantly.

Safi was slumped over on the bench, not moving.

"The conductor announced that we'll be arriving at Penta's Keep in a few minutes, so I tried to wake her up. Said her name, shook her. Nothing."

Kara bent over the girl. Her chest rose and fell in a reassuring rhythm.

"She's deep asleep," Kara said. "That's all."

"You try to wake her, then. Go ahead."

"Safi?" Kara asked.

There was no reaction.

"Safi?" Kara shook her shoulder this time. "Safi?"

Her chest continued to rise and fall, but other than that Safi appeared lost to the world.

"What happened to her?" Taff asked.

"I don't know," Kara said. "She's not dead. But she's more than asleep."

She lifted the girl a few inches off the bench and let her fall. Her body landed like a rag doll and would have rolled to the floor had Kara not stopped it.

"What do we do?" Taff asked.

Kara felt panic rising in her chest but tried to appear calm for her brother's sake. "There must be doctors in Penta's Keep. Someone who can help us."

"It's the grimoire, isn't it?" Taff asked. "It's punishing her for not using it. We should have gotten rid of it when we were on the—"

Safi opened her eyes, causing both Taff and Kara to jump with surprise.

"We have to get off the Swoop," she said.

Taff helped his friend to a sitting position.

"We couldn't wake you up," he said. "I was so scared!"

"I'm sorry. That's what happens when I have a vision. I should have warned you."

"What do you mean we have to get off?" Kara asked. "Why?"

"There are graycloaks waiting for us at the next station. I saw them." Safi hesitated. "Only this vision was different somehow."

"How so?"

"Hard to explain. Just different. But that doesn't make it wrong. We need to get off this thing. Now."

"How?" Taff asked. "You know how fast we're moving? And how high? What are we going to do—jump?"

Safi shrugged and turned to Kara.

"I'm going to need my grimoire back," she said.

Kara closed her eyes the whole way down. She landed hard in the branches of an evergreen tree, Safi's magical shield protecting her from instant death but doing remarkably little to combat nonfatal scratches and general bruising. Kara fell to the snow-packed ground and lay on her back for a few moments, regaining her breath.

She heard two *thunks* in quick succession as Safi and Taff landed beside her.

"That was not one of your better spells," Taff said.

"It worked, didn't it?"

"Depends on what you mean by 'worked.'"

Kara flipped over on her stomach and pushed herself up. Cold air snapped its teeth at her. She helped the others to their feet and they started down a narrow path lined with evergreens. Unlike the enclosed canopy of the Thickety, which always seemed in the process of swallowing its inhabitants, Kara could clearly see the dark sky above the trees: two moons and a breathtaking tableau of sparkling light.

"Pretty," Kara said.

"Cold," replied Taff, rubbing his hands together. Kara gave him his mittens and wool hat, which she always kept in the pocket of her cloak because he would lose them otherwise. "Which way?" he asked.

"Just follow the Swoop line north," Kara said. "That

will lead us to Penta's Keep."

"What about the graycloaks?" Safi asked. "Won't they be waiting for us?"

"Once they see we're not on the Swoop they'll move on." She placed her hand on Safi's back. "How was it? Using the grimoire after all this time?"

"It was easy. The spell was just sitting there waiting for me."

"That's good. Right?"

"I'm not sure. There's something about this I don't like."

"Kara," Taff said.

He raised a single finger and pointed into the woods, where a large wolf, charcoal-gray with sharp blue eyes, watched them with keen interest.

Safi raised her grimoire.

"No," Kara said. "Let's keep walking, show him that we don't mean any harm. Remember, we're trespassing in his home here."

She continued along the path, Taff and Safi to either side of her. Pristine white snow crunched beneath their feet. The wolf kept pace with them, loping through the trees. Soon four more wolves, two on either side of the path, joined him. The children walked faster and the wolves matched this new pace, though they showed no inclination to attack. Branches cracked and groaned as two mammoth animals pushed their way free of the trees. Their heads were long and narrow, their antlers cupped to the sky like giant leaves catching rain. Kara was certain the wolves would attack these new arrivals, or vice versa, but they simply walked together like old friends, the wolves dancing between the hooves of the massive creatures.

"My father had an old book for children with pictures of animals from the World," Safi whispered. "I recognize that one. It's called a moose."

"What's happening?" Taff asked.

The elk came next, followed by an entire family of

reindeer, a dozen red foxes, and two black bears awoken early from hibernation. Squirrels and chipmunks danced along the treetops; flapping wings thickened the sky. Evergreens shook clumps of snow to the ground as animals spilled onto the path, the menagerie growing at such a rapid pace that it was impossible to keep track of them all. The animals filled the spaces behind them, blocking any sort of escape, and forced the children off the path to a darker part of the forest. Taff fell behind the girls, and something that looked like a large cat nudged him forward.

"Sometimes I really miss your powers," he told Kara.

"Me too."

"You want me to cast a fireball?" Safi asked. "Maybe that would scare them away."

"Or cause a wild stampede with us in the center."

"Well, we have to do *something*. Why are they chasing us?"

"They're not chasing us," Kara said. "They're herding us."

They came to a clearing with a red tent at its center. The tent was huge, larger than even the Bindery back in Kala Malta, with three peaks like the spiny ridges of some great beast. From each of these peaks waved a black flag bearing the image of a double-fanged spider.

"It's *her*, isn't it?" Taff whispered.

Kara nodded.

The forest animals took positions on the outskirts of the clearing, granting the children entrance to the tent but cutting off every other avenue of escape.

"That's why the vision felt strange to me," Safi said. "She put it in my head. There were no graycloaks at the next station. It was all a trick to get us here."

"It's not your fault," said Kara. "She's good at tricking witches."

To either side of the tent's entrance stood two smiling girls, identical in every way. They were about fifteen, with moon-gray eyes and strange glaucous hair brushed so violently straight it could give bristles nightmares.

Between nubs of half-grown teeth Kara glimpsed misshapen black tongues.

The twins pulled back the entrance flaps and the children entered the tent.

THIRTEEN

A bone-white banquet table set with elegant dishes ran down the center of the tent. It was lined on either side by females ranging in age from a sullen four-year-old to an ancient woman so wizened she looked like a skeleton that had been painted with a thin coat of skin. They came from all corners of Sentium, as different in appearance as the grimoires held on their laps.

At the head of the table, on a crystal throne piled with silk pillows, sat Rygoth.

"Please," she said, indicating the three empty seats closest to her. "Join us."

As Kara made her way past the seated witches—their eyes regarding her with as much jealousy as hatred—she noted that the tent had been decorated with beautiful works of art displayed as apathetically as cheap souvenirs. Breathtaking tapestries hung crooked on the wall. Dirty boots lay across an elaborately engraved chest. A tall, gilded mirror was too clouded with filth to provide Kara with a reflection. These treasures had been taken simply because Rygoth desired them, not because she appreciated their beauty. There was no joy in the ownership save the ownership itself.

Kara took the seat closest to Rygoth. Taff sat between his sister and a middle-aged witch with bulging eyes. Safi sat across from Kara, on the opposite side of the table, her hand just touching the grimoire inside her satchel. Behind Rygoth, curled on a fine rug, lay a wolf with silver fur and the raised tail of a scorpion. Kara recognized the creature from Kala Malta. He had been hers first, before Rygoth stole him.

No one spoke.

After closing the entrance flaps, the still-smiling twins took the two seats at the other end of the table, placing a grimoire the color of grave dirt between them. The other witches remained focused on Rygoth, their hands folded primly over the covers of their own grimoires like a class terrified of disobeying its teacher.

Rygoth snapped her fingers.

From another part of the tent came the clatter of silverware, the rushing of footsteps. Shabbily dressed servants entered the room, balancing tureens and platters on silver trays. They set out a mouthwatering feast: creamy soup with thick slices of sausage, buttered yams, fried taro, wild mushrooms, roasted venison, and dozens of other foods Kara didn't even recognize. The servants moved in an odd, jerky fashion, like marionettes on a string. Kara looked into the eyes of a bearded man pouring wine into the witches' goblets and saw the caged desperation there. Rygoth, who enjoyed using her *wexari* powers on humans as well as other animals, was controlling these servants with her mind, a manner of enslavement far more effective than shackles and chains.

"You must be tired from your long journey," Rygoth said. "Eat."

Kara saw Taff look hopefully in her direction.

"No thank you," she said.

The enslaved servants weren't the only reason for her lack of appetite. Half-masked by the aromas of the feast was a far less pleasant smell, sickeningly familiar. She reconsidered their surroundings: the smooth white table like a section of some great rib, the fleshy walls that billowed in and out as though breathing.

"We're inside Niersook, aren't we?" Kara asked.

"How astute of you to notice," said Rygoth. "One of my finest creations. Quite adaptable. Also makes a good wagon when the need arises. You really should eat."

"I'm not hungry."

The inside of the tent was warm enough for Kara to

remove her cloak, but despite this her body had grown numb with cold. She had read in the Path that prisoners condemned to die were sometimes granted a last meal. Perhaps this was hers.

"I realize now that my attack on your ship was completely misguided," said Rygoth. "And to send a magnificent beast like Coralis to perform such an insignificant task! How embarrassingly overzealous of me. Like sending a dragon to swat a fly. I'd been trapped in that cave for so long—I admit I overreacted. This time, I promised myself I would be more civilized." Rygoth sipped her soup. "I know your plan. Sneak into the Well of Witches through the old entrance to Phadeen. Retrieve the white-haired witch. Undo the curse on your father. Quite daring! But it ends now."

Rygoth listed their secrets as though they had been blazoned across the sky. Safi looked away, ashamed that the spell she had cast to shroud their conversations had failed so miserably.

"I'm doing you a kindness, children," Rygoth said. "Have you truly stopped to consider what you might find waiting for you in the Well of Witches? An eternity of torment, if the stories are to be believed." Rygoth crawled her gloved fingers across the table. "I have to confess, though, that despite the risks I'd love to see it for myself. Minoth Dravania's blessed paradise blackened to purest evil." The witch scoffed. "You have no idea who he even is, of course."

"The headmaster of Sablethorn," Kara replied, relishing the flicker of surprise in the *wexari*'s eyes. "He forced you to leave the school. That must have been quite a blow."

Rygoth bit her lower lip and regarded Kara with a petulant glare, the wounds as fresh as if this had happened yesterday and not two thousand years ago.

"Sordyr told you," she said, a hint of betrayal in her voice. Despite the fact that she had transformed her friend into a Forest Demon, Rygoth apparently still expected him to honor her secrets. "Minoth never liked me. I was a lowborn girl, just a simple miller's daughter. Not one of his *chosen*. I showed him, though. All the other students agreed to be Sundered and sent off into the world like docile little sheep, but I refused! Perhaps *they* needed to prove themselves, but why should I have risked losing my powers and donning the green veil? Even in my youth, I was more powerful than any of them, including the teachers. Minoth called me insolent and dangerous, but the real reason he sent me away was because he *feared* me! And now look! He's nothing but bone dust and I've become the most powerful *wexari* that Sentium has ever known!"

Rygoth's painted lips curled upward, a wasted smile of triumph for a man long dead.

"But let us not spend any more words on *Minoth Dravania*," she said, spitting the name out like a spoiled piece of meat. "You were about to promise me that you would stop this ill-advised attempt to restore your father's soul."

Kara ran the words through her head a second and third time, wondering if she had misunderstood.

"You want me to *stop*?" she asked. "*Why?* If I undo the curse on my father, Timoth Clen will be erased from existence—which rids you of your greatest enemy."

"Nonsense. I want Timoth Clen to forge onward! Why search for witches myself when he'll do all the hard work for me?"

"He's going to kill them!"

"It won't get that far," Rygoth said. She sliced a small piece of rare meat from a nearby platter and slid it onto her plate, making sure not to get any blood on her white gloves. "I'll wait until all those iron cages are filled and he's about to perform his public execution—and then I'll swoop in and rescue them all. How grateful they'll be! Witches who might have resisted the idea of helping my cause will fall at my feet with gratitude. Timoth Clen is not only gathering my army, he's building their loyalty to me. I'd be lying if I said I did not appreciate the irony."

She cut a tiny slice from her meat and chewed it slowly. "I'll kill him afterward, of course, and all his graycloaks. Timoth Clen is not the only one who can arrange a public demonstration of power. But that's nothing you need to worry about. Just abandon this hopeless quest to help your father, and I'll leave you and your brother in peace. You have my word. But if you continue along this path, expect something truly unfortunate to happen." She glanced down at their empty plates. "I really would prefer it if you three ate *something*."

"We don't want your stupid food!" exclaimed Taff, slamming his fist on the table so hard the silverware rattled. "You talk about killing our father and all those other people like it's nothing you . . . you . . . *witch*!"

Rygoth's perfect features darkened, the anger held at bay thus far spreading across her face like an ink stain.

"Of course you want my *stupid food*," she said. "You want it more than you've ever wanted anything in your entire life."

"I don't," said Taff, even as he took a turkey leg and began to chew it ravenously. "I don't want any of it," he mumbled, the words barely discernable through a mouthful of meat.

"Stop it," said Kara.

"Or what?" Rygoth asked. "Even when you *had* powers you couldn't stop me. What are you planning to do now?"

Tossing the turkey aside, Taff stuffed his mouth with anything else he could get his hands on: globs of mashed potatoes, green beans, yellow custard. Kara tried to stop him but he danced out of her hands, crawled onto the table. Kept eating. The witches laughed with childlike glee. A cold fury, absent since the days she had used the grimoire, coursed through Kara's body. She eyed a carving knife leaning against a silver platter, wondered how fast she could get ahold of it and plunge it into Rygoth's chest.

Taff started to gag.

"Release him!" Safi exclaimed, rising to her feet, the grimoire already open in front of her.

Thunk! Thunk! Thunk!

The other witches slammed their spellbooks on the table and watched Safi eagerly, daring her to speak a single word.

Taff's gagging grew louder. His face began to turn red.

"Calm down, girls," said Rygoth. "No need to waste your pages."

Rygoth glanced at Taff and the spell was broken. He spit out the mound of food clogging his throat and gasped for breath.

"You didn't need to do that," Kara said, rubbing his back. "This is between me and you."

Rygoth laughed.

"'Me and you'? Is that what you really believe? That there's some sort of storybook battle looming between the two of us, the forces of good and evil?" She reached over and patted Kara on the head. "You're not a threat to me, love. You're just a plaything."

Kara felt something slither inside her mind. She wanted

to fight back against this uninvited presence, but she was no longer a *wexari* and had no means to do so. Rygoth laughed softly, covering her mouth. "Such confusion! Such sorrow! And something else. What *is* that?" Rygoth smacked her lips together as if tasting an unfamiliar food for the first time. "Ahh," she said. "Guilt. You still have nightmares about him. The boy you killed. Simon."

Beneath the table, Kara clenched her fists together.

"Get out of my head."

"I've seen *wexari* who fail the Sundering go mad after losing their magic and donning the green veil," Rygoth said. "But you . . ." Kara felt a clawing inside her brain, scooping out her innermost thoughts. "You miss it, of course, but you seem almost . . . grateful. Like you wanted to be punished for the things you've done. Killing the boy. Failing to protect your father. Forcing mindless animals to do your will." Rygoth's nose twitched as though she smelled something unpleasant. "Even the white-haired witch who tried to kill you . . . You feel

guilty you couldn't save *her*." Kara felt a slackening in her head as Rygoth pulled away, the *wexari* looking almost as relieved as Kara to be free. "Are you *always* burdened by such feelings? How do you even *live?*"

Kara, her body shaking with silent tears, was unable to respond.

"Pathetic," Rygoth said. She snapped her fingers and a servant brought over a new pair of white gloves, which Rygoth quickly exchanged for the old ones. "You're nothing but a weak fool. Magic requires control, concentration, focus. I'm glad I took away your powers—you don't *deserve* to be a witch."

She's right. All that power and I couldn't save Father or Mother. . . . The villagers were right all along. . . . I'm no good . . . no good . . .

"You did set me free from that infernal cave, though," Rygoth continued, "and I'm grateful for that. Without you, none of these wonderful things could have ever happened. I want you to remember that when the end comes."

She dismissed Kara completely and pivoted toward Safi. "Now you, on the other hand, are an interesting one. You stopped Coralis, which is impressive enough, but I know that's not the extent of your talents. You see things, don't you? The future? Had any visions recently? Maybe something about a grimoire stitched back together from four different parts?"

Rygoth knows what Safi saw inside her cell, Kara thought. *That's the real reason we're here.*

"I haven't seen anything about a grimoire," Safi said, but she didn't put much effort into the lie. It was useless to try to keep secrets from a woman who could poke around your mind.

"Now, Safi," Rygoth said. "That grimoire is very special. It was Princess Evangeline's. The first. All other grimoires taken together are but a shadow of its power. So I'm going to ask you a very important question. Do you know where the four parts of the grimoire have been hidden?"

Safi shook her head.

"I believe you. But you *could* find out for me. I could teach you how to focus your gift. With my guidance, you could become a powerful seer. We could help each other. I hope that this dinner has shown you that I am not without mercy. I could hurt your friends. I could make you do my bidding. But I have not."

"So you're just going to let us go?" asked Safi.

"If you wish it. But there's no need for you to go back into the cold. You're better than these two. Stay here where you belong."

"I belong with them."

Kara was afraid that Rygoth would erupt in anger, but instead she smiled—which was somehow worse.

"You're free to go, then. The city gates are just an hour's walk away." She leaned forward, meeting Safi's eyes. "I'll give you one day to change your mind. After that—I may just change it for you."

FOURTEEN

Penta's Keep was madness, a maelstrom of smells and noises and people. Kara's head began to pound the moment they passed beneath the city gates. There was far too much to keep track of at once. Black clouds spit from the chimneys of low-slung buildings, cloaking the streets in a coughing mist. Wagons rattled. Babies cried. Talking, shouting, screaming. Frying meat, roasted fish, unwashed bodies. They were shoved along by a tidal wave of people. Stopping, changing direction, slowing down—none were possible. They could only move along with the crowd and try not to lose one another. Vendors strolled the streets, shouting their wares. *Pretty mirrors! Sweet candy! Feathered hats!* The prices were an affront. Kara longed to swat the vendors away but she was afraid of letting go of the children's hands, the enthralled glow in their eyes a promise to wander. They drifted down one street then another, no idea where they were going; water sluiced from pipe to pipe. Dark alleyways loomed, populated by shadowy men wearing wide-brimmed hats. What confused Kara the most was the impossible coexistence of wealth and poverty. A woman wearing a fur-lined coat and glorb-earrings stepped over a starving man shivering on the ground. A newly constructed building stood next to a dilapidated shack. The confluence of expensive perfume and rotting trash birthed a profane stench.

How can people live like this? Kara thought. She wanted to bury herself with forest leaves and drink in silence for a week or two.

Finally the crowd began to thin out somewhat and they found themselves in a less congested part of the city. Against walls of splintered wood sat men, women, and children—mostly children—with gaunt faces, their hands outstretched, begging for coin. Taff reached into Kara's pocket but she stilled his hand.

"There's too many," Kara said. "We can't help them all."

"So we'll just help some of them."

"What about the ones we *can't* help?"

Taff shrugged. "They won't be any worse off than before we came. But the other ones will be better!"

In the end, she allowed him to take three coins, which he surreptitiously slipped into the hands of the most needy-looking. As he did, he asked them about the location of the Forked Library. The first two stared up at him with uncomprehending eyes and murmured nonsensically. The third one, however, a young woman cradling a baby in her arms, offered to guide them.

"Thank you," Kara said. "We'll pay you for your trouble."

"You already did."

"That was just a single copper."

The woman took Kara's hands in her own. Her fingernails were crusted with dirt, her eyes pretty beneath a haggard face.

"You could have walked past us, but you didn't," she said. "You've paid me."

Even with the baby in her arms, the woman was fast. She led them through narrow alleyways and half-flooded streets, into shambling buildings and out back entrances, past luxurious houses that shone with dangling glorblights and along a row of lean-tos where barefoot denizens fought tooth-and-nail for a spot closest to the fire.

Finally, the woman stopped. The baby in her arms instantly began to cry, as though it were only the rhythm of its mother's movement that had kept it asleep.

"We're here," she said.

In front of them a tower rose so high that Kara was certain they would have seen it from miles away were it not for the gray clouds of smoke that polluted the air. The base was constructed from some kind of red metal and gleamed brilliantly even in the minimal sunlight. From here, the tower split into four parts, like a candelabra. The first section was made of glass, and though its surface was covered with a thin layer of soot, Kara could still see rows of books inside and small moving shapes that might have been people. From the gray, metallic surface of the second tower extended long rods like antennae. These were punctured with holes that caught the wind as it passed, creating a humming sound that rose and fell like birdsong. A rising spiral of glorb-lights wound about the third, a wooden tower, providing illumination for the entire building. The fourth tower, painted entirely in black and constructed from a strange, organic-looking material, was considerably smaller than the other three. It stuck out of the base at a slightly different angle, like a thumb.

"It's amazing," Safi said, her eyes, for a few moments at least, regaining their former splendor.

The woman nodded, holding up her baby to see the pretty lights. It cooed softly. Kara couldn't tell if it was a boy or a girl. There was no pink or blue in this child's world.

"Why are the towers so different from one another?" Taff asked.

"One for each region," the woman said. She pointed to each of the towers in turn, and Kara used this distraction to slip a handful of coins into the folds of the baby's blanket. "The Glass Tower for the mirror-makers of Lux. The Tower of Rods for Auren. The Glorb Tower—formerly the Tower of Wind; before that the Burning Tower—for Ilma." The woman covered her baby's ears with her hands. "The Black Tower is for Kutt, the body snatchers of the north."

The Forked Library was indeed impressive, but Kara

was far more interested in the way it rose above the rest of the city as though upon the burial ground of some fallen structure.

We've found it. Sablethorn.

Before they entered the library, Kara wanted to contact Lucas and tell him what she had learned. The children found a spot as far away from the crowd as possible, and Taff dug the conch out of his sack.

"So how does this work?" Kara asked. "Do you have to shake it, or say some special words, or——"

Taff placed the shell to his mouth.

"Hello?" he asked. "Lucas? Are you there? Helllooo?"

Passing pedestrians didn't even give Taff a second glance. Apparently insanity was woven comfortably enough into the fabric of Penta's Keep that it could be ignored with ease.

Taff raised his voice, finally drawing some curious glances.

"Hellooo? Luuccccaass? My sister wants to talk to youuuuu."

"Taff?" Lucas asked. "Is that you?"

Kara couldn't tell if he was whispering or if the softness of his voice was simply a result of the great distance between them, and she really didn't care. She was just thrilled to know that he was alive.

"Where are you?" Kara asked.

"A place called Yandyre. Used to be a big mining town before we learned how to harness glorbs. Now it's not much of anything. Especially after the witch got done with it."

"Another one?"

"And not like Bethany—this one was *bad*. There was something wrong with her even before she started using a grimoire. I asked afterward. She liked to set things on fire. Only, when she used the grimoire, her fire shed no light. It was dark, and hot enough to melt steel, and alive. Like nothing I've ever seen. I know you don't want to hear this, Kara, but Timoth Clen *saved* this town. People would have died if he hadn't shown up when he did."

"Why wouldn't I want to hear that?" Kara asked. "I don't want anyone to die! That's why I have to restore Father to his body before Timoth Clen executes all those witches!"

A long silence stretched between them.

"Where are you?" Lucas finally asked.

"Outside the Forked Library."

"You made it! Sablethorn's underneath, right?"

"If what your grandfather said is true."

"He made no promises."

"No, he didn't."

A gentle rush of ocean waves, like the echoes that formed inside the curved surfaces of a real seashell, filled the silence. The magic allowing them to speak to each other was weakening. Unsure how much time they had remaining, Kara talked fast, saying only what needed to be said.

"Rygoth is planning to free all the witches and kill Timoth Clen and his graycloaks."

"How do you know?"

"She told me over dinner."

"*What?*"

"Doesn't matter. Rygoth is going to wait until Timoth Clen is about to perform his public execution. Wherever that is. Have you found out?"

"Not yet. They're heading north. I need to warn him!"

"No! It's too dangerous!"

The sound of the waves was stronger than ever now, and they could feel time growing short.

"Lucas?" Kara asked.

"I'm here."

She brought the shell close to her lips and whispered, "I'm sorry I got you involved in all this. You found your family. You were happy. And I ruined it."

"*Rygoth* ruined it. Besides, I wasn't that happy."

"Why not?" Kara asked.

Before Lucas could respond the waves crashed loudly in her ear and were immediately followed by an empty silence, the distance between them finally too much for even magic to undo.

After a short walk through a jostling crowd, the octagonal gates of the Forked Library loomed in front of them.

"Sablethorn must be right below us," Kara said. She laid a hand on the stone pavement, as though she could feel the heartbeat of the forgotten school.

"Why bury it?" Safi asked. "Why not just knock it down altogether?"

"Because they couldn't," Kara said. "Sablethorn was built by Minoth Dravania himself. It was his pride and joy, protected by all manner of powerful spells—that's what Sordyr said in his letter. The king wanted his people to forget that magic ever existed, but he wasn't able to destroy the school—so he buried it and hoped that as the years passed people would forget there had ever

been a school there at all."

"Which they did," said Safi.

"But on the other hand," Taff said, "Minoth wouldn't want any bad witches to ever find Sablethorn. There're probably all sorts of secrets inside. That's why my rabbit broke! There's a spell protecting Sablethorn from being found by magic!"

"But even if this place is still there," Safi said, "how do we get inside? Was there anything in Sordyr's letter?"

Kara shook her head. "The library was built after Rygoth transformed Sordyr into the Forest Demon. As far as he knew, Sablethorn was still standing."

"If there's any sort of entrance, it will be in the basement," Safi said. "Since the school's underground, that only makes sense."

"Does it?" Taff asked. "The king wanted to *destroy* Sablethorn. That was the whole purpose of the Forked Library. Why would he build a way to get inside of it?"

"You're right," Kara said. "The *king* would have never

built an entrance. But I don't think that Minoth would have allowed his beloved school to just vanish forever. There'll be a way."

Taff gasped with excitement.

"A *secret passageway!*"

Kara saw the idea of hinged bookcases and dark tunnels glowing in her brother's eyes. She took his hand and they started toward the great doors. As they neared the entrance, however, Kara realized that Safi had not followed them.

"What's wrong?" Kara asked, making her way back to the girl.

"What about Rygoth?" she asked, her hands nervously clutching at her skirt. "You were warned not to save your father. She'll know. She always does."

"You're probably right."

"I'm scared."

"You have nothing to worry about. Rygoth needs you."

"It's not me I'm scared about! It's you and Taff! Maybe if

I went to her she would leave you alone like she said. . . ."

Kara knelt so she could look straight into Safi's eyes.

"Don't talk like that. We're going to get through this together. Got it?"

Safi gave a brief, unconvincing nod. Kara wanted to say more but Taff, lingering along the edges of what he sensed to be a private conversation, finally lost his patience and interrupted them.

"Could we *go* already?"

A few moments later, the three children passed through the giant doors.

Kara knew, of course, that the library was an imposingly large structure, but nothing prepared her for the complexity of how this massive space had been used: four iron stairways winding upward to the other towers, floor hatches opened by red-robed librarians balancing stacks of books beneath their chins, a multitude of steel doors that held the threat of even more areas to explore, labyrinthine shelves stacked with books, more books than

Kara had ever seen; more books than she thought could possibly even exist.

It was a forest, a kingdom, a world.

Kara loved it.

Knowing that a place such as this could flourish amid the chaos of the city filled her with a strange sort of hope. No, not hope. *Gratification.* She had always believed that beauty could be found everywhere, in even the unlikeliest of places, and here was all the proof she needed.

Kara longed to explore the upper towers, but that wasn't why they were here; the entrance to Sablethorn would be located beneath them. They descended ladders and staircases, each floor more poorly lit than the one before it, until they found themselves in a section of the library packed with dust-covered volumes that looked as though they hadn't been read in eons. Occasionally the group would be forced to slip into the shadows to avoid a passing librarian, but other than that they had the entire floor to themselves. After being thwarted by a few dead

ends they found an unusual iron door with no knob or handle. There was, in fact, no way to open it at all. Next to the door stood an ancient stone tablet with boxes, circles, and seemingly random lines carved into its surface. Kara thought they might be letters, but if so, they were unlike any letters she had ever seen before.

"It looks old," Safi said. "Really old. Maybe this is written in a language that nobody uses anymore."

"It might tell us what's behind the door," Kara said, running a finger over the mysterious grooves. "Or how to open it. But that's no help if we can't—"

With a sudden shout of excitement, Taff swung his sack to the floor and began digging through its contents. "I know what to do!" he exclaimed. After tossing a dozen toys to the library floor—wooden paddles, a recorder with three extra holes, red yarn tangled into a misshapen ball—he finally found what he was looking for: a long kaleidoscope painted with colorful shapes. The beads sealed in its interior rattled together as Taff raised it to his eye and looked at the stone tablet.

"I found some old books in Kala Malta," he said, slowly twisting the outer cylinder on the end of the kaleidoscope. "Nobody remembered how to read them, but Mary taught me how to use this kaleidoscope." He twisted the cylinder clockwise, grunted, turned it in the opposite direction. "It can change any language into something you can read." He was turning the cylinder so slowly now that Kara could barely see it move. "It's just a matter of finding . . . the right way of looking . . . *There!*"

"What's it say?" Safi asked.

Taff hesitated, slowly forming the words with his lips. The kaleidoscope had done its job translating the ancient words, but for Taff the most difficult part still remained; reading was one of the few things that had never come easily to him.

Kara squeezed the back of his neck.

"Take your time," she said. "Do the best you can."

A few minutes passed. Safi paced back and forth

impatiently. On the floor above them Kara could hear the muffled footfalls of librarians and patrons.

Finally, Taff spoke.

"It says there was a 'black sickness' while the library was being built," he said. "Many workers died. Their bones are sealed in a crypt past this point, but no one can enter here because they can still catch the disease."

"I guess this direction's out, then," Safi said.

Taff shook his head, smiling.

"Don't you get it? This is Minoth's doing. He knew he couldn't stop the king from burying his school, but he didn't want all his hard work to be lost forever, so he created this 'sickness' to scare people away from the lowest level. And once they were scared away, I bet he built a passageway from the library into Sablethorn. This Minoth guy is *smart*."

"How could he build an entrance by himself?" Safi asked. "It would take hundreds of workers to do something like that."

"Minoth was a powerful *wexari*," Kara said. "He could do it."

"Or there really is a disease down there," Safi said.

"Let's find out!" said Taff.

He removed the wooden hideaway from his sack. Using the penknife, he filed away a fingernail's length of the door's surface and placed it in the box.

He closed the lid and opened it again.

They heard a muffled *thunk* from the other side of the door as something heavy dropped to the floor. The door creaked open with a loud grating noise. They entered and shut the door behind them. Their new location was pitch-black, so Taff removed the ball that Mary Kettle had used to guide them through the Thickety and tossed it up and down until it began to emit a soft blue glow. They were in a narrow tunnel of stone, as though they had stepped out of the Forked Library and into some sort of cave. At Kara's feet lay a steel bar as thick as a plank of wood.

"Look," she said, pointing to L-shaped brackets driven

into the stone just beyond the outer edges of the door. "The bar was holding it shut. It would have been impossible to open from the library side—without magic, at least."

"And no skeletons," Taff said, raising the ball high enough to reveal the entire tunnel. "That whole disease story was made up." He grinned at Safi. "Told you."

At the end of the tunnel was a second door, almost identical to the first one. Taff opened it. Beyond this lay a circular room, empty save for a single hatch at its center. Just like the other doors, the hatch lacked a knob or a handle. Taff used the hideaway, and they heard something fall from the other side of the hatch, followed by a longer-than-expected silence before it crashed to the surface.

"There's a drop on the other side," Kara said. "Be careful."

Gripping Taff's shoulder for balance, Kara stomped down on the hatch door. It fell open, releasing a geyser of stale air. They peered into the darkness, Kara holding Taff as he lowered his ball of light as low as he could reach. They saw the iron bar that had kept the hatch locked lying on top of a red surface, the drop not nearly as far as Kara had thought.

"I'll lower you two down first," Kara said. "Then I'll just hang down and drop. Easy."

She started with Taff, since he had the light. Just as she was about to lower him into the darkness, however, his eyes narrowed, as they did whenever an interesting thought popped into his mind.

"Who locked all these doors?" he asked. "It had to be done from the inside, and they wouldn't be able to get back out again. They'd be trapped down here forever."

"That's horrible," said Safi.

"It doesn't matter," Kara said. "Whoever it was, they're long gone by now."

She hung over the edge of the hole and lowered Taff gently into the darkness. Safi went next, landing awkwardly on her ankle but with no serious harm done, followed by Kara herself. The roof was surprisingly small. She peered over its side. Taff's light revealed a wall of giant rectangular stones that sloped downward in a widening series of steps.

"It's a pyramid," Kara said.

But neither Taff nor Safi seemed to hear her. They were too busy gazing up, mouths agape. The earth and stone that made up the foundation of the Forked Library lay just above them, suspended in the air, some sort of invisible force keeping it from crushing the building beneath it.

"What kind of magic is this?" Safi asked.

"*Wexari* magic," Kara said. "The most powerful kind."

They found the entrance easy enough, a plain wooden door that did not even require Taff's hideaway to open. After descending a long set of stone stairs, they entered a wide hallway lined with doors. Suddenly they could see. There were no torches, no glorb-lights (though Kara supposed that the last time Sablethorn had been open, glorb-lights hadn't even been invented yet). It was as if the school, recognizing that there were visitors, had breathed light into the very air itself.

Taff slid the magical ball back into his sack.

"What now?" he asked.

Kara was suddenly giddy with excitement. *We're in Sablethorn!* After reading Sordyr's letter time and time again the place had taken on a mythical quality in her mind. She longed to explore every room and learn its secrets.

Except there wasn't enough time.

"We need to find where students used to enter Phadeen," Kara said. "That should take us right to the Well of Witches."

"Any helpful information in that letter of yours?" Safi asked.

"Actually, yes. Sordyr said the entrance to Phadeen happened to be on the lowest level of Sablethorn."

"'Happened to be'?" Safi asked.

"Those were his exact words. I thought them strange as well."

"More stairs," said Taff. "Swell."

The hallways were wide and lined with countless doors. Kara imagined hundreds of students pressed together, making their way to their next class. Unlike De'Noran, magic would not be forbidden but a never-ceasing topic of conversation.

It must have been wonderful.

"Why isn't this place falling apart?" asked Taff. "It's been buried underground for the last two thousand years."

"They used magic to preserve it forever," Safi said. "Maybe they hoped that one day Sablethorn could be opened again."

"Or maybe they just loved it," said Kara. "Sometimes it's that simple."

There were no cobwebs, no scurrying insects. The floors weren't even dusty. Kara opened a door, wondering if she might see students still sitting inside, their curious expressions frozen in time. All she saw, however, were rows of desks and chairs, and something that looked like a large glass sphere in the center of the room.

"Whoa," said Taff. "What's *that?*"

Kara closed the door.

"I have a feeling that if we start investigating these classrooms we're going to get very distracted. Let's stay focused."

At the end of the hallway they reached a large stairwell that wound its way down to an open area, presumably the lobby. Safi found two gigantic red doors—the main entrance—and opened them to reveal packed dirt held back by the same magic that kept the Forked Library from crushing the roof. Painted directly on the wall across from these doors was a portrait of an odd-looking man wearing a green robe. He had no hair or eyebrows, and a dark birthmark swelled across the left side of his face like a half-completed mask.

The stone below the portrait was engraved *MINOTH DRAVANIA, HEADMASTER.*

"He's not what I expected," Taff said.

Safi shrugged. "He has to look like something. Why not this?"

They passed a few statues on marble pedestals, the names unfamiliar to Kara but presumably famous graduates of Sablethorn. Her favorite was a woman named Azorean, who rode a giant wolf while brandishing a wooden staff in one hand. The children passed through a large archway into a long dining hall. Circular tables were still set with empty plates and silverware. Fire pits had been dug into the walls. From a black stand in the center of the room hung a cauldron so large that any sort of cooking would require the stepladder that rested next to it. A painting of the dining hall covered the back wall, giving Kara an idea of what it must have been like here: hundreds of students packed into the benches, some talking quietly amongst themselves, others with books stretched open before them. Green-veiled figures poured water into goblets and ladled out food.

Kara's heart sank.

"Remember what Rygoth said about not wanting to wear a green veil?" she asked. "That's what she meant. Those who failed the Sundering became servants! They weren't even allowed to show their faces!"

Kara didn't want to even consider the possibility that Rygoth might have been right about something, but the thought of a student being punished with a life of servitude seemed . . .

She heard footsteps.

The sound came from somewhere above them, carrying well through the empty halls. Boot heels clicked against the stone floors. *More than one person—maybe two or three. Getting closer.* Luckily, the dining hall was dimly lit, with plenty of places to hide. Kara pushed Safi and Taff toward the back of the hall and folded herself behind the cauldron stand; she wanted a position close enough

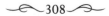

to see their pursuers as they passed through the archway. The footsteps grew louder. Kara heard Safi remove the grimoire from her satchel.

They waited.

Against the far wall of the hallway came two shadows stretched as tall as giants. Kara was reminded, momentarily, of the darkeaters back in the Thickety, and then the twins from Rygoth's tent stepped into the light. They shared a single grimoire, held open between them.

Kara turned, her back pressed against the cauldron. She was certain there was no way the twins could see her, not from their current position, but she tried to keep her breathing as quiet as possible. At the back of the hall she saw a pair of green eyes peeking out from beneath a table and waved her hands frantically: *Not yet, not yet! Don't cast a spell!* Perhaps Kara was wrong, perhaps a surprise attack would have been the best plan, but the idea of engaging the twins in a magical battle terrified her. Out of all the witches in her army, Rygoth had assigned these girls to guard the entrance to her tent and then follow them to Sablethorn. Clearly Rygoth felt the twins were special. Kara had no desire to learn why.

She risked a peek and saw that the twins had entered the dining hall. All their attention was focused on the grimoire, which was good, because when Kara looked back Taff was crossing to a wide door at the rear of the hall. Hiding behind a nearby table, he motioned for them to join him. It was a short distance for Safi but still a risk. Kara, on the other hand, would have to cross an open expanse to get there. The twins would notice her for sure.

Go, Kara mouthed to Safi. *I'll catch up.*

Safi shook her head. Kara pointed to the back door insistently, and then, struck by an idea, held up her finger: *Wait a second.* Searching the ground at her feet, she found a small piece of wood that had originally been intended to burn beneath the cauldron. Like everything else in Sablethorn, it hadn't changed much in the intervening millennia. Keeping her arm rail straight, she arced the wood over the cauldron, toward the front of the dining hall. It clattered across a table, taking a pewter cup with it. The twins were distracted only for a moment, but it was enough. Safi dashed out of her hiding place and slipped through the door with Taff, who paused to look back at his sister with concern. Kara smiled and waved him along: *Go! I'll be right behind you!*

He left. Kara sighed with relief.

Taking a cautious peek around the cauldron, she saw the twins looking at their grimoire like a map, as Bethany had done. They marched down the center of the dining hall, their footsteps perfectly in sync, until they were standing just to the right of Kara's hiding place. She slipped around to the left side of the cauldron, keeping it between them. Took another peek. The twins rotated the book, like someone turning a map to understand their location better, and nodded with recognition.

They started toward the door at the back of the room.

Safi is the one that Rygoth wants. That's why they're here. That's who the grimoire is tracking.

I can't let them get her.

Kara ran.

Her footfalls fell heavy on the floor, but that was okay—that was, in fact, the point. Kara was trying to make as much noise as possible in order to distract the twins. *This is a big place. I can lose them, double back, find Safi and Taff. Once I get through the archway, I'll break left toward the stairs. If I'm fast enough, they won't even know what floor I'm on.* She heard the twins read from the grimoire together, not in unison but each completing the other's incantation, their deformed tongues producing slurred, impossible words. Kara thought, *This is the only language they speak,* and then one of the circular dining tables rolled in front of the archway, blocking her exit. She tried to push past it and jumped back when the wooden surface of the table parted, revealing a mouth composed of jagged splinter-teeth. Benches slid across the room and joined the table, became legs and arms; tin plates embedded themselves in the places eyes would go. As the new creation got unsteadily to its feet, these plates burned themselves into the wood and then fell away, leaving horrible black stains that blinked with abrupt cognition.

The wooden monster roared.

It swung a bench at Kara and she dropped to the floor just in time, feeling the makeshift arm skim over the top of her body. The monster swung its other bench-arm high into the air and brought it downward with hissing speed. Kara rolled out of the way. The bench shattered. Splintered wood pricked the back of her neck.

The monster stared stupidly at the place where its arm had been and tottered to one side, as though unsure how to compensate for this sudden change in equilibrium. Kara tried to use this opportunity to escape, but the twins spoke more words and something cold and wet grabbed her ankle, throwing her off balance. She slammed to the floor. Pain ran up the length of her arm and numbed it.

Turning on her side she saw a whiplike tongue wrapped around her ankle, from a shadowy mouth that used to be a fire pit. It yanked her across the floor toward the hungry darkness. The twins spoke more words. Kara heard a loud rattle, like a clapper rolling around inside a bell, and saw long, jointed legs emerging from the body of the cauldron, heard the gentle *clink* as they touched down on the stone surface of the floor. The tongue of the fire pit dragged her closer.

She sat up——and found herself inches from the gaping mouth of the wooden monster.

It roared, and without thinking Kara reached into its mouth and snapped off a wooden tooth. The monster threw its head back, hollowing in pain, and Kara stabbed the tongue around her ankle, again and again, until the fire pit finally released her.

She ran out of the dining hall.

Before she could head toward the stairs, however, the cauldron skittered through the archway on spiderlike legs, blocking her path. Kara turned right, opened the first door she saw, and dashed into the room. It was a kitchen. Tables piled with pots and pans, racks of knives, metal basins. There was a door on the far right that, Kara guessed, had been the one that Taff and Safi had passed through, and a small set of stairs in the back of the room, leading down. The knives came to life first, folding and reshaping into tiny metallic insects with serrated wings and needle-sharp antennae. Kara didn't need to see anything else. She ran for the stairs, trying to ignore to deafening rattle to either side of her as cookware and cutlery shifted into unexpected new things. Something buzzed past her and she felt a sharp pain in her earlobe. And then she was through the back door and into the narrow stairwell, latching the door shut just as hundreds of metal knives thudded against it and clattered to the ground in defeat.

Kara ran down a winding, narrow staircase, listening carefully for the sound of a door opening behind her.

Though her fingertips came away wet when she touched her ear, the pain was no worse than a bee sting. The stairs went down and down and down, finally emptying into another dining hall, this one smaller but with fancier furniture: marble tabletops, crystal goblets, fine cutlery.

Safi was running toward her.

"Where were you?" she asked. "You said you were coming! We were so—"

"They're right behind me," Kara said, out of breath. "Where's Taff?"

"Come on," Safi said, pulling her forward. They broke into a run. "We found the entrance to Phadeen."

"Great!"

"Not great. There's a problem. Taff's working on it."

"What kind of problem?"

Kara heard the door at the top of the stairs creak open, followed by soft footsteps in no particular hurry. She followed Safi, running hard now, into a gargantuan hallway framed by stone arches. The walls were covered with

large tapestries: cloaked figures sitting in a field of flowers; a still lake glistening beneath a lavender sky; tranquil
animals with splendid wings grazing in a field of grass.

These are depictions of Phadeen, back when it was a paradise.

Suddenly the tapestries began to rattle on their hooks
like wild beasts eager to be uncaged. The girls exchanged
a look and ran faster. Kara could see a pair of double doors
in the distance now, a crack of light between them. *Keep
running. Don't look back.* Tapestries fell around them like a
flock of bats, their edges tearing and shaping into jagged
wings that enabled them to sail through the air.

We're not going to make it, Kara thought, the door still
painfully small in the distance.

The tapestries attacked.

Safi stopped running and read from the grimoire. Her
voice was soft but navigated the strange syllables with
confidence. The tapestries fluttered upward and began to
unspool with impossible speed. Colored thread streamed
through the air like confetti.

"I did it," Safi said, laughing. "I actually did—"

"Watch out!" Kara screamed.

Safi started to look up but it was already too late. The last remaining tapestry, out of range when the spell was cast, swooped down and *absorbed* her, spreading across the ground as flat as a rug.

Safi was gone.

"No!" Kara screamed.

She flipped the tapestry over and stared at the picture. A majestic waterfall crashed into the banks of a river. On the shore stood a gorgeous tree with buds of delicate mauve, providing shade for a small girl holding a book.

"Safi?" Kara asked.

The girl didn't reply. She was just thread.

Fluttering its false wings, the tapestry pulled itself from Kara's grasp but could not quite propel itself into the air. Instead, it slunk along the stone floor of the gallery, as though the girl caught inside its world now made it too heavy to fly.

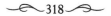

It came to a stop at the feet of the twins.

The left twin picked it up, and her omnipresent smile reached new heights as she saw Safi within the tapestry's borders. She showed her sister, who clicked her teeth together in appreciation, some sort of strange language they shared.

A tear zigzagged across the surface of the tapestry.

Kara shielded her eyes as rays of purple light burst forth from the tear and sent the twins flying. The light quickly vanished—and there was Safi, trying to crawl out of the tapestry. Kara grabbed her hands and pulled backward, taking a moment to eye the twins.

Still breathing.

Kara and Safi ran through the double doors and quickly pushed them closed. Together, they slid a wooden beam through two brackets in order to secure it.

"I'm not sure that will hold them if they wake up," Safi said. "Maybe I can make the door stronger." She opened the grimoire and winced at the spell she saw. "Except it doesn't want me to. It wants me to attack them. Finish them off. Of course."

Kara touched her arm. "Show it who's in charge."

She turned and examined the room. The floor was covered with gears: small gears and big gears; hexagonal and square and round gears; silver, bronze, and stone gears. A case of books leaned against the wall nearest her. Across the room was a single door embedded with countless pegs. Gears hung from almost all of them. In the place where a doorknob would go was a large wheel that would only turn, Kara assumed, when the gears were in their proper places.

Taff, trying to find the right gear for one of the empty pegs, grunted in frustration.

"Sordyr mentioned there was a puzzle," Kara said. "So only the worthy could cross into Phadeen."

Taff brightened.

"Did he give you the answer?"

"No."

"So he told you about the puzzle but didn't tell you how to solve it?" Taff asked, combing through the gears. "I think I liked him better when he was a Forest Demon."

"You can do it."

"I know. But I need more time. I'm not completely sure if all the gears I used are the right ones."

"One of the twins just moved!" Safi exclaimed, her eye pressed to the crack between the doors. "We have to hurry!"

Taff hung the last gear on the door and, pausing a heartbeat, turned the wheel. The gears grinded together, did not move. He nodded, took off a single gear, replaced it with another one. Still no luck. Taff stepped back, taking in the entirety of the door, and then smacked himself in the forehead before quickly switching two gears.

When he turned the wheel this time all the pieces of the door spun like clockwork.

"I've got it! I've got it!"

He continued to turn the handle, but the door did not

open. Instead, a cheerful song began to play, a tune for dancing around the fire. Taff spun the handle faster and the pace of the music increased.

"The door will open when the song is over," Taff said. "That must be it."

The final note played, and the pegs retracted into the door. The gears fell to the floor, some clattering directly in front of Taff's feet, others rolling across the room. The pegs returned to their usual position.

The door did not open.

"But I did it right," Taff said. "That's not fair!"

Something crashed into the double doors and the wooden beam rattled in its brackets. Safi remained intent on her grimoire, beads of sweat rolling down her temples. "Come on! Give me the spell I want! Come on!"

"Any other bright ideas?" Kara asked Taff.

Another crash. A crack split the beam.

"Got it!" Safi exclaimed in delight.

She spoke the words of her spell and the double doors

glowed purple with magical reinforcement.

"That should buy us a little more time," Safi said.

"Great," said Taff, "but it doesn't help us with our other problem."

Ask the right question, Kara thought. *Ask the right question.*

"Why is that shelf of books there?" she asked.

"I already thought of that," Taff said. "They just contain a bunch of names and dates. Nothing important at all."

"Then why did Minoth store them in the most important room in Sablethorn? Unless they're a lot more important than they seem."

Taff, seeing her point, ran over and started pulling books off the shelf. Kara joined him. She didn't see anything special inside their pages—Taff was right, just records of some kind—but on the fourth book she noticed a thick line burned across its leather cover, like a brand. The fifth and sixth books had no such distinguishing marks, but the eighth and ninth books did: a straight line and a curved one. She found another line, this one L-shaped. . . .

"I know what to do," Kara said, kicking gears away to make an empty space on the floor. "The *books* are the puzzle we need to solve. Put them together the right way and they form the entrance to Phadeen."

"What about the door with all the gears?" Taff asked.

"It's a giant music box. Apparently this Minoth has a sense of humor."

The three children worked together, laying the books on the floor and connecting the black lines burned into their covers. A perfect outline of a door began to form. Safi slid the last book into place and the stone floor within the borders of the book vanished, replaced by a portal of black liquid.

"Yuck," said Taff, eyeing the dark portal nervously. "We really have to go through that to get to the Well of Witches?"

The purple light surrounding the double doors began to dim as the twins pummeled it furiously with magic.

"They're going to break through," said Safi. "And then they'll follow us into the Well. How are you going to find your father with those two on your tail?"

"We'll figure it out," Kara said.

"No," Safi said, straightening. "It's *me* they want. That's why they tried to trap me in the tapestry. So they could bring me back to Rygoth. They won't hurt me. I know it."

The double doors rattled, the purple light almost gone now.

"We have to go!" shouted Taff.

"*You* have to go," said Safi. "After you're gone I'll put the books back. I'll tell the twins you went through the door with the gears. They might try to figure it out, but they don't seem like the smartest pair, and eventually they'll give up."

"We're not leaving you behind!" Kara exclaimed. "Rygoth might not hurt you, but there are other things she can do to make you help her. She'll *change* you."

"Safi," said Taff. "Please come with us."

But the young witch refused to look in his direction. Instead, she tore a page out of her grimoire and pressed it into Kara's hand.

"You'll need this to save your father," she said, and pushed Kara through the portal.

BOOK THREE
THE FACELESS

*"It is how we address
the questions without answers
that makes us who we are."*

—Minoth Dravania
64th Sablethorn Lecture

FIFTEEN

When Kara opened her eyes she was staring at a sand-colored sky splotched with dark brown. Her head felt heavy. *Where am I? How did I get here?* Beneath her fingertips the ground felt strangely smooth, the air as musty as the bottom of a well. Kara heard a steady scratching, the sound of quill on parchment, and slowly pushed herself up to see what was making the noise. The ground, as impossible as it seemed, was cream-colored paper, and across it the words *Where am I? How did I get here?* were in the process of being written. Kara recognized the neat, steady penmanship, the stubborn flourish on the hanging tail of the *g*.

It was her handwriting.

What is this? she wondered, and the three words scratched themselves into the ground as she thought them. Kara tried to touch the letters but they were located just beneath the paper ground like veins. Her two earlier thoughts began to glide away as though caught on some unseen current, rising over a slight hill and then slipping out of sight.

She remembered.

Safi pushed me. I'm in the Well of Witches.

These new thoughts scrawled themselves into the ground, followed by an additional one: *TAFF!* Kara jumped to her feet—too fast!—and the world spun for a moment. Her brother was lying next to her. He groaned as he got to his knees. No doubt he was suffering from the same disorientation as Kara, but other than that he seemed fine.

"My head," Taff said, rubbing it with his knuckles. "Safi pushed me. Did you know she was that fast? I didn't know she was that fast." His face flashed with anger. "I can't believe she did that!"

Kara watched the words I thought she was my friend! etch just beneath the ground. The handwriting was Taff's, a childlike, blocky print.

"She *is* your friend. She was trying to keep us safe."

Although Taff didn't reply, Kara read his next thought: But who's going to keep her safe?

"She's on her own until we get out of here," admitted Kara. "But she's a strong witch, and an even stronger girl. I wouldn't underestimate her."

"I guess you're right," Taff said. And then, shaking his head in surprise, added, "Wait! How do you know what I'm thinking? Are you magic again?"

Kara showed him the words on the ground, and explained, as best she could, what little she had learned. Taff proceeded to waste several giggling minutes making the ground inscribe random thoughts such as *Mashed potatoes!* and *My shoe is leaking!* and *Yellow-globbyflowything!*

"Are you about done?" Kara finally asked.

"Absolutely," Taff said, but his true thoughts spilled across the ground: *I'll just do it when she's not looking.*

Kara raised her eyebrows.

"Nuts," said Taff. "This might not be as much fun as I thought it would be."

Behind them a huge rose-colored wall towered into the sky, cutting off any travel in that direction. Kara ran her fingers along its surface, which was strangely wet to the touch.

"It feels like the cover of a grimoire," she said.

"And the ground and the sky are like pages," Taff said. "What does it mean? Are we *inside* a grimoire?"

"I don't know. But I don't like it."

"My toys!" Taff exclaimed. "I took the satchel off because it kept banging against the gears! I still have my

slingshot, but I left everything else in Sablethorn! Can we go back?"

"I don't think so."

She pointed to a black rectangle on the wall, the same size and shape as the door through which Safi had pushed them. It looked as though it had been burned into the surface.

"Safi closed the door," Taff said. "Just like she said she would. The twins can't follow us now. That's good, at least."

"In a way," Kara said, "but Safi forgot one thing. Now that she's closed the door, how are we going to get out of here after we find Grace?"

"You're right," said Taff. "For all we know, that could have been our only way out. We're trapped!"

"There's always another way," Kara said.

She held Taff close so he couldn't read her frantic doubts.

Although they seemed to be walking on paper it was as sturdy as regular ground, and Kara quickly got over her initial fear that they would fall straight through it. The land, for the most part, was blank and featureless, punctuated only by a series of paper-thin walls that were ten times the height of the children but as easily pushed over as a page in a book. Taff took great delight in this. Everything was the same sandy hue, and Kara quickly found herself hungering for the colorful variety of the real world. The utter *sameness* of this place was dizzying.

They came to a small waterfall that emptied into a narrow river. Instead of water, however, light-brown pulp the consistency of quicksand fell over the cliff. Paper trees lined the shore, and there was a small patch of flowers carefully folded like origami.

"I bet this used to be beautiful back when it was Phadeen," Kara said. "Before dark magic corrupted it."

"Just like the Thickety," Taff said.

Kara nodded. Beneath the ground she saw, in her own

handwriting, *Does magic ruin everything?* The words slid into the pulp and vanished in its currents. She saw other words floating there. They had been written in dozens of different hands, the letters linked together like a line of toy rafts: *How come she gets to be a Whisperer and I'm stuck here on the barge? Trina claims she's been through a Burngate but I don't believe her; her tail is almost complete—won't be long now before she becomes one of them.*

"What does it all mean?" Taff asked.

"It means we're not alone," said Kara. "The Well of Witches is gathering everyone's thoughts."

"Why?"

"Not sure. Maybe the thoughts are feeding it somehow?"

"It eats *thoughts?*"

"Imogen ate memories. It's not much different."

"But Imogen was a person. Well, sort of a person. This is a place. It's not alive." He threw his hands into the air. "Unless it *is* alive. I give up."

"The important thing right now is to find Grace as quickly as possible. Any ideas?"

Taff shrugged his shoulders. In the distance, the lower half of the horizon darkened to a familiar rose color. "Look," he said. "There's another wall, just like the one we came out of. It's so tall—I think it touches the sky, or at least what passes for the sky here."

As Taff talked, his thoughts continued to flow in a steady stream about various other topics: How can we be walking on paper? Where are they going to take Safi? This place is nothing like a well. What did that glass globe in Sablethorn do? Kara's hair is a mess. What happens if there's a fire?

Kara knew her brother had been gifted with an unusual intelligence, but seeing it on display here made her smile.

"Let's follow the river," Kara said, straightening her hair as best she could. "Keep walking against the current. The thoughts floating there now must have entered at some point upstream and flowed in this direction."

"So our plan is to *search* for the evil witches."

"That's where Grace will be."

"Now that we're actually here, the idea of seeing her again scares me."

"Me too."

"Even if she agrees to help us, we can't trust her. Not even a little bit. The first chance she gets—"

"You don't have to tell me that," said Kara.

"This is completely different than Mary Kettle. I could tell there was good in her. Grace Stone never had a drop of goodness. Even before she became a witch."

Kara nodded, and then watched with surprise as her mind leaked a thought she didn't even know she had into the ground.

There is good in everyone.

It slipped into the sludge and flowed away.

There was no morning or night in the Well of Witches, no paper sun and moon. Just the rose wall, growing incrementally closer with each labored step. Kara and Taff did not feel the need to sleep. They were not hungry or thirsty. These changes made traveling easier on a practical level, but they still made Kara uneasy.

What will happen to us if we don't escape this place soon?

They followed the river of words until—at long last—they saw other inhabitants.

Kara pulled Taff behind a nearby Page—as they had started calling the easily moved walls that populated the landscape—and the two children peeked their heads out for a closer look. Dozens of girls and women worked in a forest of paper trees standing as tall as the Fenroots they resembled. The witches all wore the same attire: blood-red cloaks that would make them incredibly easy to see from a distance, especially against such a uniform backdrop. Encircling the tree closest to the children were three witches holding hands, their faces hidden beneath their hoods. At first Kara had no idea what they were doing, but then she saw the words gliding along the ground toward the trunk of the tree: *Cut, chop, saw; cut, chop, saw; cut, chop, saw.* Two witches sent their thoughts at blurring speed, but the third witch, her hands withered and covered with purple veins, was slower. Finally, however, Kara saw physical gouges appear in the bottom of the tree, as though an invisible woodcutter were taking an ax to it.

A few minutes after this the tree crashed to the ground.

The Cutters did not take a moment to celebrate; they simply moved to their next assignment. Meanwhile, another set of women dragged the tree away to an unknown destination. Other groups were partnered in the same fashion.

"Look at that," Taff whispered, pointing to the ground between the trees and the river. Some of the words were slipping away from the sludge and gliding toward the trees, where they vanished into the ground. "I think the words are helping the trees grow. Like water."

This idea made no sense, of course, but it did not make it wrong.

All of a sudden, an argument erupted among the three witches. Kara wasn't close enough to hear the words, but the gist of it was clear enough: The young witches were unhappy that the older woman was taking so long to send her thoughts, thus slowing down the pace of their work. The argument escalated. The old witch pleaded that she would try to do better, but the younger women, arms crossed, were having none of it. The rest of the workers gathered in a loose circle to see what would happen next.

Taff covered his mouth, stifling a scream, and squeezed Kara's arm.

A figure made entirely of paper was approaching the witches. It had the general shape of a human, with parchment skin and gangly arms and legs like thinly rolled scrolls. From its neck protruded an additional seven arms, each as tiny as those of a child.

These arms had no fingers or hands. Instead, they ended in masks.

While the rest of the thing's body was the same flat color as the ground, its masks were each a different shade. Kara was reminded of the papier-mâché masks she had seen during the Shadow Festival, flour-hardened ghouls and goblins painted garish colors. These masks, however, were far more horrible, because they were literally the monster's *face*. The one it currently wore was rust-orange with bulbous white eyes and a long snout. As soon as the creature reached the witches, however, and saw the older woman kneeling on the ground with her hands in the air, its neck arms swiveled and provided a new mask, this one a staid expression, with two slits for eyes and a noncommittal half smile.

If the first mask was for watching, this one was for making judgments.

The monster peeled a strip of paper from its own torso and the old woman, knowing what was coming, turned

obediently. Attached to the back of her cloak was a large ring fitted with hundreds of similar strips. With stiff fingers, the creature threaded one more through the ring and tied it tight. Kara noticed that all the witches had these rings, though none with as many paper strips as the old woman. As she walked away they dragged along the ground like chains.

The monster switched back to its rust-orange mask and glared at the other witches until they went back to work.

Finally, it left.

"What was *that*?" asked Taff.

"I think it's a guard," said Kara. "Something that the Well created to keep the witches in line."

"If you don't work hard enough, they attach paper strips to your back?" Taff asked. "That's a strange punishment."

"I don't think it's normal paper," Kara said. "It doesn't look like it rips. Just like the ground and the sky."

"But *why?*"

Kara was about to answer when someone stepped behind them.

"Fools!" a woman said. "You hide but make no attempt to conceal your thoughts. I've been watching them water the trees below, like footprints leading back here. I will be well rewarded when I report you to the Faceless. They might even remove one of my strips."

"Please don't," Kara said. "We'll leave right now."

She turned around. Before her stood a red-cloaked woman with a pudgy face and pretty blue eyes.

I know her.

The woman shuddered.

"Not you!" she exclaimed. "It can't be!" She pressed her hands to Kara's cheeks and gazed into her eyes with unsettling intensity. "You would never be so foolish as to cast your Last Spell. Never!"

The woman's mouth fell open as she saw the locket hanging around Kara's neck. She grabbed it in two trembling hands and ran a thumb across the seashell embossed in the wood.

"Helena," she said. "It's really you."

Kara jumped at the sound of her mother's name, but it allowed her to make the final connection her memory needed.

"Hello, Aunt Abby," she said.

SIXTEEN

Before the conversation could progress any further, Aunt Abby insisted on leading them to a spot farther downstream. Kara and Taff followed her at a distance in order to conceal their rampaging thoughts.

"Do you remember who she is?" Kara asked.

Taff nodded, his cold stare piercing the woman's back.

"You told me all about *her*," he said. "She killed people. Mother tried to stop her but couldn't in time, so Aunt Abby ended up here and Mother got blamed for what she did. If it wasn't for her, Mother would still be alive and

everything would be different."

Kara understood why he was angry; in many ways, Mother's death *was* this woman's fault. What Taff wasn't old enough to remember, however, was the other side of Aunt Abby: the tireless player of hide-and-seek, the baker of treats, the teller of jokes that went over little Kara's head but made Mother and Constance blush and then burst into laughter.

"She's not a bad person," Kara said. "The grimoire sunk its teeth into her and bit deep. She's as much a victim as Mother." Taff seemed about to contradict this point but Kara took his hand and squeezed it. "You never felt the grimoire's pull. It's hard for you to understand. Blaming Abby for her actions would be like blaming Father for trying to kill us on De'Noran."

"I guess," Taff said. His voice was quiet, but the point had hit home. "It doesn't mean I have to like her, though."

"Fair enough."

Aunt Abby led them to three tall Pages that had fallen

against one another, forming a pyramid that would protect them from prying eyes.

"I can only stay for a few minutes, Helena," Aunt Abby said once they had entered. "If they find out I'm gone . . ."

Her hand reached back and shook the ring attached to her cloak. There were no more than a dozen paper strips there, and Aunt Abby clearly wanted to keep it that way.

"First we have to get something straight," said Kara. "Helena was my mother. I'm her daughter, Kara."

Squeezing her eyes shut, Aunt Abby shook her head.

"That's right! Poor Kara. You've left her all alone. Darling little thing."

"Will you look at me, please? I'm *thirteen*. How could I be Helena?"

"Time works differently in the Well of Witches," Aunt Abby said.

Kara couldn't argue with this; though it had been seven years since she last saw Aunt Abby, the woman had not aged a day. Of course, there was no reason why

Helena should appear *younger* than she had been in the real world, but Kara did not think logic had much place in this woman's world anymore.

Aunt Abby placed her hand on Kara's stomach. "What happened to the baby?"

Kara pointed to Taff.

"Right there."

"No," said Aunt Abby, her eyes scanning Taff. "No, no, no. That's not a baby. Besides, you said the baby was going to be a boy."

Taff crossed his arms.

"I *am* a boy!"

Abby shook her head. "There are no boys in the Well of Witches. Everyone knows that. The Faceless wouldn't allow it. You're just an ugly girl. That's the only explanation."

"Hey!"

"Would you rather she call you pretty?" Kara asked.

Aunt Abby examined Taff closely, her words coming

in short, breathless chunks.

"This little girl . . . looks so much like your husband, Helena. How is that? Shouldn't be possible. Unless . . . Could you be telling . . . Could I have been in this wicked place for that long? No. No."

Aunt Abby bit down hard on her thumb to control her hand's sudden shaking. She stared straight ahead, her eyes no longer seeing Kara and Taff but sliding toward a place from which she might never return. . . .

Kara grabbed Aunt Abby by the shoulders and shook her until the woman's eyes regained focus.

She's not ready to believe the truth yet, and I need her help.

"You're right," Kara said. "It's me, Helena. I'm sorry I told you otherwise . . ." She started to say "Aunt" and caught herself just in time. ". . . Abby. I just got here, and I was confused."

Aunt Abby sighed with relief and took Kara's hands.

"I knew it," she said. "I knew it the whole time. I'm so sorry for what I did." Tears ran down her cheeks. "Peter.

Constance. I never meant to hurt anyone."

"All of that is in the past. Right now I need your help." Abby straightened.

"Anything," she said, her voice resolute. "I can never atone for what happened, but I'll do what little I can." She pointed at Taff. "But tell me first—who's this little girl?"

"Really?" Taff asked.

"I found her wandering all alone. She's looking for her friend. I'm trying to help her."

"That sounds like the Helena I know," Abby said. "But how did you come to be this far from the Spellfire? You're not Cutters, like me, otherwise I would have seen you before." Noticing Kara's look of complete incomprehension, Abby added, "Surely the Faceless assigned you a job, right? That happens the moment you get here."

"We entered a different way," said Kara. "Nobody knows we're here except you."

Abby backed away slowly, a look of horror on her face.

"If that's true," Abby said, "and they find you—they'll

take you to the Changing Place and turn you into one of the Faceless on the spot." Her eyes grew wild. "I need to go. Right now. If we don't hurry back they'll know I'm gone!"

Kara grabbed her arm.

"Can you help us find the girl? Yes or no?"

"I don't know. This place is a lot bigger than it looks, and the Faceless are always watching. Chances are I've never even seen her."

"You'd remember, if you did. Her name is Grace. She's thirteen and she has long white hair and bright blue eyes."

Aunt Abby froze in place. Kara saw a single thought—written in sharp, De'Noran cursive—form beneath her feet: *The one with the bad leg.*

"Yes!" exclaimed Kara. "That's Grace! Can you take us to her?"

"Did you just read my thoughts?" Abby asked. Her mouth was wide with shock.

"Is that bad?"

"It's the *rudest* thing there is," Abby said. "We expect the Faceless to do it, but another witch . . ."

"I'm sorry," Kara said, her face flushed. "I didn't know the etiquette."

"All right. Just don't do it again." She leveled a finger at Taff. "You too, girl."

Taff looked as though he were about to object, then just shrugged his shoulders and nodded.

"So you've seen her, then?" Kara asked. "Grace?"

Abby nodded.

"I helped pull her into the Well myself."

"I remember."

"Are you sure you really want to find her?"

"It's very important," said Kara. "Why?"

"Because she's a Whisperer," Abby said. "The youngest one there's ever been."

"What does that mean?" asked Taff.

"I'll show you, and then you'll understand." Abby

chuckled nervously. "A Whisperer. Even us witches find them a little scary."

Kara and Taff, now wearing red cloaks that Abby had found them, tried to blend in with the other Cutters as they shuffled their way out of the forest. Two Faceless corralled the group. One of them rode a long beast that looked like a giant caterpillar with great leathery ears. Its feet rustled gently against the paper ground, and its long mouth, stretching from one ear to the other, seemed made for smiling. It wasn't smiling now, however—paper strips that looked as strong as rope had been knotted around its midsection. As the creature walked it emitted a pained moaning sound, and Kara felt her face flush with anger.

This poor creature has more legs than just the twelve, but the others are bound to its body. Perhaps that's how they keep it from escaping.

They walked away from the forest until they reached

a second river, this one flowing toward the rose wall instead of away from it. Docked at the shore were three large barges, little more than flat decks with towering paper sails. Two of the barges had already been loaded with the day's quota of trees. The Cutters crossed a short plank onto the third barge, passing right by one of the Faceless. Kara kept her head bowed and tried to stay with the crowd. Although Abby had promised Kara that they had nothing to worry about, she felt her heart racing beneath the itchy cloak.

Finally, the craft started to move. Abby found them a seat as far away from the others as possible. Their only companion was the old woman from the forest, her train of paper spilling across the floor of the barge.

"That's Landra," Abby said. "I wouldn't worry about her, poor thing. She's too far gone to hear us anymore. It won't be long for her now. Just one more strip, maybe two. Then they'll take her to the Changing Place and she'll become one of them."

"She won't be a person anymore?" Taff asked with a horrified expression. "Not even underneath the paper?"

Abby shook her head.

"Just a mindless monster like the rest of them. The Well will lose her thoughts, of course, but she'll help keep the Cutters cutting, the Whisperers whispering. Efficient, no?"

The craft moved faster than Kara had first anticipated. This river was different than the last one, more like cloudy water than pulp. Words waded along its surface, keeping pace with the barge: I acted like I didn't know where they were hiding so it would last longer. He was beautiful, even after I turned him to glass. I wish I remembered what it was like to be hungry.

Seeing how Kara's gaze followed the words, Abby said, "Food for the Spellfire. Our thoughts. Not all of them, of course. Memories. Wants. Fears. The ones it can use. The other thoughts, the day-to-day ones, aren't strong enough to be used for fuel. They follow the Sludge to the forests downstream and make the trees grow."

"What's the Spellfire?" asked Kara.

"That's our main duty here—to keep its flames raging. Remember how you told me that Phadeen drained witches' souls and used them to power the grimoires?"

I didn't tell you, Kara thought. *My mother did.*

She nodded anyway.

"You were close, but it's not exactly like that. There's no such thing as a soul. At least, not the way you were thinking of it, as this exhaustible life force that could be mined for energy. The true soul is both simpler than that and far more complex. It's the memories and experiences and feelings that make us who we are. This is what the Spellfire takes. It feeds best on the darker thoughts, of course. Plenty of those to go around in a place like this. Some witches remember their days of evil with fondness; others despair over the things they have done. The Spellfire isn't picky. It can use both. A source of energy that constantly replenishes itself."

They had arrived at the rose wall, as sheer and mountainous as the first one but with a large gate at its base. This was guarded by a Faceless wearing a gray authoritative mask, strands of confetti dangling from its chin in a mockery of a beard. The Faceless shifted a lever that lifted the paper-trellised gate, and the barge passed beneath the wall and into a new area.

Kara heard Taff gasp.

Perhaps they had only been on the outskirts of the Well of Witches, for the world that stretched before Kara now was infinitely larger. The sky and the ground still resembled parchment, but they were darker, as though they had been formed from pulp mixed with coffee grounds. In the center of all this sameness spiraled a funnel of black fire that shot upward, disappearing through a hole in the sky.

It made no sound.

"The Spellfire," Kara said. She noticed that the sky closest to it was blackened and shriveled, like paper held too close to a flame. "Is that where these trees are going?"

Abby nodded.

"To feed its flames," she said. "The thoughts you see scurrying beneath the ground are useless until they're burned."

"And then they turn into magic?" asked Taff.

"Not at all," said Abby. "The Spellfire powers the Well's *hold* on the grimoires, its ability to tempt future witches and draw them further toward darkness. It cannot create magic, only focus a girl's natural ability."

"And turn it evil."

Abby absently stroked her neck.

"You speak true," she said.

In time they came to a fork in the river. The ships packed with the most trees continued toward the Spellfire, while Kara's barge and several others followed the alternate route. Around Kara the other witches engaged in hushed conversation about various aches and pains they had been experiencing—crimped necks, sore backs—and who would be the next to turn into a Faceless after Landra.

It's like I'm back in De'Noran, listening to the farmers talk about weather and the local gossip. She almost laughed. No matter what the situation, people would always find a way to pass the time with idle conversation.

Kara was half dozing, her downturned head bobbing with the motion of the raft, when she heard shouts of surprise. She opened her eyes and saw that they had just passed through another gate, the Spellfire now concealed from view. This section of the Well was mustier than the others and smelled of old books.

I must have slept longer than I thought.

Around her, witches were pointing into the sky, the arms of their red robes sliding down bone-thin arms. Kara followed their fingers to three charcoal smears like small, dirty clouds in the parchment sky.

"What the heck are those?" Taff asked.

"We call them Burngates," said Abby. "Their appearance means that new witches will be arriving soon. After they cast their Last Spells, their grimoires will open and allow them passage into our world. For a few moments, we will all be granted a sliver of real sky, possibly even a taste of sunlight. Witches will travel from all the different parts of the Well to see it. There is nothing more exciting."

Abby smiled at the thought, and Kara suddenly remembered how she had fed her uncooked dough when Mother turned her head.

"How does the Well know that new witches are coming?" Taff asked. "Can it see the future?"

Abby shook her head. "No, but the Spellfire knows all about its grimoires. There are at least three out there that are nearing completion. The Last Spells can be expected soon. Still, we usually only see one Burngate at a time. Three is unprecedented. And so close together!"

Kara and Taff exchanged nervous glances.

"There's going to be a great battle," Kara said. "Between an army of witches and an army of men. Could that be the cause?"

"Possibly," Abby said. She whistled softly. "Three Last

Spells. I wouldn't want to be a soldier in *that* army."

And those are just regular witches. Who knows what horrors Rygoth herself has planned? The graycloaks are going to be slaughtered.

Father.

Lucas.

"How long before these Burngates open up?" Taff asked.

"The usual measures of time have no place here," Abby said. "A day? Maybe two? Soon the ground will rise to meet them, allowing the chosen to climb up and pull the new witches down into the Well."

Too soon. We'll never be able to find Grace and escape in time. The thought drained all the energy from her body, which was why she was so surprised to see a big grin plastered across Taff's face.

"What?" she asked.

"You don't know?"

"I don't know."

He whispered in her ear, "Gates open both ways."

She reconsidered the black smears in the sky. *Why not?* If a Burngate could allow a new witch to enter the Well, then Kara and Taff could use it to leave.

They docked shortly afterward. Abby pulled them behind a cracked fountain, a once-stunning remnant of Phadeen with small snatches of stone still peeking out through the paper facade.

"This is where we part ways," Abby whispered. "There's another forest up ahead and much work to do. The Spellfire burns low these days." She leaned closer to Kara and pointed into the distance. "Wait until you see the backs of the Faceless and then run that way and keep on running. Eventually you'll come to a garden. Your friend will be there."

"A garden?" Taff asked dubiously.

"You'll know it when you see it," Abby said. "You'll be safe from the Faceless, at least. They are not allowed there."

"Why not?" asked Taff.

"Whisperers must not be disturbed. They need complete and total concentration."

The last of the Cutters disembarked from the barge. The group started toward the forest.

"I have to go," Abby said.

"Come with us," Kara whispered. "We're going to escape this place."

"Oh, Helena. It means so much to me that you would even ask. But I can't do that."

"Why not?"

"Because this is where I deserve to be."

"That's not true. What happened wasn't your fault."

The words brought instant tears to Abby's eyes.

"Do you mean that?"

Kara wondered if she truly did. Yes, the grimoire had been at fault, but without this woman her mother would still be alive.

Except Abby doesn't think you're Kara right now. She thinks you're Helena. The real question is: What would Mother do?

The answer came easily.

"You're my friend," Kara said. "You always will be. I forgive you."

Abby smiled.

"Thank you," she said, hugging Kara tight. "That means so much. The trouble is—I can't forgive myself."

Abby slipped out of Kara's grasp and joined the other witches. They formed two lines and vanished around a nearby bend, their paper strips dragging along the ground.

SEVENTEEN

The ground crinkled beneath their feet like a school-master crumpling dissatisfactory work into a ball. Kara's thoughts etched themselves into a torrent of curli-cued worries: *What if we can't find Grace? What if she won't come with us? What if the Burngates open before we're ready?*

Their footsteps grew muffled as the surface began to change, Kara's thoughts vanishing beneath a thin layer of soil that looked and felt like pencil shavings.

Taff stopped moving.

"Listen," he said.

Hushed voices drifted in their direction. It was difficult to distinguish how many people were whispering at once. It might have been only a handful. It could have been hundreds. Following the sound, the children crept to a rise so unnaturally sharp it was as though the ground itself had been folded and creased.

They scaled it on their forearms and peeked over the edge.

A cold sun had been sketched across the parchment sky. Beneath it stretched a garden of paper flowers immaculately folded into irises and soneybuds, roses and lannies. Despite the lack of color the garden could have been beautiful in its way, were it not for the black-cloaked girls whispering to its flowers.

"What are they doing?" Taff asked.

"Nothing good."

Kara lifted both legs over the peak and slid to the other side. She inched closer to a paper chrysanthemum and the girl stretched along the ground before it, who was about fifteen with bushy hair and a nose that looked as though it had been broken at some point. The girl's eyes were closed, and she seemed completely unaware of Kara's presence. Kara caught snippets of the words she whispered: "Wake up, Claudia. Wake up. How can you sleep when such wonders await you? Just one spell. A small one."

Kara looked down at the chrysanthemum and saw the witch's final words—*"Just one spell. A small one."*—scrawled within the folds of its paper petals. The chrysanthemum seemed to breathe in and the words vanished.

Where did they go? she wondered.

Kara didn't understand, and she wasn't sure she *wanted* to understand. She took Taff's hand and led him onward. There was all manner of paper flowers in the garden— roses, canadrils, sunflowers, and many other species that Kara didn't recognize—but one thing remained consistent: the words spoken by the Whisperers were inscribed into the petals and quickly vanished. After a while Kara stopped looking at the flowers, but she couldn't escape the whispers: "They deserve it. . . . Think about how much fun it will be. . . . This is what you're made for. . . . Just peek inside the grimoire and see what's waiting for you. . . ."

Kara realized the purpose of the garden.

She was surprised by how angry she felt. She had certainly never imagined witches as being members of a loyal sisterhood, obligated to help one another simply because of the power they shared, but this still felt like the worst sort of betrayal.

And Grace is a part of it. Why am I not surprised?

"What is it?" Taff asked, sensing her malaise.

"These flowers allow the Whisperers to communicate with witches in Sentium," Kara said. "Each flower connects to a specific grimoire in the real world. That lets the Whisperer speak directly to the mind of the witch who has that grimoire, especially while they're sleeping. Tempt them into using magic, draw them further into darkness."

"I thought the grimoire did all that."

"So did I." Kara shook her head. "When it comes to magic, it feels like I'm never going to stop being wrong."

It was bad enough when she had thought it was the grimoire trying to corrupt her, but the idea of a real person inside her head was even worse. Kara scanned the garden, wondering if her Whisperer was still here, or maybe a flower with her face on it, the petals wilted from disuse?

She heard a familiar voice, honey smooth with a hint of playful arrogance.

"Remember that calico cat you passed by the river?" the voice asked. "You convinced yourself it was just sleeping, but we both know better, don't we? Little Kitty is gone, gone, gone! But don't worry—you can still fix it! In fact, you can make that mangy old fur ball into something exciting and new! What possible harm could come from such a helpful little spell?"

Kara followed the voice to a red lily. Grace lay beneath the flower, her closed eyelids fluttering with concentration. A paper bow secured her white hair in a neat ponytail.

"Get up," Kara said, squeezing her arm.

Grace's eyes opened. They were even bluer than Kara remembered. She stared at Kara for a long time before rising to a sitting position, a few errant strays of white hair falling over her eyes, and hesitantly touched Kara's cheek.

"Are you real?" she asked.

"It's me."

"It's been a long time, I think. I don't know actually. I don't . . . The days slide together because there are no days. Or nights. Is my father still dead? I suppose he is. You can't change things like that. I think you might hate me, Kara. Yet sometimes when my mind is my own I remember us as being great friends. Should we hug?"

"We're not friends, Grace. We never were. We never will be."

Kara's statement was like a bucket of ice thrown in

Grace's face, shocking her memory into working.

"Ahh," she said. "That's right. But how did you get here? Wait—I know. You cast your Last Spell and this time it wasn't all magical fire and fluttery little bird pages. You were dragged into the Well of Witches just like I was."

"Actually, I haven't used a grimoire since our battle."

"Our battle," Grace said. A smile lit up her beautiful face and she clapped her hands beneath her chin. "That was grand, wasn't it?"

"I don't remember it that way."

"Then you don't remember it."

There were dark circles under Grace's eyes and her cheeks were gaunt. The tone of her voice remained the same as always, however, as though she understood a joke that would always be lost on the rest of the world.

"If you didn't cast your Last Spell," Grace asked, "then how are you here?"

"I came a secret way."

"You came to this place of your own accord? *Why?*"

"To rescue you."

Grace released a short sharp yelp of laughter.

"I find that difficult to believe."

"Imagine how we feel," muttered Taff.

"Oh, look," Grace said, noticing Taff for the first time. "You brought the whelp."

"Maybe *rescue* is the wrong word," Kara said. "This is nothing more than a simple exchange. We help you escape, but in return you need to undo the spell on my father and send Timoth Clen back to his grave."

Grace rose to her feet, using a tightly rolled paper staff to support her bad leg. The ring on the back of her cloak had only a single paper strip tied to it.

"You truly plan to escape?" she asked.

"Yes," Kara said. "And you can come with us, leave this place forever. You just have to undo Father's spell when we get back to the real world. After that, you're on your own. We'll never see each other again."

"You'd really give me a grimoire to use?" Grace asked

dubiously. "After everything I've done?"

"A page. No more."

At first Kara thought that Grace might refuse, but even the possibility of casting a single spell again was enough to rekindle the embers of her obsession. Her eyes burned an intense shade of blue difficult to look upon.

"Can I see it?" she asked, grasping Kara's forearm. "Do you have it with you?"

"No," Kara lied.

Grace nodded, though Kara could tell she didn't quite believe her.

"Tell me your plan for this great escape," Grace said. "Are we using this secret entrance you spoke of?"

Kara shook her head. "It's been closed to us."

"We're going through the Burngates!" exclaimed Taff.

Grace regarded him with a flat, unreadable expression.

"The Burngates," she said.

"There're three of them in the sky right now," continued Taff. "All we have to do is wait until they open up and

slip through. I figure everyone will be so distracted by the new witches that they won't notice us."

"That makes sense," said Grace. "It's amazing that no one has ever thought of that before. It seems so obvious."

"So you'll come with us?" Kara asked.

Grace shrugged.

"The restoration of your father seems like a small price to pay for my freedom. Why not?"

Kara had played this conversation many times in her head, rehearsing all the possible ways she could convince Grace to join them. She hadn't expected her to simply *agree*. It was unsettling. Grace was doing exactly what Kara wanted her to do, but Kara couldn't stop thinking that it was really the other way around.

They sloshed through a shallow part of the river— thoughts bouncing off Kara's shins like blind fish—and continued across a featureless expanse of paper ground. Now that they had left the garden soil behind, Kara's and

Taff's thoughts were revealed once more, streaming just beneath the ground and emptying into the nearby river. They made sure to walk behind Grace so she could not read them, which also allowed the siblings to have a silent conversation:

We can't trust her, thought Taff.

Of course not, Kara answered. *But she's not going to try anything until we get back to Sentium. She needs us to escape.*

Did you see her eyes when you told her about the grimoire page?

Taff's next thought was communicated as a picture: a pair of eyes bursting with flames.

Magic always had the deepest hold on her, Kara thought. *That hasn't changed.*

Once the page is in her hands how can we be sure she'll use it on Father and not on us? asked Taff.

Kara tried to focus her thoughts in a more positive direction, but her true feelings escaped first.

We can't be sure. That's why she can't know I've lost my powers. Especially once we get back to the world. If she finds out . . .

Grace's head started to turn and Kara quickly rushed forward, blocking the girl's view of the words trailing along the ground.

"It feels like we're out in the open like this," Kara said, flinching at the unbidden thoughts that skimmed beneath the ground: *Make conversation. Distract her until those thoughts are out of sight.* "What happens if we run into any Faceless?"

Though Kara's primary intent had been to distract Grace, her concern was real enough. A paper desert stretched before them with little in the way of Pages or elevated ground. They would be visible for miles.

"There's nothing to worry about," Grace said. "Faceless patrols are very regular. There won't be any here for hours."

"You've thought about this a lot."

"I think about everything a lot."

"Doesn't seem it," Kara said, indicating the blank ground. The girl shed no thoughts at all.

Grace smirked with some of her old arrogance.

"I'm the only witch in the entire Well who's learned to control her thoughts," she said. "Except for when I sleep, of course. I can't do anything about that. The Spellfire takes what it needs." She smiled. "Are you worried about whether or not you can trust me, Kara Westfall?"

"The thought has crossed my mind." Kara pointed to the words *Can't trust her* being scrawled across the ground. "See?"

"I don't need to read your thoughts," Grace said. "I can see the doubt on your face. I understand. I make no excuse for the things I've done, but my time here has made me realize the error of my ways. And though I may have occasionally been cruel, it was the grimoire that turned me into a monster. You must believe that, at least. I want to help you, Kara. I know what it's like to lose a father."

Kara studied the girl's face but found no signs of duplicity. *Does that matter? Grace's mask of innocence fooled an entire village. There's no way to tell if she's lying or not.*

"You claim you've changed," Kara said, "but I heard you whispering to that girl in the flower, trying to convince her to use her grimoire."

"I didn't have a choice! I have to follow orders. If not, they'll drag me to the Changing Place and . . ." Grace raised a hand to her mouth, as if just the thought of it was enough to make her physically ill. "Disgusting freaks. The only good thing about working in the garden is the Faceless aren't allowed anywhere near it. I won't become one of them. I *won't*."

They continued to walk. Kara tried the conch again to see if she could reach Lucas, but it still didn't work. *I hope he's okay. I'll never forgive myself if something happens to him.* The memory of how he had almost kissed her fluttered along the ground. She heard Taff stifle a laugh.

"Stop reading that!" she said, blushing. Behind Taff's smiling face she saw a hint of movement in the distance: five figures sitting astride long, low creatures. They hadn't seemed to notice the children yet.

"Grace," Kara whispered, touching her arm. "We have to hide. Faceless."

"Finally," Grace said.

Kara could see what was about to happen but although she offered a soft "Don't," there was really nothing she could do; Grace was already waving her arms in the air and shouting, *"Intruders! I've found intruders! Over here, over here!"*

Kara and Taff ran. They didn't get very far at all.

EIGHTEEN

The Faceless threw Kara into a domed cage that seemed to have risen from the very ground itself. There wasn't enough room for Kara to stand at her full height, so she balanced herself on her knees and shook the bars. They were made from paper but as sturdy as iron.

A second paper cage stood right next to hers. Taff was crouched inside.

"You okay?" she asked.

"I'm fine. I just feel a little stupid."

"For trusting Grace?"

"Oh, I never *trusted* her," Taff said. "Not for a moment. I just figured she would try to trick us *after* we escaped, not before. Doesn't she want to get out of this place?"

"I honestly don't know what she wants."

"I feel stupid because I kept my hideaway in the sack and not in my pocket. It would be really useful right now. I should have thought of it."

"You're absolutely right," Kara said. "You should have entertained the possibility that masked monsters might imprison us in paper cages."

This made Taff smile.

"You never know, with us."

Just outside the cage, the Faceless gathered in a circle. Their tiny neck-arms rotated until each face was fitted with the same mask, a small mouth open wide in a grotesque mockery of talking.

For the first time, Kara heard the Faceless speak, a strange concoction of clicking sounds.

"What are they talking about?" Taff asked.

"I don't know. Maybe what to do with us?"

"I sure hope not," Taff said. "That sounds like angry clicking."

Finally, the Faceless all nodded in agreement and changed back to their bulbous-eyed masks. Kara watched the closest one carefully, trying to catch a glimpse of what its *real* face might look like, but as the masks rotated, the creature lifted its hands to hide the face beneath. All Kara caught was a brief flash of white between paper fingers, nothing more.

A few moments later, she heard Grace scream.

"No! What are you doing? I helped you! *I helped you!*"

Dragging Grace by one arm, the Faceless opened the door to Taff's cage and tossed her inside. She shoved Taff out of the way and pressed her face against the bars of the cage, continuing her entreaties: "You're making a mistake! Let me out of here! Let me out!"

The Faceless ignored her.

"Is this one of those times when it's okay to laugh at

someone?" Taff asked Kara.

"You'll get no scolding from me."

Taff opened his mouth and shook his head. "I missed my chance. Now I'm just mad again."

Any pretense of cooperation had vanished from Grace's face. Strangely enough, this made Kara feel more comfortable. At least she was on familiar ground again.

Grace asked, "Did you really expect me to help you?"

"No," Kara said. "But I thought we could have helped each other."

Grace's hair had come undone. She took a deep breath, regaining her composure, and began to steadfastly fashion it back into a ponytail.

"Perhaps," said Grace, "if there had been the slightest chance of your plan succeeding. But the Burngates? Honestly, I expected better. Any witch who's ever had a single thought of escaping has tried that. *Hundreds* of Faceless gather together to guard them when they open. You wouldn't have been able to get close."

Kara saw Taff look away to hide his blushing face. If there was one thing he hated, it was being accused of having an unoriginal idea.

"What about the chosen?" Kara asked. "The ones who pull the new witches into the Well. Surely they have a good chance to slip away."

Grace sighed with impatience.

"They're tethered around the ankles. Trust me, the Faceless have thought of everything. There's no escaping this place." She shrugged. "The most reasonable course of action seemed to be to turn you in."

"Why?" Kara asked. "What did you possibly hope to get in return?"

Grace indicated the single paper strip hanging from her ring.

"They remove them sometimes, when you do a particularly good job. For a long time I was the only one with an empty ring, and I wanted to be perfect again. I wanted to be the best witch of all. But these Faceless have made a terrible mistake. They seem to think that I was actually helping you two." Grace clapped her hands together as an idea occurred to her. "Maybe you can tell them the truth! My plan from the beginning was to turn you in, I promise. Tell them that! It could really help me."

"All your talk about changing, regretting the past," Kara said, "I actually started to believe you a little bit."

"But that was all true," Grace said. "I *do* feel bad about the way things turned out. If I had done a better job conserving the pages of my grimoire, I would still be in the World right now, casting spells."

"What about the people you killed?" Taff asked. "Do you feel bad about them?"

"*Of course I do*," said Grace, insulted that Taff would think otherwise. "I should *never* have hurt them. I was wrong. If I could go back and change things I would."

"Oh," said Taff.

"I wasted so many pages on people who were not the *least bit* important. Once I have a grimoire again I'll only kill the people who *absolutely* need killing—I promise you that." She turned to Kara. "And whose fault was it that I lost control, anyway? Let's not forget that *you* were the one who stole the grimoire from me. The need to use it built up and up—you know how it works—until I couldn't help myself. If you had just minded your own business, Kara, then maybe none of this would have happened. 'We are all at fault for evil.' That's from the Path itself."

Kara spoke quietly through gritted teeth. "Just be glad you're in the cage with Taff and not me."

"Goodness, Kara!" Grace exclaimed, clapping a hand to her chest. "When did you become so *violent?*"

"What are they doing?" Taff asked, watching the Faceless through the bars of the cage. They had arranged a large rack on the ground, like something one might use for drying clothes, and were currently pulling long strips of paper from their bodies and draping it over the rods.

"Oh no," said Grace. "This is just what I was afraid of."

"What?" asked Kara.

"They're going to change us," Grace said, her voice trembling. "Make us like them. I've seen it done before. We were all forced to watch as a warning. They prepare the . . . skin first. Lay out the paper in strips. They'll need a lot of it, especially for three of us. After that, they'll rest so their own bodies can regenerate what they've torn away. When they wake up they'll bring us to the Changing Place."

"What's that?" Kara asked.

"A building. A temple, some say. We'll go in, and when we come out . . ."

"We won't be us anymore," Taff said.

Grace nodded, her eyes wide with terror.

"You have to get me out of here," she said. "I'll do anything. I'll undo the curse on your father. For real this time. Just don't let me turn into one of those things."

Kara watched the Faceless take turns flaying one another. The paper peeled away from their bodies with a slight sucking sound, like a foot removed from a stubborn boot, exposing gray skin. Soon dozens of strips dangled from the rack. One of the Faceless, the skin of its chest mostly exposed now, knelt down in front of their cage. Neck-arms spun until a new mask fitted onto its face: eyes closed, mouth open in an exaggerated snore. Its arms fell to its side, like it had instantly fallen asleep. The other Faceless did the same thing, until all five were kneeling before the cages in a neat line. Kara could already see their paper skin regenerating, the remaining strips growing taut and then lengthening to cover the missing spaces.

"How long will they stay like this?" Kara asked.

"An hour," said Grace. "Maybe two."

"Can they see us?" Taff asked. He waved his hand back and forth in front of the bars, checking for a reaction.

"I don't think so," said Grace. "It's like they're hibernating. But they can still hear, loud noises at least. That much I'm sure of."

"Why should we believe anything you say?" Taff asked.

Grace clapped her hands and two of the Faceless whipped their heads in her direction. They stared for a moment—as much as one could stare with closed eyes—and then returned to their previous resting position.

"I was going to suggest rocking the cage back and forth," Kara said, "but clearly that's out. Any quieter ideas?"

"What about using the grimoire page?" Taff asked.

Grace curled her long fingers around the paper bars of the cage. *"What?"* she asked, her eyes blazing. "You have a page from an actual grimoire here?"

So much for keeping it hidden from her, Kara thought.

"It's for Father," said Kara. "We can't waste it."

"We only need one spell for that," Taff said. "There are two sides. It's worth a try, at least."

Since she didn't have any better ideas, Kara reached into the inner pocket of her cloak for the page. She knew something was wrong the moment she touched it.

"No," she said. "No, no!"

It was practically falling apart in her hands, like an old letter left to molder in a trunk for decades.

"*That's* from a grimoire?" Grace asked.

Kara nodded.

"Odd," Grace said. "When I tore a page out of *my* grimoire it worked just fine. Must have been something you did."

"You used it just a few seconds after you tore it out," Kara said. "But this one's been out of its grimoire for quite some time. I wonder if that makes a difference."

"Like a leaf," Taff said. "It can survive for a little while on its own, but eventually it'll die if it's not attached to a tree."

"Great," said Kara, looking down at the crumbling page. "Something else to worry about."

"Give it here," Grace said. "I'll set us free. Come on. It's useless to you anyway. Your spells only work with animals. You're *limited*."

Kara started to slide the page through the bars but

held it back at the last moment.

"Oh, come on," Grace said, reaching her hand as far as it would go. "We don't have time for this. All I want to do is get out of here, just like you." Grace reached farther, her fingertips practically brushing the page now. "Come on, Kara. Just give me the page. Give it to me."

"No," Kara said. "This is a mistake. I can feel it."

She folded the page carefully and returned it to the inner pocket of her cloak. Grace glared at her with icy fury.

"It isn't nice to *tease*. And exactly how do you expect me to fix your father if you won't let me cast a spell?"

It's a good question. I'm going to have to trust her eventually— but not yet.

"Any others ideas?" Kara asked Taff.

"Nothing. How about you?"

"Sorry."

The skin of the Faceless was nearly complete. The centermost one had begun to twitch slightly, as though having a bad dream. It wouldn't be long now before they woke.

What will it be like? Will I be trapped inside my new body? Or will only the monster remain?

"Isn't anyone going to ask me if *I* have an idea?" asked Grace.

"Do you?" asked Taff.

"Yes, as a matter of fact. And unlike your idea, this one is going to work. Now let's hold hands."

"Huh?"

"Oh!" said Kara, brightening. "I know what she has in mind. Like what we saw them do in the forest to cut down trees."

Taff tapped his knuckles against his head. "I should have thought of that!" he exclaimed.

"Only you didn't," said Grace.

"Will it even work? I'm a boy. I can't do magic."

Grace did not bother to conceal her impatience. "It's not magic. It's thinking. Boys can think." She shrugged her shoulders. "Sort of."

Getting as close to the bars as she could, Kara reached her long arms into the next cage. Taff took her right hand and Grace took her left. Kara saw her brother grimace as he intertwined his fingers with Grace in order to complete the circle.

"I was a Cutter for a little while before the Faceless realized my true talent was in Whispering," Grace said. "It's not just a matter of thinking about the right word. You need to attach an image to it to give it strength. So if you're using the word *chop*, make sure you attach a memory of someone chopping firewood. Sounds and smells work too—sometimes even better. My thought-cuts are going to be flawless, of course, but it has to be all three of us for this to work. Understand?"

"Can we just start?" Taff asked Grace. "The quicker we get this over with, the quicker I can stop holding your hand."

"Fine," said Grace. "Let's begin."

Kara closed her eyes, just like she had done when she

was first learning to be a *wexari*, and imagined *slicing* a potato, heard the *tap-tap-tap* of the knife on the cutting board. She felt the two hands tighten in hers and the mind pictures sharpened, became more concrete—not just images anymore but a tool to be wielded. She peeked between half-shut eyelids and saw her SLICE moving across the ground toward Taff's CUT and Grace's CHOP.

It's working, Kara thought, a smile breaking across her face. *It's really working!*

"Kara," Grace said. "You can stop now."

She opened her eyes.

A sizable gap had appeared along the bottom of their cages. With nothing to hold them in place the bars folded outward with ease.

"We did it," Kara said. "That was a brilliant idea, Grace."

The girls exchanged an unexpected smile before they remembered their history together and looked away.

"We have to hurry," Taff said, nodding toward the

Faceless. Their skin was completely regrown now, and they were all twitching like soon-to-burst chrysalides. There wasn't enough room between the cages for the three children to slip out at the same time, so Kara had to wait for Taff and Grace to make their exit before crawling free. They crept past the Faceless, Grace leaning on Kara's shoulder to avoid scratching the ground with her cane. Although an inviting paper horizon beckoned the escapees forward, Kara stopped at the place where the Faceless had tethered the creatures they used for transportation.

"What are you doing?" Grace asked. "We need to keep moving! We can find a boat by the river. Lose them."

"We'll never make it. And we can't outrun them on foot."

"And you can't get these rustle-feet to do your bidding," Grace said. "Not without wasting a side of the grimoire page."

Kara smiled.

"I don't need magic to get animals to like me."

She crossed over to the first rustle-foot she saw. Its amber eyes, deep-set within folds of hooded skin, watched her with curiosity. The rustle-foot's long body was segmented into five bulbous parts, allowing it to carry a like amount of riders, but its neck had been tethered to a hook so tightly that it could barely lift its head off the ground. Kara stroked behind its leathery ears and unhooked the rope fastened around its neck. The creature, more surprised than anything, made a sound like a baby's rattle.

"Good morning, beautiful one," Kara whispered in the rustle-foot's ear. "My name is Kara. I wish I had more of a chance to introduce myself, but time grows short. We'd like a ride. Do you think that would be all right with you?"

The rustle-foot rose to its full height and shimmied back and forth. It repeated the rattling sound, louder this time.

"I like the way you talk," Kara whispered. "May I have

the honor of giving you a name? How about . . . Rattle?"

Kara's voice calmed the creature. She held her hand to its nose and it sniffed her open palm greedily.

"Why aren't we leaving?" Taff asked.

"She's afraid that if she helps us she's going to get punished. I need a moment to convince her otherwise."

One of the Faceless rose to its feet and looked in their direction. It placed a hand on the masked creatures to its right and left. Both stood. Their neck-arms began to rotate.

"Stop messing around, Kara!" Grace said. "Just tell the giant caterpillar we need to move or we're *all* going to get punished."

"Set the other creatures free," Kara said. "We need a distraction."

Grace crossed her arms. "I am not touching those things."

"I always knew you were bad," said Taff, "but I didn't realize you were such a *girl*."

He set to untethering the rest of the beasts, and Grace, with a grunt of exasperation, began to help. Kara continued to rub Rattle's flank. Paper rope had been coiled so thickly around its torso that it was difficult to make out the other legs pinned to its sides, but the pain in the rustle-foot's eyes was crystal clear. "Look what they've done to you," Kara said. "You poor, marvelous creature. No wonder you're afraid. But you don't need to trust me. I know that's too much to ask. Trust *yourself*. They can't punish you if they can't catch you." Kara placed her hands on Rattle's face and gazed directly into its eyes. "I just want to go along for the ride."

The rustle-foot rattled faster than ever and lay flat on its belly, allowing Kara to mount it. Grace quickly did the same, wrapping her arms around Kara's stomach, with Taff taking the rear.

They took off.

As the parchment landscape began to blur past them, Kara risked a glance over her shoulder. The Faceless camp was in complete disarray. Four of the monsters were chasing the errant rustle-feet, trying to grab on to their whipping tethers with little success, while the fifth Faceless stood in place and watched Kara depart. Its long arms were folded behind its back in an unsettling show of calmness, but its neck-arms rotated to fashion a new mask over its face: oval-shaped with a gaping black hole at its center.

The Faceless screamed, a thunderous roar that shook the ground and echoed throughout the Well. Rattle stumbled, and Kara, who had thrown her hands over her ears, would have fallen had Grace not straightened her.

"What was *that?*" Kara asked.

"What do you think? It just called for help. We need to hide."

Where? Kara thought, scanning the horizon. She saw nothing but flat emptiness. When she turned to her right, however, she saw hazy outlines in the distance. She thought, at first, that these were Pages, or hills, or maybe just large boulders, but as Kara's eyes focused she realized she was mistaken.

They were buildings.

Back when this was Phadeen that must have been some sort of town, a place where students could purchase food and new clothes and magical ingredients for their spells. Kara's face brightened. *There will be pantries there. Cellars. Storehouses.*

Places to hide.

Leaning forward, she put her arms around Rattle's neck and turned it toward the buildings, whispering, "Faster! Faster!" into its ear. The creature grunted in pain as it struggled to follow her command. *If only it could use all its legs*, Kara thought. She tried to unknot the bindings around its torso without any luck. The material looked like paper but was as strong as sailors' rope.

Grace, seeing the approaching town, gripped Kara tightly and exclaimed, "No! We can't go there! That's where they—"

Swish-swish-swish.

A large group of mounted Faceless was approaching on Kara's left. Almost all of them wore forest-green masks with black spirals painted on the foreheads. The sole exception was a Faceless much larger than the others, its face covered by a gleaming red mask. This was, apparently, the only mask it needed; the six other ones had been torn from its neck-arms and impaled on the giant antlers sprouting from its head.

Kara spurred Rattle onward. The swishing sound of the other rustle-feet remained just behind them, with Redmask—as Kara decided to call the antlered Faceless— at the head of the procession.

They quickly halved the distance to the buildings, allowing Kara to make out some details. The ancient structures were composed entirely of yellowing parchment, except for the occasional stone column or glass window that had somehow escaped the transformative powers of the Well. *It won't be possible to hide anymore, at least not right away, but maybe we can lose them in the streets somehow. . . .*

Grace screamed.

Redmask had managed to drive its rustle-foot next to them, reach across the gap between the mounts, and grab Grace's arm. Taff pounded the five jointed scrolls of its hand and tried to pry them off, but they were as strong as iron. Kara felt Grace start to slide away. In just a few seconds Redmask would pull her off altogether.

"Kara! Do something!"

Half rising from her seat, Kara twisted toward their assailant, hooked her fingers through the eyeholes of its red mask, and snapped her wrist back hard. The mask flew off. Kara caught a glimpse of maggot white before the Faceless covered its real face in shame and stopped chasing them entirely.

"Took you long enough," Grace murmured.

"You're welcome."

Kara turned her attention back toward the rapidly approaching town and gasped in surprise.

There were Faceless everywhere. They filled the

streets and stood in open doorways. A few held long spears with curved blades at the ends.

"I don't understand," Kara said. "Why are they all here?"

"They *live* here," Grace said. "*That's* what I was trying to tell you. Not that you listened."

A phalanx of Faceless marched out and encircled them. Rattle weaved back and forth, awaiting further orders, but Kara saw no point in trying to escape. Their enemies were too many, and the poor rustle-foot would only get hurt. Kara slid to the ground, Grace and Taff right behind her.

The crowd parted and Redmask stepped into the circle. Its body tensed with fury as it grabbed a spear from the nearest Faceless and walked toward Kara.

"It was *her* idea to run!" exclaimed Grace. "I tried to stop them. . . ."

Kara gritted her teeth, expecting Redmask to raise its spear and strike her down. It walked right past her.

She felt a rush of relief, but this was short-lived once she turned and saw Redmask's true target. "Don't!" she screamed, but the spear was already whipping through the air. Rattle wailed in pain and slumped to the ground. The Faceless hit it again. Again. Again. Kara was thankful to see that Redmask had not attacked the rustle-foot with the sharp end of the spear, but the wounds were still grievous. The paper strips bound about its torso darkened with blood.

Kara dodged two guards and ran to Rattle's side.

"I'm sorry," she said, placing a hand behind its leathery ears. "I never meant for you to get hurt."

The rustle-foot rattled softly and nuzzled her hand.

Redmask pulled Kara away and tossed her to the ground. Though its expression was hidden beneath the mask, Kara was certain it was smiling. She felt a dark, murderous rage bubbling up inside of her.

"You shouldn't have hurt her," Kara said.

Redmask mounted Rattle, causing another wail of

pain. One of its back legs dragged unnaturally as the rustle-foot struggled forward, spurred onward with merciless whips of the spear. Kara herself was pulled away by two Faceless and slung, like a sack of grain, over the back of a different rustle-foot, this one smelling like a moldy stump. Her wrists and ankles were bound. Kara felt a tugging at the back of her cloak and then a sudden weight. She was unable to see it, her face buried in bristly fur, but she knew what it was.

They just attached a ring and the paper strips.

Taff and Grace were soon hung upside down beside her. The rustle-foot started to move.

"Where are they taking us?" Kara asked.

Grace's face was even paler than usual.

"The Changing Place. They're going to make us like them. And there's nothing we can do to stop it."

NINETEEN

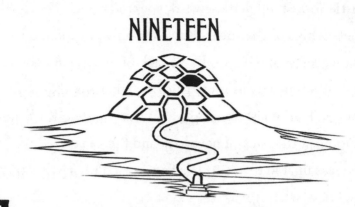

As they rode through town, bulbous-eyed Faceless lined the road, popping their scrolled fingers in what might have been their version of applause. Parchment houses lined the streets, along with a large building that Kara took to be a library. A circle of stones, now cocooned in paper, held the memory of meditative reading and quiet conversation. Long ago, before grimoires and Spellfires and Whisperers, this had been a pretty place.

They came to a sudden stop on the outskirts of town. *Good thing it wasn't far*, Kara thought, for hanging upside down off the side of the rustle-foot had already begun to make her head feel heavy and strange. She twisted her neck to take stock of their new location but could see only the backs of tightly pressed bodies. Most were Faceless, but there were a small collection of red-robed witches as well. They gave Kara a cursory glance and then returned their attention to something beyond her view.

Using a hooked spear, a short Faceless—perhaps no more than a child—cut Kara's hands and feet free and pulled her to the ground like shoddy cargo. Kara's wrists were only chafed, but her feet had gone completely numb during the journey. She pushed herself into a sitting position and rubbed feeling into them.

"Why's it so crowded?" Kara asked.

"These particular witches have all gotten paper strips recently," Grace said, her hands shaking slightly as she undid the bow in her hair and then retied it neatly in place. "They've been brought here to witness what will happen if they don't fall in line. As for the Faceless . . .

they always congregate when a Change takes place, like the way the villagers back home gathered together to celebrate a new birth."

Grace tried to stand, but without a staff to lean on she was forced to place all her weight on her good leg and wobbled as she rose. Taff slid to his right so that she could use his shoulder for support. Neither one acknowledged the assistance, though Kara thought she saw the slightest glint of gratitude in Grace's eyes.

"How did they know we were coming?" Kara asked.

"They're not here for us, though I'm sure they'll stay now that they've made the journey," Grace said. She pointed past the crowd. "See? We're not the first ones being sent into the Changing Place today."

Though her feet were still prickling her with pins and needles, Kara managed to rise.

Past the crowd, Kara saw a woman being led up a short flight of stairs to a dark tunnel. Faceless kept pace to either side of her, but the woman did not seem likely to resist; she walked with the resigned footsteps of one who had long ago accepted her fate. Behind her a train of paper strips dragged along the steps. She turned back to the crowd, as though wanting to see the world through her own eyes one last time, and then vanished into the darkness.

"Landra," Kara said, recognizing the old woman they had seen on the barge. "I guess she got her final strip."

The guards made their way to the base of the steps and stood with spears held across their chests, though there seemed little point; no one had any desire to follow the unfortunate woman. Time, which always passed so strangely in the Well, squeezed to a trickle. All was silent. Kara did, however, catch some of the witches' thoughts skittering along the ground: *Let's see if she takes longer than Karin to Change. I'll never let this happen to me. Whatever they want, whatever they want, whatever they want . . .*

The Faceless shed no thoughts at all.

Taff gripped her wrist.

"The turtle!" he gasped.

"What?"

"Look at the building! Look at it!"

Kara craned her neck to see past the milling witches to the building beyond them. From the main entrance a long paper tunnel, like the comb of a giant wasp nest, curved along the ground to a small dome in the distance. Its paper roof was the same color as the sky except for a stubborn hexagonal tile, shockingly green against all that sameness.

With a sharp intake of breath, Kara remembered the drawing in Sordyr's letter.

"The *queth'nondra*," she said.

"The who?" asked Grace.

"A long time ago, the Well of Witches used to be part of a school for magic," Kara said. "That building was where students took their final test. Those who passed became full *wexari*."

But this is the Changing Place. The source of all the Faceless.

How could such a good place become so evil? Or is that the point?
The greater the good, the greater it can be corrupted?

"What's a *wexari?*" Grace asked.

Kara shook her head. "Never mind." Looking at the building again, she couldn't help but smile. "It *does* look like a turtle."

"I wish Safi were here to see it," Taff said. He looked down, perhaps wondering if he would ever see his friend again. Kara was on the verge of offering some comforting words when Landra exited the tunnel. Some of the witches gasped. There was even a single, quickly muffled scream. But the primary noise was from the Faceless, who popped their fingers in jubilation.

Landra's face was a taut, flat parchment from which all features had been erased. She tottered down the steps where Faceless wrapped her almost tenderly with paper strips. These immediately adhered to her body like new skin. The Faceless fawned over the seven nubs protruding from Landra's neck like parents over a baby's smile.

I guess it takes longer to grow a mask-arm than erase a face, Kara thought. Despite the warm, stale air she felt as cold as ice.

That's what's going to happen to me. That's what I'm going to become.

Two Faceless guards pushed through the crowd and headed in the children's direction. At first Kara thought they were coming for her, but at the last moment they veered toward a different target. "Get off!" Grace screamed, clawing at their paper arms as they dragged her toward the stairs. "Not this! Please! I don't want to Change! I don't want to be a monster!" Taff tried to intervene but was tossed aside with little effort; the Faceless were far stronger than they looked. "Kara!" shouted Grace. "Kara! Please! I know you can stop them! You won't let them do this to me! You're good, Kara, good—"

The guards came to a sudden halt. In front of them, blocking the entrance to the *queth'nondra*, stood Redmask.

It looked at Grace, shook its head, and pointed to Kara. The two guards exchanged a look, momentarily surprised by this change in routine, but when Redmask took a step toward them they quickly dropped Grace to the ground and started toward Kara.

"Don't bother," she said. "I'll walk."

Kara passed through the parted crowd. Taff tried to reach her but was restrained by a Faceless. "What are you doing?" he asked. "Kara!" She kept moving. *It will only make it harder if I stop. And they'll just drag me inside anyway. Whatever my fate might be, I'll meet it standing.*

Redmask stood at the bottom of the steps, arms crossed with smug satisfaction. Kara looked away as she passed; she refused to let the foul creature see the fear in her eyes. In the distance the Burngates had grown darker and begun to swell outward like warped boards. Three helixes had risen from the ground nearly high enough to touch the parchment sky. Kara could see tiny figures making their way up the narrow slopes.

The Burngates will open soon. After that, who knows how long it will be before another witch casts her Last Spell? I won't get a second chance. I have to escape this place. I have to save Father.

She stepped forward into the tunnel and the world immediately turned black. Gelatinous air seemed to clutch at Kara, and a warm, slimy substance with the consistency of raw eggs slid up her nostrils and down the canals of her ears. Oxygen was reduced to a teasing dribble. *Is this the stuff that makes people Faceless? Is it inside me now? Am I already changing?* She kept moving forward, each footstep a struggle. Faded memories were drawn to the forefront of her thoughts like iron filings to a magnet. Images slid by at blinding speed: looking up at her parents from within the folds of a warm blanket, her first steps, Mother's death, finding the grimoire, their flight from the villagers, the Thickety, the unghosts, Safi's sacrifice, entering the tunnel just moments ago. Her life was sliced open and exposed, and Kara knew that she was not the only one watching. Something, some *entity*, studied every moment. She felt the weight of its regard like a face peering over her shoulder, learning every thought and experience, every fear and desire. By the end, it knew more about Kara than she knew about herself.

At which point she was spit out of the tunnel and sent tumbling across the ground. Kara ran her hands over her face, fearing that her fingers would meet only gruesome smoothness but feeling instead the familiar curves of eyes, nose, and mouth. She clutched her neck and was overjoyed to find it bereft of the knobby pieces of flesh that would grow into mask-arms.

I haven't changed. I'm still me.

Kara placed her hands on the ground, intending to push herself to her feet, and felt something strange beneath her palms.

It can't be!

Grass, lush and green, tickled her fingertips. Kara was not outside, however, but in a large room with a door set into the opposite wall. In the center of the room grew a beautiful tree dappled with orange and yellow leaves. Kara felt sunlight on her face. Looking up, she was surprised to find that the room had no ceiling—or no roof, for that matter. The walls simply opened up to a glorious blue expanse with fluffy clouds.

"Impossible," Kara said.

"I'm surprised, Kara Westfall," replied a man sitting against the opposite side of the tree. "After everything you've been through, I was certain you would have stricken that deceitful word from your vocabulary by now."

Kara crossed the room until she was able to see him: a small man wearing a green robe with a dark birthmark that covered nearly half his face. He looked a little older than his portrait in Sablethorn, but not by much.

"Minoth Dravania," Kara said.

"Indeed," he replied. Minoth spoke with a strange accent Kara had never heard before, his voice as raspy as burlap. "How nice to hear my name spoken aloud after all this time. I was starting to wonder if I remembered it true."

"How are you . . ."

". . . still alive? Nothing special. Hardly even magic, really. I just forced my remaining years into this one specific spot instead of letting them spread willy-nilly all over the world. People would be surprised how far a few good years could last them if they weren't so wasteful! Unfortunately, that means I cannot leave the shade of this tree without immediately perishing. A fair trade, I think. It's a rather nice tree."

Minoth gave her the faintest trace of a smile. Kara thought he might be having fun with her, but she wasn't certain.

"How is it possible to see the sky from here?" Kara asked. "Have I left the Well of Witches?"

"Unfortunately not. This place is all I could save of the original Phadeen. The eye of the storm, if you will."

He traced his fingertips along the bark of the tree. "You should have seen it in its prime, Kara. My life's work. Do you know what happened?"

Minoth watched her expectantly, and Kara straightened like a schoolgirl standing before the class.

"Evangeline's Last Spell," she said.

He tilted his hand from side to side, as though she had given a response that approached the answer without truly hitting the mark.

"It was indeed the princess who cast the spell," he allowed. "Still, I've always found it hard to believe that one little girl could have been responsible for transforming a magnificent place like Phadeen into the Well of Witches." He folded his hands in his lap and fixed Kara with a knowing stare. "You might want to think on that at some point. But today we have a more immediate concern. You've made it a long way without magic, my dear, and not without your share of travails. I'm quite impressed."

Kara blushed at the unexpected praise.

"Thank you," she said with reflexive politeness, before considering the implications of his comment. "Wait . . . how do you know all this? How do you even know my *name?*"

"In the tunnel, all that sticky stuff like blackberry jam? That was the mind of the *queth'nondra* learning everything it could about you." Minoth twirled his thumbs together guiltily. "I confess I might have peeked a little. You've led an interesting life! Witch duels, tree monsters, shadow creatures . . . though it must have been a fearsomely hard thing to be Sundered like that."

Kara recognized the word from Sordyr's letter but did not understand how it applied to her. Minoth, seeing the confusion on her face, added, "What Rygoth did. Sundered you. Took away your magic. Speaking of which, how'd you like to get it back?"

For a few moments, Kara was too stunned to answer.

"I didn't think it was possible," she said quietly.

"It's not. But that's never stopped me before. So I'll ask one more time: Would you like to be a witch again?"

Kara wondered when she had given up the possibility of regaining her powers. At the banquet table with Rygoth, perhaps? Or was it even earlier than that, as long ago as the *Wayfinder*? It didn't matter now. Long-suppressed hope surged through her body, bringing tears to her eyes.

"Yes," Kara said. "I would like that very much. Can you really do it?"

"I wish it were that easy, Kara," Minoth said, with genuine regret in his eyes. "But even I cannot restore a *wexari*'s magic." He indicated the door behind her. "Only the final chamber of the *queth'nondra* can do that. The good news is you've already walked your Sundering. All that remains is to answer the riddle without a question."

Kara's head spun.

"I'm a little lost here," she said. "I know that the Sundering is some kind of test—"

"More than that, my dear. *Much* more. The Sundering was a rite of passage that could have lasted anywhere from a few months to several years. To start, a *wexari*'s powers were taken away——"

"On purpose?" Kara asked, shocked.

"It didn't hurt," Minoth said. "There was a potion. Or maybe an ointment. It's been a long time and the details escape me. In either case, sundered *wexari* were sent out into the world, penniless and with only the clothes on their backs, to learn what life was like without magic. Some wandered. Some learned trades. Some——"

"But that doesn't make any sense! Sablethorn was a school for magic! How can you teach someone how to be a *wexari* if you take away their power?"

"Sablethorn would have been a very poor school indeed if we focused only on *how* to use magic and spent no time on the *when* and *why*. In my day those with the gift were revered and admired from birth. They were exalted above all others. Imagine if you had been told your entire life that you were more important than other people. Something truly terrible might happen. You might start to believe it! You might begin thinking, 'Why should I help any of these sheep around me?' For those with true power, such thoughts are the first steps down a dark, dark path. That's why it was crucial that students experience firsthand what it was like to be powerless, poor, downtrodden—to understand life from a different perspective. Nothing quells the dark temptations of power better than empathy. Do you understand?"

Kara gave a slight nod.

"It's just—a world where people admired those who could use magic is hard for me to imagine," she said.

Minoth patted the ground and Kara sat beside him. He smelled of mothballs and butterscotch.

"I saw how the people of your village treated you," Minoth said, his lips clamped together with restrained anger. "An entire religion dedicated to the notion that magic was evil. I've never heard of such a ridiculous thing."

"But are they so wrong?" Kara asked. "I've seen what grimoires do. They change people. Make them do bad things."

Minoth's face fell.

"Oh, Kara," he said. "You poor, poor child. Magic isn't evil. It's *sick*—and badly in need of healing." He placed his dry fingertips against her forehead. "Let your mind whittle away at that for a time, and come back to it after it has taken shape. For now you need to understand the second purpose of the Sundering. Yes, *wexari* were meant to learn empathy and humility, but they were expected to meditate on their greatest fault as well. Everyone has one. Envy. Laziness. Greed. When they returned from the Sundering, students were required to enter the final chamber of the *queth'nondra* and prove that they understood this weakness, for recognizing our faults is the first step toward correcting them. Only then would their magic be restored."

"But how can you prove such a thing?" Kara asked.

Minoth smiled.

"The riddle without a question," he said. "It's different for everyone. That's why you must pass through the tunnel. The *queth'nondra* needs to learn everything about you in order to know what riddle to pose. If students gave the correct answer, their powers would return on the spot and they would graduate from Sablethorn as full-fledged *wexari*. If their answer was wrong, however . . ."

"They lost their magic forever and donned the green veil," Kara said, remembering the painting in the dining hall of Sablethorn. "Just because students failed to solve a riddle, you made them hide their faces in shame and become servants? That was beyond cruel."

Minoth's face colored slightly.

"When I became headmaster I did try to abolish that particular rule, but the oldest traditions are hardest to change. And I found, quite to my surprise, that many students were *relieved* to fail the *queth'nondra* trial. Being a *wexari* is a dangerous life, not for everyone."

"So instead you made them *servants?*" Kara asked, her voice rising. "They did nothing wrong. Why did they have to hide their faces behind—"

Kara gasped.

"That's why the witches who enter this place are changed into Faceless. The *queth'nondra* is confused. It thinks anyone who steps through the tunnel is here to be tested, like back in the Sablethorn days, only these poor girls don't know anything about that, so of course they fail. They don't have a chance. Used to be they were only punished with a green veil, but now they're punished with a different sort of mask, aren't they?"

Minoth shifted uncomfortably.

"You are correct," he said. "The *queth'nondra* was not totally immune to the corruptive influence of the Well. I warned the first witches who wandered in here that they should not enter the final chamber, but there's no going back through the tunnel and no one ever heeds me anyway. When they failed the trial—as is inevitable for any

who are not *wexari*—they should have simply been given green veils to cover their faces, but the *queth'nondra,* poisoned by darkness, grew confused and overzealous in its duties, and—"

"—took away their faces instead," Kara said.

Minoth nodded. "You would have made a fine addition to Sablethorn. You have a quick mind."

"You should meet my brother."

Kara eyed the door set into the opposite wall. All of a sudden she wanted to get out of this room as quickly as possible.

"How can I solve a riddle when I don't know the question?"

Minoth *tsk*ed.

"But the riddle *is* the question, my dear; figure that out and you're halfway home. The general idea of the chamber is the same for each student, however. It will be filled with objects, and you must leave with *only what you need* to prove to the *queth'nondra* that you understand

your greatest fault—what you must overcome in order to become a good *wexari*. Do that, and your powers shall be restored."

"And if I'm wrong?" Kara asked.

Minoth met her eyes but did not answer. They both knew what would happen to her if she were wrong.

"What was your greatest fault?" Kara asked.

The old schoolmaster's eyes widened in surprise.

"Interesting," he said. "All these years, and no one has ever asked me that. I suppose I can tell you. As you can see, I'm an unusual-looking man. At this stage in my life I've grown quite accustomed to it, but when I was young I was sensitive and bristled at the slightest stare. I walked my Sundering for three years before I finally realized that my outward appearance was spectacularly unimportant. I left the chamber wearing a jester's cap and shoes with tiny bells."

"Which proved you didn't care anymore if people mocked you for how you looked," Kara said.

Minoth held his hands out to her, palms up: *Now you get it.*

"How do you know all this will still work?" Kara asked. "Like you said, the Well corrupted the *queth'nondra*, made it turn all those witches into monsters. Even if I answer the riddle correctly, are you sure it will still give me back my powers and not do something . . . less helpful?"

The smile slipped from Minoth's face.

"No," he said. "To tell you the truth, I'm really not sure what it will do. All you can do is *believe*. Are you ready to do that, Kara?"

"I hope so."

"Do more than that. The *queth'nondra* does not take well to uncertainty. Make sure you're positive before you leave the chamber. You'll have great need of your powers in the coming days, Kara Westfall. As I said before, magic is sick. And I suspect you're the one meant to heal it."

Taking a deep breath, Kara faced the door and placed her hand on the curved handle. Though her lavender dress

remained dry, her red cloak, covered with the sticky substance from her journey through the tunnel, had begun to stiffen. *No sense trying to blend in with the other witches anymore*, Kara thought. She shed the cloak like an unwanted skin and opened the door.

TWENTY

A thousand Karas greeted her, the mirrored surface of the dome reflecting her image over and over again in its endless depths. The stone floor was covered with chests of every size and description. Some were taller than Kara and had to be opened from the front, like a wardrobe. Others were small enough to hold in the palm of her hand.

There was a sound behind her like a window slamming shut, and when Kara turned around the entrance to the room had vanished. She turned back—and saw that it

had reappeared on the other side of the chamber.

Only one way out . . .

Ignoring the chests for now, Kara regarded herself in the nearest mirror. Her long black hair was sticky and tangled, her skin pale, her dark eyes haunted. *Is that really me?* She touched her cheek to make sure she was looking at her own reflection and not that of a sunken-eyed impostor.

"Who are you?" she asked her other self. "What is your greatest fault?"

Kara jerked away, suddenly terrified that her reflection would break the mirror-rules and reply. It didn't. She saw her horrified expression in the mirror and laughed quietly.

"Frightened of my own reflection," she muttered. "Perhaps it's courage I lack."

But did she? Kara remembered following Watcher into the Thickety for the first time (the thought of her old friend and how they had parted sending a pang of regret through her midsection). *I broke the most important rule in De'Noran that day. And since then I've always done what needed to be done, whether I was scared to do it or not.*

No. It wasn't courage that she lacked.

Then what?

She began opening lids, hoping to get some ideas. Each chest, regardless of its size, contained one—and only one—object. In a few cases the fault addressed by these contents was obvious. Kara found beggar's threads in a bronze chest, no doubt intended for a *wexari* too attached to the comforts of gold. In another chest—this one constructed from vermillion crystal—she found a sword broken in twain. *For a* wexari *overly enamored of violence,* thought Kara. Most objects suggested multiple possibilities. *A spyglass? Could be for a* wexari *who spends too much time looking at books and not the world outside. Then again, it might be for one who needs to think more about the future and not just the present day.* A claw hammer? *Perhaps for a* wexari *who needs to learn how to fix problems—or, just as easily, a*

peaceful sort who needs to learn that force is sometimes neces-
sary. And finally there were those objects whose relevancy
eluded her altogether. *Painted rock? Piece of string? Cheese
grater?*

She continued her search.

At first Kara was worried that she would find no
objects that applied to her, but soon the opposite was
true; the stone floor, now littered with the chests' contents, offered an endless array of possible solutions. She
picked up a small clock and held it loosely in her hands.
I am often impetuous, Kara thought. *Rushing into things on
the spur of the moment without considering all the possible
consequences first.* She thought the clock might represent
her need to take more time before acting. It wasn't a
bad answer, but it didn't feel exactly right. She placed
the clock nearby—in case she changed her mind—and
picked up a swaddling blanket. *I'm the closest thing Taff will
ever have to a mother. And I need to do a better job. He's been in
constant danger. I don't check often enough that he's bathed or*

brushed his teeth. *And it's been months since he's seen the inside of a schoolhouse. . . .*

She supposed this was as good an answer as the clock, but not necessarily a better one—and she didn't want to leave the chamber until there were no doubts left in her mind.

Minoth said to take "only what you need." Can I take both of them?

Even as Kara considered this her eyes were drawn to a pair of half-moon spectacles. *I was so easily fooled by Rygoth. Perhaps I need to see clearer in the future. . . .*

Could she bring three things? Four? All of them?

Kara slumped to the ground.

She could see her many faults reflected in nearly all the objects littering the floor. *I'm lacking in so many ways,* she thought. *I can't possibly pick just one.*

I wish Taff were here. He would know what to do.

Countless reflections stared back at her, countless Karas doomed to failure.

She sat up.

I'm not good enough, she thought, the idea maybe not perfect yet but with a comforting feel, like finally finding a familiar path after hours lost in the woods. *I always fall short in the end. I wasn't a good enough witch to keep my powers. I wasn't a good enough daughter to save Mother and Father. I'm not a good enough sister to keep my brother safe. Even now I want Taff here because I'm not good enough to solve this riddle on my own!*

She picked up the clock and hurled it across the room. It struck the mirror with a resounding clatter but did not crack the glass.

"I'm not even good enough to break that mirror!" Kara screamed. "I don't deserve my powers!"

But could this really be the fault that the *queth'nondra* was seeking? Surely her powers would not be returned to her if she did not deserve them in the first place. Was this all some kind of cruel jape?

She heard Mary Kettle's voice, as close as a whisper:

You must learn to ask the right questions.

Kara stared at the place where she had thrown the clock. *Another mirror that refuses to crack*, she thought, remembering Bethany's grimoire and how it had swallowed Lucas's arrow. The unfortunate girl was no doubt in an iron cage right now, or maybe even dead. Yet another person she couldn't help.

Kara noticed her defeated expression in the mirror and grew suddenly angry.

"But I *did* help her," she said. "I saved her from doing wrong. I saved all those children too."

And then Timoth Clen came and snatched her away and . . .

"Yes. But I still saved them." She jabbed a finger at her chest. "*Me*. I did that."

Kara took a seat on a feathered trunk as a stunning new idea blazed to life. What if she was thinking about this all wrong? What if she *did* deserve her powers after all? What if her fault was . . .

Self-doubt.

Minoth's words rang in her ears: *"All you can do is believe. Are you ready to do that, Kara?"*

"That wasn't just talk," Kara said. "That was a hint!"

She rose to her feet, shaking with excitement. *I'm close. I can feel it.* All she had to do was find an object that demonstrated . . . what, exactly? That she trusted herself? That she was worthy of having her powers returned to her? Kara had no idea how a single object could prove this; nevertheless she began to sift through the chests' contents for a second time. As she did, Kara remembered the good she had done, hoping that one of these accomplishments might point her in the right direction.

I rescued Taff when Simon tried to kill him.

I overcame the dark power of the grimoire.

I saved De'Noran from Grace, though the villagers were cruel to me and hardly deserved such help.

I stopped Imogen.

I freed Kala Malta.

I brought Mary Kettle back into the light.

I traveled to the World. Found Sablethorn. Entered the Well of Witches.

For the first twelve years of her life Kara had been told, through both words and actions, that she was evil and worthless. This litany of good deeds, however, acted as a balm for the thousands of unseen wounds she had accumulated as a Child of the Fold.

She suddenly felt stronger. Lighter. Free.

They were wrong about me. All of them.

"I've done good things!" Kara exclaimed. "I've helped people! I'm not worthless!"

Suddenly, she knew the answer to the *queth'nondra's* riddle. It was unorthodox, and would require ignoring Minoth's instructions completely, but it felt *right*.

I need to have complete faith in myself.

She opened her hands and the objects she was holding clattered to the floor.

"My name is Kara Westfall," she said, making her way toward the exit to the room. "Daughter of Helena and

William. Sister of Taff. And I don't need anything from this room to prove that I deserve my powers back. I know I do. I am—and always will be—what my people claimed was impossible: *a good witch!*"

Empty-handed, Kara stepped through the door.

It was Redmask who noticed her first. The antlered Faceless was listlessly poking its spear into Rattle's flank, the piteous whines of the rustle-foot causing the surrounding monsters to pop their fingers in appreciation, when it glimpsed Kara approaching from the far side of the *queth'nondra*. Redmask tilted its head in confusion. *It wasn't expecting to see me like this*, Kara thought. *All the witches before me exited the same way they entered. And none had kept their face.* Kara's reappearance—*smiling*, no less— clearly made Redmask uneasy. Its paper fingers tightened around its spear. Kara knew that if she got too close the creature would drive it through her chest without hesitation. In Redmask's mind, any witch who could escape the *queth'nondra* unaltered was too dangerous to live.

Other Faceless began to turn in Kara's direction. She heard the rustle of cloaks, the crinkle of spinning heels against the paper ground. Taff shouted her name. She tuned out the sounds and remembered a sunny day, the heat gracing her skin with warmth so tender it was like a caress, and used that memory to build a mind-bridge to the rustle-foot. *This is my world*, Kara told it. *Light. Life.* For a brief, heart-stopping moment Kara felt nothing— and then Rattle opened itself up to her, eager to embrace any show of kindness.

All of this happened in the flutter of a heartbeat. While Kara's mind wandered to the rustle-foot, her dark eyes remained on Redmask.

"I really don't like you," she said.

She sent her command and Rattle followed it glee-fully, opening her long mouth and swallowing Redmask in a single bite. The rustle-foot chewed thoughtfully for a moment, enjoying the new flavor of this unexpected treat, before spitting out a pair of antlers. They skittered along the ground and came to a stop at Kara's feet.

After this it was chaos.

Kara didn't even need to build mind-bridges to the other rustle-feet; Rattle's action had given them all the courage they needed. Many Faceless were devoured on the spot. Those that escaped were hunted down by a rampaging horde of rustle-feet that crushed masks beneath their feet with playful abandon. Kara felt their joy—their *freedom*—and she rejoiced in it.

Taff ran into her arms. She rejoiced in that as well.

"I guess you got your magic back," he said.

Grace arrived just in time to overhear this. Her mouth dropped open and she shoved her right hand against her hip.

"What's he talking about?" she asked. "Are you telling me that this entire time you haven't had any *powers*?"

"Long story," Kara said. She turned to her brother. "I met Minoth Dravania! He was wonderful! And I learned a few things that we should probably——"

"No time," Taff said, pointing past her. "Look!"

One of the Burngates had opened, exposing a small circle of sky. Sunlight spilled across the Well of Witches, red-cloaked figures clawing at one another for a taste of its embrace. The ground below the Burngate spiraled upward like a staircase, allowing five witches—their ankles shackled by long paper chains—to climb through the hole itself. From this angle, their bodies—half in the Well and half in the real world—seemed to vanish at the waist. A few moments later a struggling figure was dragged into the waiting arms of the Faceless. Though it was faint at this distance, Kara could hear the witches chanting, "One of us, one of us, one of us!"

The Burngate closed, leaving the parchment sky unchanged, and the ground descended to its original position. The other two Burngates swelled like blisters ready to pop. It wouldn't be long before they opened as well.

"The battle between Rygoth and Timoth Clen is

happening right now," Kara said.

"That's impossible," said Taff. "We've only been gone a week at most, and last we checked the graycloaks were still near Nye's Landing and Rygoth was on the other side of Sentium."

"Rygoth has Niersook," said Kara. "She can get places fast. Or maybe witches are casting their Last Spells for a different reason altogether. I don't know. The important thing is those Burngates are about to open. Who knows when we'll get this chance again?"

"You'll never make it in time," Grace said.

"I didn't come this far just to give up now," Kara said.

As much as she hated to admit it, though, she saw Grace's point. It would take them at least an hour just to reach the place where the ground rose into the sky, and then hours more to climb to the hole itself . . . not to mention all the Faceless and witches standing in their path.

One of the remaining Burngates made a sizzling noise,

like oil touching a hot pan, and a beam of sunlight speared the ground.

Dark despair began to worm its way into Kara's body.

No, she thought. *I can do this. There must be a way! But how?*

Inside her mind she felt a warm nudge, a forgotten cat pressing against her legs for attention.

I help. Cut free first. Go fast-fast!

With a wide smile, Rattle rolled her hooded eyes toward the thick ropes wound about her torso.

The majority of its legs are bound just like all the other rustle-feet, Kara thought. *It will take some precious time to free them, but once I do we should be able to move much faster. . . .*

"All right," Kara said. "Let's see what you've got."

As the second Burngate burst open, she snatched Redmask's spear from the ground and used it to cut at the ropes. Taff followed suit, and even Grace—much to Kara's surprise—picked up an abandoned blade and began to help.

A few minutes later the rope fell away, and Kara realized that it wasn't Rattle's legs that had been bound at all.

It was her wings.

Freed at last, they sprang out from her body like a compressed spring, knocking the children to the ground. Twice as long as the creature herself, the wings were the drowsy blue of an early-morning sky with tips of purest gold.

Kara, mouth agape, rose to her feet.

"This ugly thing's a *bird*?" Grace asked.

The rustle-foot shook her wings proudly and rattled with joy.

Come, Rattle thought. *Fly*.

It flattened itself as low as it could, allowing the children to climb onto its back. Kara assumed that Rattle would immediately take off into the sky, but the rustle-foot still had one surprise left for them that day: balancing on the tips of its wings, it raised itself high and dashed across the ground. Kara had just enough time to notice that the second Burngate had closed, then she held tight and pressed her face close to the creature's body as the Well blurred past them in a quickening rush.

Grace screamed. Taff laughed.

Rattle took flight.

The rustle-foot was fast—impossibly, improbably, storybook fast. Through eyes slitted against the stinging air, Kara saw the final Burngate peel away and drift to the ground like a diseased cloud. A large hole revealed the world beyond the Well, the moon hanging pale in the night sky. *How can it be dark already?* Kara thought. *It was just sunny out two minutes ago.* There was no time to think about that now; five witches standing at the peak of the skyscraping ground stretched into the other world, the widening hole large enough to fit them all with ease. Kara saw their bodies tense as, she imagined, their quarry was doing her best to escape their clawing hands. The witches climbed even farther until only their feet, shackled by paper chains, were still visible.

Just a few more moments, Kara thought, willing the doomed witch who had just cast her Last Spell to dodge their grasp for as long as possible. They were nearly there, but Rattle was beginning to tire; it had been a long time since she had last used her wings.

Come on, Kara pleaded with the rustle-foot. *Please. For me. . . .*

And then the witches had their prey: a middle-aged woman with long auburn hair and a shirt drenched with blood. Kara could not tell if her screams came from pain or horror. Perhaps both. The witches dragged her down, none too gently, and she was passed to a group of waiting Faceless.

The hole began to close.

"No!" Kara shouted. "No!"

Hold tight, thought the rustle-foot. It gave its wings one last ferocious swoop and tucked them tight against its body. Kara felt like one of Lucas's glorb arrows as they shot through the air at blinding speed, knocking witches and Faceless from their sky perch and shooting through the open Burngate into the cold, rainy night.

Taff whooped with delight.

We made it, Kara thought. *We made it!*

Her jubilation was short-lived, however, as the first creature crashed into them, a large bird with teeth-lined wings and a snout as long as an alligator's. It snapped at Rattle, who extended her wings and knocked the grotesque animal into a flock of flying lampreys. These tore the bird to bits and then darted toward the children with long undulations of their eel-like bodies, as though sky could be swum through as easily as air. Right before the lampreys reached them, however, their path was blocked by a massive reptilian form. Kara assumed, as high as they were, that this new arrival was airborne as well, but looking down she saw that it was simply huge, its massive feet making craterous footprints in the earth below them.

Get us out of here! Kara told Rattle.

Before Kara had finished her sentence the rustle-foot

was on the move, gracefully dodging creatures large and small in a sky teeming with life. *What is going on?* Kara thought. Deafening noise stretched out in all directions: screeching, squawking, fluttering. *These are Rygoth's creations. Just like Niersook. Life that was never meant to be.*

Cold pebbles of rain pelted the children as Rattle swooped lower. Below them stretched a scene even more chaotic than the one in the sky. Hundreds of graycloaks armed with shields and ball-staffs fought all manner of creature: shambling monstrosities that stunk of grave dirt, icy shadows hovering low to the ground like mist, six-footed beasts with manes of fire. Witches read from open grimoires and created golems of dirt and stone, fireballs, waves of black energy. A wizened old woman stood in the midst of all the chaos and brought forth bolts of black lightning from the sky, so engrossed in her conjurations that she did not hear the graycloak approach her from behind. His ball-staff flashed in the moonlight and the black lightning ceased.

"I'm glad you rescued me, Kara," said Grace, hugging her from behind. "This is great fun!"

Kara pushed Grace away.

"Rygoth freed the witches," Taff said, pointing to the empty iron cages scattered across the field.

"At least Timoth Clen didn't kill them," Kara said.

"Except they're fighting for Rygoth now!"

"I don't think so. The witches down there look more experienced. They're probably the ones from Rygoth's tent. Don't forget, three of them just used their Last Spells, otherwise the Burngates wouldn't have opened. New witches wouldn't be that far along in their grimoires yet."

"We have to help the soldiers," said Taff. "They're getting slaughtered down there!"

"Right now we have to find Father!"

"Listen to your sister," said Grace. Her eyes, drawn to the carnage below, glowed like twin moons. "Graycloaks don't *want* help—especially from two witches. This is what the Children of the Fold have been praying for—a great battle against the forces of darkness! It would be unfair to rob them of their glory."

They heard the screams of a man far below them and then tearing sounds, like two dogs fighting over a piece of meat.

"We can't just let them die—" said Taff.

"Sure we can!"

"—because even though they're graycloaks, they're still *people*. Father would want you to help them first. You know he would."

Kara looked over her shoulder at him. "But he's so close, Taff. I can feel it."

"Father's waited for us a long time. A few more minutes won't matter. You *have* to do this, Kara."

Taff's right. If I have the power to save these men, it's my responsibility to use it.

"Is anyone going to ask me what *I* think?" Grace chimed in.

"No," said Kara and Taff in unison.

The rustle-foot landed in the center of the field. Shadowy shapes—perhaps man, perhaps beast—noted their arrival and crept closer.

Kara slid to the ground and reached out with her mind.

She was afraid, at first, that she would be unable to control Rygoth's creations; their minds felt different from natural animals, vacant, like the soulless creatures of the Draye'varg. It turned out, however, that slipping inside these monsters required little effort at all, and Kara soon found herself flitting from one mind to the next with surprising ease. *Their thoughts are completely unprotected. Rygoth made them that way so they'd be easy to control. She never imagined that another* wexari *might take advantage of it. She didn't even stay to make sure they were doing what she asked; she just sent them in the general direction of the graycloaks and allowed their violent tendencies to do the rest.*

Rygoth's initial order—*KILL EVERY HUMAN YOU SEE*—was too deeply entrenched for Kara to remove;

these creatures had been engineered for the sole purpose of death and destruction. However, she was able to *tweak* the order by adding a single word, a change the monsters willingly accepted because they would still be allowed to hurt things.

Kill every NOT-human you see, Kara ordered them.

As she expected, the creatures attacked each other.

The night was filled with the sounds of snapping jaws and snarling, frothing mouths. Oft-bitten bodies slumped to the ground. Winged predators dug their talons into the flanks of unsuspecting monsters and hurried them away. The witches, confused by this unexpected development, tucked their grimoires beneath their arms and fled. Graycloaks set off in hot pursuit.

"How are you doing this without a grimoire?" Grace asked, mouth agape.

"I don't need one," said Kara. "I can do magic anytime I feel like it. Best remember that, in case you're thinking of crossing me tonight."

For the first time Kara could remember, Grace Stone was at a loss for words. She simply nodded.

"Good," Kara said. "Be ready to do your part."

The field grew eerily quiet. Motionless shapes, both great and small, were cast in nets of silver moonlight. A dozen graycloaks, feeling more confident now, encircled Rattle and the three children in a tightening coil. They were younger than Kara expected—little more than boys, really.

"Who are you?" one of them asked. He had the large build of a farmer's son and stared at the rustle-foot with a stupid, flat-eyed expression. "Why were you riding one of her monsters?"

"This is not a monster," Kara said. "This is Rattle. And as you might have noticed, I stopped these creatures from attacking you."

"How?"

"I think we both know the answer to that."

He scowled and thrust his ball-staff into the air.

"Witch!" he exclaimed, and the other graycloaks followed his lead. "Witch! Witch! Witch!" They started forward, raised weapons ready to strike.

"Stop this nonsense right now," Kara said. She had barely raised her voice, but there was something in her dark eyes that froze the men in their tracks.

"Listen and listen well," she said. "I know you're followers of Timoth Clen and have been taught that anyone who uses magic is evil. But I'm a *good* witch. And if you don't believe me, consider this: I just wiped out a field full of monsters without breaking a sweat. Do you really think that I would have much trouble with a handful of *boys*?"

Suddenly unable to meet her eyes, the graycloaks lowered their weapons.

"Thank you," she said. "Now someone tell me what's going on—"

A figure wearing a bow on his back pushed past the soldiers. Kara glimpsed familiar brown eyes.

"Lucas!" she exclaimed.

Kara realized it was probably unwise to take her eyes off the graycloaks, but she threw her arms around him anyway.

"I thought I'd never see you again," he said. "The shell you gave me stopped working. Every day I tried to reach you but—"

"It was because I was in the Well of Witches."

"This whole time?" Lucas asked with disbelief. "That can't be!"

The farmboy stepped between them.

"You're *friends* with this witch?" he asked, sneering as though some secret suspicion had been realized. "The Clen won't like that."

"You're wrong," Lucas said. "He *needs* her. We all do. Most of the seasoned soldiers are dead. We're only alive because the youngest graycloaks were bringing up the flank when they attacked. Kara here is our only chance to save our leader from certain death."

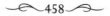

Lucas grinned at her. The smile was the same, but there was something different about his face.

She noticed, for the first time, that he wore a gray cloak.

"Lucas," she said, a sickening feeling spreading through her stomach. "What's going on? Why are you wearing that?"

"A lot has happened since you left," Lucas said. His voice sounded deeper than the last time she heard it. "I promise I'll explain everything but right now we need to move. Rygoth has freed all the witches." The other gray-cloaks stiffened, their eyes wandering far afield as though simply saying Rygoth's name might cause her to appear. "Timoth Clen is her prisoner. We can't get close, but maybe with your help . . ."

"I don't understand," Kara said, her mind spinning. "How are you one of *them*? How could this have happened so quickly? I've only been gone a few days. A week at most."

Lucas shook his head.

"You've been gone almost a year, Kara."

She staggered backward. *A year?*

"No." She felt dizzy, the world spinning out of control. "This is some kind of trick. An enchantment. Rygoth's work—it has to be!"

"It's not," Lucas said, his eyes filled with sympathy. "Time happened. I know. I was there. Why does it seem so strange to you?"

"It's only been a week."

"That's impossible."

"Do I look any older than the last time you saw me?"

"No," Lucas admitted. "Different, somehow. But not older."

"Time doesn't move the same way in the Well of Witches," Taff said. "It's the only thing that makes sense. That's why the Burngates changed from day to night in minutes, why Aunt Abby looked barely older than the day she died. Time moves faster. Or slower, depending on your point of view."

"Taff," Lucas said, smiling as he noticed the boy for the first time. "I see you haven't changed. Still smart as a whip." Lucas's eyes played over Grace, but he did not acknowledge her presence. Kara wasn't sure what to make of that.

Lucas's eyes narrowed with concern.

"Where's Safi?" he asked.

"She helped us get away from these really bad witches," Taff said. "Twins."

The graycloaks grumbled among themselves, using words that Kara would have rather they kept to themselves in front of her brother.

"We know all about the twins," said Lucas. "I'm so sorry for your loss."

"No!" Taff exclaimed. "She's not dead! The twins were about to find us so Safi stayed behind to distract them. She's Rygoth's prisoner. We'll save her!"

Lucas knelt to one knee and placed his hands on the boy's shoulders.

"Rygoth doesn't take prisoners, Taff."

"She took Timoth Clen."

"To be executed in front of her followers. It's nothing long-term. We have scouts who have seen her camp. They would have told us if there were any captives."

"Well, they just didn't see her, then. Safi has to be somewhere. Rygoth needs her."

"Listen," Lucas said slowly. "I just want you to be prepared—"

Taff pushed him away.

"You think she's dead," he snapped. "I can see it in your eyes. But you're wrong. She's alive. She's my best friend and she's still alive!"

"I hope so," Lucas said, rising to his feet. "If she is, I have no doubt you'll save her." He turned to Kara. "We need to hurry. Rygoth took your fa—" He paused, eyeing the other graycloaks. "Timoth Clen several hours ago. She's in the graveyard up ahead, the place where the original Clen is buried, distributing grimoires to those who swear their allegiance to her. My guess is she's forcing the

Clen to watch, just to gloat. She'll kill him afterward, though—I'm sure of it. We have to save him."

But after so much time, does any part of our father still remain? In her last dream of Father he had taken another—perhaps final—step toward madness, spinning a conversation with empty air. At the time, Kara imagined she had only a week or two before he was lost to her forever. That had been nearly a year ago.

His mind must be completely lost by now. What will he be like if we bring him back? Will he even know who he is? Will he remember Taff and me at all?

She had to try, even if there was only a small chance of ever having a father again. Kara had come this far; she would see this through to the end—for good or for ill.

TWENTY-ONE

The graveyard sat on top of a small mountain. Rattle flew the group most of the way, setting down on a large boulder shielded from view by a tight thicket of trees. Kara didn't want to risk getting any closer. If Rygoth had posted guards, the rustle-foot would be hard to miss.

"Stay here," she whispered into one leathery ear. "And be ready. When we come back we may need to hurry."

In the distance Kara could make out flickering torch-lights and rounded tops of stone. The low angle prohibited

her from seeing any people, but Kara knew they were up there: the silence was periodically broken by voices raised in a dark chant of exultation.

She tried not to think about what could make Rygoth's coven so happy.

A narrow path led uphill between windblown trees battered by rain. Lucas took the lead, followed by Kara, Taff, and Grace. Kara had insisted on the small group. More bodies meant more noise, and right now their only advantage was the element of surprise. Kara had no illusions about her chances of beating Rygoth in a straight fight, but if she struck fast and unexpectedly it might provide enough of a distraction for the others to rescue Father and Safi.

But first I need Grace to try to undo the curse, because if she can't, that changes things completely. The last thing I want to do is risk my life to rescue Timoth Clen. Kara remembered the animal skeletons hanging from the Fenroot tree, the scarecrow meant to be her with a ram's skull and black school dress. *Timoth Clen is a madman who will try to kill me the moment he's free. If there's no chance of returning Father to his body, it might be best not to rescue him at all.*

Grace muttered something beneath her breath as she nearly slipped and fell. Though she had found a branch to use as a walking stick, the muddy ground remained difficult for her to navigate.

"Grace," Kara whispered, waiting for her.

"Yes," she grunted breathlessly. Her pretty features were pinched tight with frustration. "What?"

"Things may get tricky once we reach the graveyard. It'll be best if I give this to you now."

Kara slid her hand into her cloak and carefully removed the grimoire page, pieces flaking off like burned crumbs. *I hope it still works*, Kara thought, offering the magical paper to the girl who had once tried to kill her. Grace gazed at the page with solemn reverence and then took it with two hands. The moment her fingers touched the paper she giggled with unadulterated joy.

"I can feel the power," she said. "It tickles."

"Put it away before it gets wet. We can't have it taking any more damage than it already has."

Grace quickly slipped the page beneath her cloak.

"I know we've had our little differences," Grace said, "but you held up your end of the bargain and I'll do what you asked. You can trust me."

"No, I can't," Kara said. "I'm sure that as soon as you have the opportunity you'll try to stab me in the back. You might even succeed. I know how clever you are. But if you fail, I'll throw you back into the Well myself, I promise. How do you think the Faceless will greet you, Grace? The girl who escaped and made them look like fools." Kara leaned forward and whispered in her ear. "I'm sure they'll have a special mask waiting just for you."

Grace drew back, her lips trembling, and Kara felt a momentary pang of guilt. *Did I go too far? Did she really mean it when she said I could trust her?* But then the expression on Grace's face shifted and Kara's feelings of guilt dissipated. The white-haired girl examined Kara like a butcher regarding a slab of meat, considering which angle to make the first slice.

Ah, Kara thought. *There you are.*

"You're wrong about me," Grace snapped, gripping Kara's wrist with her ice-cold hand. "I *will* do what you ask today. And I would *never* stab you in the back. I wouldn't use a knife at all. When I finally get the best of you, it'll be a spell that does it." Noticing something over Kara's shoulder, Grace canted her head and said, "Hmm. How interesting."

Kara turned around.

Lucas had notched an arrow to his bow. It was pointed straight at her.

"Lucas?" she asked.

"I can't believe you really did it," he said, stepping around Kara and swiveling his bow in Grace's direction. "You rescued her. *Grace Stone.* I didn't want to say anything until we were alone, because if the other graycloaks

knew the truth it would have been impossible to convince them you were on our side. I had to wait."

"What are you doing?" Kara asked.

Lucas pulled the bowstring back and gritted his teeth, willing himself to let the arrow fly. Grace stared into his eyes with a slight smirk on her face.

"I'm so sorry about your father," Lucas said, "but I can't let her undo the curse. You weren't here this past year. You didn't see the burning villages, the corpses piled on top of one another. Without Timoth Clen, who's going to stop the witches? Who's going to save us?"

Kara stepped between Lucas and Grace, blocking his shot.

"I am," she said.

"Move, Kara. Please."

"You need to trust me."

"I do, you *know* I do, but—"

"If today has proven anything it's that Timoth Clen doesn't have a chance against Rygoth. He's been taken prisoner. His army was wiped out. You and all your new gr.aycloak friends would be dead right now if I hadn't come in time. You know what that tells me? The world doesn't need a witch hunter. It needs a *witch*."

Lucas stared at Kara for a long time and then lowered his bow.

"I hope you know what you're doing," he said.

Kara looked back at Grace, her wet hair plastered against her skull. She was smiling.

So do I, Kara thought.

By the time they reached the graveyard the rain had finally stopped. Past three rings of massive, oblong stones half-buried in the earth, Kara could see torch-lit figures moving in the night. She carefully made her way from ring to ring until she reached the innermost circle and pressed her back against a slick wet stone. The others followed her lead, each using a different stone for cover.

Taking a deep breath, Kara peeked just far enough to see into the graveyard.

There were no tombstones. Instead, hundreds of violet pyramids, ranging in height from a kneeling child to a full-size man, created a labyrinth in the muddy ground. The pyramids had been constructed from some sort of sea glass, and in the moonlight Kara could see mummified corpses pressed against their semitransparent walls.

Between the pyramidal coffins walked the witches.

They were all dressed the same: black cloaks that reached down to their ankles and bore the crimson crest of a double-fanged spider. Hoods concealed their faces but not the grimoires in their hands.

Fifty of them, Kara thought. *Maybe more.*

Three stones down, Kara heard Taff's sudden intake of breath. Their eyes met, and he pointed to an area of the graveyard that she was unable to see from her current vantage point. She crossed behind the stone and peeked out from the other side, hoping for a better angle.

Her stomach lurched.

Near the northern edge of the graveyard stood an ancient black obelisk engraved with faded, forgotten letters. Her father was chained to it. He was barely conscious and his white robe was slashed and speckled with red. The cruel, Clenian edges cut into his face had been smoothed by exhaustion and pain; at that moment, he looked like their father again.

Kara heard a low, musical laugh.

Rygoth.

She sat on a pile of animal bones crafted into a makeshift throne, closer to Kara's hiding place than the obelisk but facing off to the side. The long dress she wore was the dark purple of a lingering bruise and embroidered with silver weblike patterns. Her long white gloves gleamed like polished ivory. By her side sat the wolf with the scorpion tail.

"I grow tired of waiting," Rygoth said, yawning into the back of her hand. "Who's next?"

At the opposite end of the graveyard a dozen girls dressed practically in rags pawed through a pile of leather volumes. *These must be the girls that Rygoth rescued from the iron cages*, Kara thought. *They're choosing their grimoires from what's left of the stock Rygoth transported from Kala Malta.* Two black-cloaked witches found a girl already clinging to a spellbook and shoved her forward. Her face was filthy, her hair dirty and unkempt.

"Did it call to you?" Rygoth asked, gesturing toward the grimoire in the girl's hands. "Did it speak your true name?"

The girl nodded.

"You feel its power, don't you? After all those months in that cage, you burn to use it. Don't fight your feelings, dear. You're absolutely right. The world *does* deserve to be punished for what it did to you. Just vow your undying loyalty to me, and you'll never be weak again."

The girl dropped to one knee.

"I, Holly Lamson, swear that—"

"Not like *that*," Rygoth said. "I have no interest in *words*. Haven't you been watching the others?"

The girl nodded subserviently.

"Then you know what to do."

Holly crossed to the black obelisk. She considered the man before her, perhaps feeling a final moment of pity, and then opened her new grimoire to the first page. Strange words poured forth from her lips. Timoth Clen screamed in pain as an invisible force whipped his chest, leaving a new tear in his shirt.

Holly gasped in childlike delight, amazed by what she had done. The other witches swarmed around her, chanting, *"Welcome, sister! May darkness embrace and empower you!"* A black cloak was pulled over Holly's head and she was folded into the coven.

Another ragged girl was shoved in front of Rygoth. The process began anew.

Kara did not want her father—her *real* father—suffering through the pain that Timoth Clen must be experiencing at that moment, but there was no more time to wait. She needed to know if all her efforts had been worth it.

Here we go, she thought, nodding toward Grace.

The girl eagerly withdrew the tattered page. Kara closely observed Grace's every movement, ready to act at the slightest sign of duplicity; she had already built mind-bridges to a pair of large vultures perched at the top of the stone, just in case.

If she gives me the slightest reason I won't hesitate to send them.

"That's not right," Grace mumbled, staring down at the page. "That's not what I need."

Biting her lower lip, Grace focused all her energy on the page. Her hands began to tremble. A ribbon of paper tore away and fluttered to the ground.

"Give me what I want," she said. "Give me, give me, give me . . ."

Grace smiled victoriously.

She closed her eyes, savoring the moment, and spoke the words.

Chains rattled as Timoth Clen jerked forward, his eyes rolling back in his head. Grace spoke faster, and then faster still, the words blending together, a sweeping of sounds. Beads of sweat rolled down her left temple.

Kara looked back at her father and saw him cough out a puff of black, polluted air.

"She's doing it," Taff whispered, his face aglow with hope. "It's really working!"

A long ripping sound tore through the night.

"No!" Grace exclaimed, far too loud. The black-cloaked witch standing closest to them raised her head and started in their direction. Kara ducked behind the stone and turned toward Grace.

She was holding two pieces of torn paper in her hands.

"The spell was too powerful," Grace said. "The page was already weak from all the time it spent away from the grimoire. It couldn't handle it." She met Taff's eyes, her

expression uncharacteristically soft. "I'm sorry."

Dirt crunched on the opposite side of the stone as the curious witch drew closer. Lucas reached for his glorb-bow but Kara shook her head. She breathed deeply, feeling each heartbeat thudding in her chest, surprisingly calm. *I know exactly what to do. It's just a matter of getting it done. Like chores on the farm.*

"Taff," she said, keeping her voice as close to a whisper as possible. "Grace needs a grimoire. When I make my distraction, sneak over to that pile and steal her one. Grace, be ready to try that spell again. Lucas, can one of those fancy arrows of yours break those chains?"

"I think so," Lucas said. "But—"

"Good. Go get my father. And keep an eye out for Safi. She has to be here somewhere." *If she's not dead, of course.* "I'll meet you all back where we landed. If I'm not there—don't wait for me. I'll figure something out."

She backed away from the stone.

"Where are you going?" Taff asked.

"To get my wolf."

Kara stepped into the open and nearly collided with the approaching witch. The girl raised her grimoire to cast a spell but Kara knocked it from her hands.

"Rygoth!" Kara exclaimed.

Robes rustled as witches spun in her direction, torchlight illuminating a sea of startled faces. *That's right*, Kara thought. *Look here! Keep those backs turned so Lucas and Taff can do their jobs.*

Dozens of grimoires opened at once. The night was filled with the sound of flipping pages.

"Close your spellbooks!" Rygoth exclaimed. "Let her come."

Kara maneuvered past the aboveground coffins, mud sucking at her boots. Desiccated faces shielded by violet glass watched her as she passed. When she reached the silent witches they parted into two sections, forming a path that led directly to Rygoth. *No escape now*, Kara thought. *I have to be prepared for anything.* She called out to more vultures, constructing mind-bridges from specific memories of death—lifeless eyes, swollen bodies—in order to tempt the carrion eaters. Soon all of the stones in the circle were topped with hunch-winged shadows.

Wait, Kara told the vultures. *Not yet. On my signal only.*

She stepped before Rygoth's throne.

To either side of the *wexari* stood the twins, their wan faces slashed with joyless smiles. *Did they really kill Safi?* Kara thought, scanning the graveyard and seeing no trace of her lost friend. Her blood raged, and the wolf seated by Rygoth's throne bared his fangs.

"My persistent little *wexari*," Rygoth said. Sparks of color glinted in her fractured eyes. "I was wondering when you would get here."

The lack of surprise in Rygoth's voice, as though Kara's arrival had been as expected as nightfall, needled her with fear.

What else does she know? Is this all a trap?

Are the others in danger?

Kara pushed that last thought away, picturing instead a clear blue sky with white clouds. *I have to keep my mind as blank as possible. If Rygoth slips inside she'll learn all our . . .*

"No need to protect your secrets from me, Kara," Rygoth said. "I already know them all."

Kara had her doubts about this. She felt a scratching at her skull, like a dog wanting to be let inside the house.

She's trying to gain entrance to my mind. She wouldn't be doing that if she knew everything already.

"I'm not afraid of you anymore," Kara said.

"Why? Because you have your powers back?" Rygoth smiled at Kara's shocked expression and clapped a hand to her mouth. "Oh dear! Were you hoping to take me unawares? Have I ruined the surprise?"

The witches erupted into laughter. Rygoth let it continue for a few moments, her pitiless eyes never leaving Kara's, and then raised one hand into the air.

The laughter stopped immediately.

"So you're not afraid of me," Rygoth said. "How inspiring. But there's a serious flaw in your logic. Being a *wexari* again should make you *more* afraid of me. Before you were just a meddlesome child. But now? I really do have to kill you."

Kara looked into Rygoth's eyes and saw not hatred or joy but something even worse: the first stirrings of boredom.

I have to stall, give the others as much time as possible.

"How did you know I got my powers back?" Kara asked.

Rygoth smiled.

"Now that's a question I'd be *thrilled* to answer."

She snapped her fingers, the sound muffled by the white gloves. A small figure stepped forward from the first row of witches and pushed back her hood.

"Safi!" Kara exclaimed.

The girl shuddered at the sound of her name but did not look in Kara's direction. Safi's green eyes, usually so full of life, were flat and dull.

The twins didn't kill her. They brought her to their queen.

She's alive!

"Allow me to introduce you to my seer," Rygoth said. "Stubborn little thing at first. But she's learned her place. Tells me all sorts of useful information—like the fact that you got your magic back, for instance. After this she's going to help me gather the princess's grimoire, piece by piece. You think you've seen magic? Just wait."

"Safi," Kara said. "I'm going to get you out of here."

Raucous laughter shook the witches.

"Is that so?" Rygoth asked. "Tell me, Seer. Do you want to leave my side?"

"Of course not," Safi intoned. "I live to serve you."

"What will you do if Kara tries to take you by force?"

"I will kill her, if my master commands it."

Rygoth smiled and folded her hands in her lap.

"Kara, Kara, Kara. I'm a bit bewildered by what you hope to accomplish here. Are you waiting for the right

moment to send these vultures you've gathered up on the stones?" Rygoth sighed. "Yes, Kara, I know about them too. They would never dare to attack me. No creature would."

Kara saw, however, the way Rygoth's eyes flickered up to the birds. She was not afraid—not even close—but there was a certain degree of weariness in the glance, as though taking care of the vultures would require more energy than she'd like to expend. Kara saw her slumped shoulders, the way she leaned on one armrest of the throne.

Creating all those creatures to attack the graycloaks must have taken a lot out of her. She's exhausted.

I have to do this now. I won't get a better chance.

"I met Minoth," Kara said.

Rygoth raised her eyebrows in surprise before quickly regaining her composure.

"Of course," she lied. "I already knew this." Rygoth straightened in her throne and smiled widely. "Did he admit his mistake in forcing me to leave Sablethorn? Now that he can see the greatness I've achieved, did he—"

"Actually, he didn't mention you at all. Oh, wait. Yes he did! After I went into the *queth'nondra* and passed the Sundering test—that's how I got my powers back, but *I'm sure* you knew that—Minoth told me that you were too scared to take it. He said that I was a better witch at age thirteen than you'll ever be."

Rygoth's lips tightened with simmering rage.

"That's not true."

"If you say so," Kara said. She clapped her hands together, as though she had just thought of an idea on the spot. "I'll give you a chance to prove it. A challenge. How does that sound?"

"I don't need to prove *anything* to you. If I wanted to, I could—"

"Oh," said Kara. "Looks like Minoth was right. You *are* scared."

A murmur of shocked whispers passed through the

witches. Rygoth regarded them with fury, a hint of color rising to her cheeks.

"Name your challenge!" Rygoth screamed.

Kara nodded. She was relieved to have made it this far in her plan, but now came the hard part.

"That wolf by your side came to me first," Kara said, "and you stole him. I want him back. That's the challenge. The wolf sits between us and we both call to him. If he comes to me, you let me and Safi go. If he goes to you, I will pledge my loyalty and serve you as you see fit."

Rygoth smiled at this.

"I accept your challenge, child. This should be quite amusing, while it lasts."

She waved a hand and the wolf trotted to a point between them. It sat back down, its scorpion tail arcing high into the air. The witches pushed together for a better view, forming an alley between the two *wexari* with the wolf right at the center.

"Shall we begin?" Rygoth asked.

Kara already had, trying to *listen* for what the wolf needed—so she would know how to build her mind-bridge—but his thoughts were blocked by dark walls. Rygoth smirked, clearly sensing what Kara was attempting to do, and sent forth a whip-strike across the wolf's mind. Kara felt it as well, a fiery bolt of pain. She screamed. The wolf whimpered. The witches cheered. Head down, the wolf started in Rygoth's direction. Kara shook her head and tried to pierce Rygoth's walls, looking for an opening, a weakness, anything. They were impenetrable.

Finally, she got down to one knee and called the wolf to her.

"Here, boy." Kara thought for a few moments and then added, "Here, Darno. That's what I'm going to call you, okay? I hope you like it. All creatures deserve to be named."

The witches thought this was the most hilarious thing they had ever heard, and the resultant laughter was deafening. Kara ignored them. *I don't need to see his thoughts.*

I know what he wants. I'm sure of it. She laid the images of freedom on the ground between them like a trail of food—*standing on the edge of the* Wayfinder, *the ocean breeze whipping through my hair, dashing through the trees of the Thickety, flying on Rattle's back. . . .*

Darno took a few steps toward Kara.

The witches stopped laughing.

And then Rygoth struck out again with lashes of pure, seething hatred, and the whimpering wolf backed away from Kara and toward his master. *Freedom is not enough,* Kara thought, and she flooded the wolf's mind with memories of love and companionship. The wolf reversed direction, took a few steps toward her. *Yes,* thought Kara. *Come with me. I'll take you away from here! We can be great friends, you and I.*

He was almost within her reach now. Kara held out her hand, waited for his warm nose to greet—

Rygoth rose from her throne and screamed with fury.

Darno howled in excruciating pain. His eyes became

watery, his stinger shook. He took a few steps toward Rygoth, but Kara's hold on him was still strong and he hesitated. He wanted to be with her. Kara could feel it. He wanted to be loved.

But if he resisted Rygoth much longer she was going to kill him.

Enough! thought Kara. *I don't want her to hurt you anymore. I release you. Go!*

The wolf scampered across the graveyard and did not stop until he was cowed before Rygoth's feet.

The witches applauded.

"I have taken countless lives," Rygoth said. "At first it's thrilling, but as the years pass it becomes routine, like blowing your candle out at night. But your death is one I shall truly savor."

Kara, her mind elsewhere, hardly heard the words. She had never really thought she had a chance to beat Rygoth. Her primary goal had been to build a connection to the wolf so he would do what she wanted when the time came.

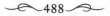

488

Now!

Darno's scorpion tail shot down like an arrow and pierced Rygoth's hand.

The *wexari* stared at the wolf in complete disbelief, and then her hand began to swell, the glove cracking open at the seams and finally tearing away altogether, revealing a swollen mass of flesh. "What have you done?" Rygoth screamed, raising her deformed hand into the air. "What have you done? *Kill her! Kill her!*"

All around Kara, grimoires began to flap open.

"Attack!" she commanded, looking skyward.

A cloud of dark feathers descended upon the witches. The vultures would have no doubt preferred the tender flesh of carrion, but the grimoires had the stink of death to them and were an acceptable substitute. Razor-sharp talons snatched the books and carted them away.

Amid the chaos, Rygoth hunched over her still-ballooning hand; Kara pushed her way to Safi.

"Come on," Kara said, grabbing the girl's wrist. "Let's get out of here!"

Safi shoved her away.

"I will never go with you!" she screamed. "Never! I serve only the Spider Queen!"

Safi spoke a few words from her grimoire and a gust of wind slammed into Kara, thrusting her through the crowd of witches. She tumbled and rose just before the inner circle of stones.

Safi was nowhere to be seen.

The witches had begun to gain the upper hand in their battle against the vultures. Fire lit the night and winged bodies dropped from the sky. A woman pointed in Kara's direction and screamed, "There!" Sparks of magical energy chipped the stone to Kara's left.

She ran.

Kara had always been a fast runner, but exhaustion was overtaking her body and the witches slowly gained ground. She reached out to the creatures of the forest for help and heard leaves rustle, screaming, fewer footsteps than before. Finally, she reached Rattle, wings extended,

ready to leave. There were only three shapes on the rustle-foot's back.

"Where's Grace?" she asked, quickly taking stock.

Lucas shook his head and pulled Kara onto the rustle-foot's back.

Her strength was finally failing, the world growing dim. Wings flapped. The ground grew smaller. The twins stepped out of the trees and into the clearing, the grimoire held between them. Kara couldn't hear the words of the spell from that distance but she saw boulders transform into great snapping birds of prey and launch themselves at the rustle-foot. Kara reached out with her mind to stop them but she was too tired; magic was beyond her. She was about to throw her arms in front of her face when suddenly the sky *shimmered*. The rock monsters instantly reversed direction, as though they had bounced off some kind of invisible surface, and plummeted toward the startled figures far below them. The twins barely had time to flee into the forest before the boulders crashed into the surface and a geyser of earth shot into the air.

As the dust cleared, a black-cloaked figure holding an open grimoire stepped out from the shadows and pushed back her hood, revealing a stubborn clump of short brown hair.

Bethany, Kara thought. *She's dressed like the others . . . but she saved us.*

Bethany quickly slammed her grimoire shut as a mob of witches swarmed into the clearing. Luckily, these new arrivals were too distracted by the departing rustle-foot to wonder what Bethany was doing there, and the young witch donned her hood and vanished into their numbers.

Be safe, my friend, Kara thought as Rattle stretched out her wings and sailed into the night. Kara squinted at the unconscious figure in front of her, roped securely to his seat. Even in the darkness she recognized his familiar form. "Father?" Kara screamed against the raging wind. "Father?" He didn't move. "Father? Is it you?" Kara reached out a hand to touch his shoulder but a sudden rush

of dizziness nearly caused her to topple into the night. Heart pounding, she grabbed the folds of Rattle's skin.

Please be you, she thought. *This can't have all been for nothing.*

Kara closed her eyes, held tight, and hoped.

EPILOGUE

They landed just outside the graycloak camp. By the light of the flickering campfires, Kara saw dozens of soldiers heading in their direction. "It'll be fine," Lucas assured her. "These are my friends." Kara still felt uneasy—these were *graycloaks*, after all—but Rattle was too exhausted to carry them much farther, and Father had wounds that required attention.

Kara helped Taff to the ground.

"What happened to Grace?" she asked.

"I brought her a grimoire, just like you told me to," Taff said. "She opened it up and read from the first page.

Then she said, 'Thank you, whelp,' and vanished."

"What about Father?" Kara asked. "Did she undo the curse first?"

There was no need for Taff to answer that question. Father had finally regained consciousness. He saw Kara and his mouth curled into a scowl.

"Imprison this witch!" he exclaimed to the approaching graycloaks. "And her brother, too! I'll see them both killed come sunrise."

They shackled Kara to an iron hook driven deep into the earth. The sky was still dark but with a hazy tint to it as dawn began to stir. At most they had two more hours to live.

Lucas had tried to save them, of course, but he had been restrained by the other graycloaks and dragged away. She had no idea where he was right now. Taff sat right next to her, shackled as well, his mind working out a way to escape.

"Any chance you can create one of those monsters like

Rygoth did?" Taff asked. "Maybe something that can bite through chains?"

"Sorry, brother," Kara said. "I don't think I could enchant a worm right now."

It was true. Her head pounded fiercely and her whole body ached. She had used too much magic in too little time.

"I can't believe Grace left us like that," he said.

Kara gave him a bemused look.

"Okay. Maybe it's not so hard to believe."

"Some people can't change who they are."

Kara considered telling Taff about Safi, but then wondered what would be the point.

Let him believe his friend was true to the end.

Timoth Clen entered the clearing. He was wearing new robes and his face had been scrubbed clean of blood and dirt.

"Leave us," he barked at the guards. "There are things these two need to tell me before they swing from a tree."

His face was set in a furious grimace as he knelt before Kara. He reached into his cloak. Kara drew back, expecting some sort of knife.

Instead he produced a key and unlocked her manacles.

"What's going on?" she asked, rubbing her wrists.

"Oh, Kara," he said, wrapping her in a tight embrace. "How can you ever forgive me?"

"Father?"

He hugged her tighter.

"It's not . . . some kind of trick . . . a spell . . . an enchantment . . ."

"Shh," he said. "It's me. Just me. Your father who loves you more than anything in the world."

He unlocked Taff's shackles and embraced him as well.

"I'm confused," Taff said. "Delighted, but confused. I never saw Grace cast a spell on you."

"*Grace* helped you?" Father asked.

"It's a really long story."

Father squeezed his head between two hands.

"I don't know what happened. One of the witches we captured cut me—her name was Holly, if I remember true—and the next thing I remember I was in the gray-cloak camp."

Kara laughed.

"The first spell that Grace cast worked," Kara said. "But Grace wanted an entire grimoire, so she pretended that it didn't. She probably tore the page in two herself."

"So she *did* help us," Taff said.

"In her fashion."

And now she's out there in the world, with a grimoire. I set her free, just like Rygoth. . . .

But those thoughts could wait. Her father had returned to them. Right now that was all that mattered.

"I wanted to tell you right away," he said, gathering them into his arms. "But if the graycloaks knew that I wasn't the real Timoth Clen, they wouldn't listen to my orders. They might think Kara had bewitched their leader. They would probably kill you two, and—"

"They might kill you as well," Taff said.

Father nodded.

"We have to go," Kara said. "Before the guards come back. Where's Rattle? The creature I was riding?"

"She flew off before the graycloaks could restrain her."

"That's good," Kara said. "She's free. Once I'm strong enough I can call her back and she can carry us anywhere we want."

Kara had no idea where they would go, and she really didn't care. The thought of being a family again filled her with warmth.

"No," Father said.

"I don't understand."

"I can't come with you. I have to stay here and pretend to be Timoth Clen. If I leave, the graycloaks will be without a leader. They'll scatter, fall apart. I can't allow that to happen. Someone has to stand up against Rygoth."

"Let *me* fight her," Kara said. "I'm the *wexari*. It's my duty. I got the best of her tonight. I can do it again."

The words sounded brave, but even Kara could hear the doubt in her voice. *I escaped tonight mostly because of tricks and luck. It won't be as easy next time.*

"You have a more important task to perform," Father said. "When Timoth Clen was controlling me he saw my memories, but I saw his as well. I know what Rygoth's plan is. She's after a grimoire so powerful that it was split into—"

"—four parts and hidden across Sentium," Taff said. He shrugged. "Sorry. We know these sorts of things."

"I see," said Father, holding back a smile. "Well, if Timoth's memories can be trusted, there's a man who may know the location of all four pieces. A *dangerous* man."

"He's a *wexari?*" Kara asked.

"I don't know what he is, exactly. But it's important that you talk to him. If we can find out where the pieces of the grimoire are we can stop Rygoth from getting them."

Father told Kara where she could find this man—or rather, *when*. It didn't make a lot of sense. In fact, it made

her wonder if Father had not gone mad after all.

When he was done explaining, Father placed the shackles back around their wrists but did not lock them.

"You need to wait until dawn before leaving," Father said. "I'm going to drug the morning gruel. Should knock everyone out until noon at least."

"Won't they be suspicious afterward?" Kara asked.

"Absolutely not," Father said, a hint of Taff in his grin. "As their leader, I always eat along with my men. I'll wake up with the rest of them, and we'll all blame magic for our unusual slumber. By then you should have gotten a good head start. Your mare is waiting at the edge of camp with supplies for your trip."

The thought of seeing Shadowdancer again brought a smile to Kara's face.

Father said, "I'll lead the search team east."

"And we'll go west," said Taff.

Father nodded. He placed his hands on his son's shoulders.

"*Kara* will go west," he said. "Your place is with me.

We can convince the graycloaks that you were under some kind of spell and——"

But Taff was already shaking his head.

"I go where Kara goes."

Father looked deeply into his son's eyes for a moment and nodded.

"You've grown older," he said.

"What about Lucas?" asked Kara. "Is he coming with us?"

"I haven't told him," Father said, shifting uncomfortably. "He still thinks I'm Timoth Clen and you two are scheduled for death. I had to lock him up for the time being. He'd insist on coming with you if he knew the truth, but that wouldn't be wise. His sudden disappearance would create a cloud of suspicion that could undo the whole plan. If the graycloaks realize I'm not really their leader——"

"Of course," said Kara, trying to ignore the quivering in her voice, the sudden certainty that she would never see Lucas Walker again. *Don't be so selfish. It's safer for both of them this way.* "Just watch over him, okay? Keep him safe."

Father nodded and rose to his feet.

"Wait—" Kara started.

"We've no time for long good-byes. Let's not make this more difficult than it already is."

"It's not that," Kara said. "It's just—there's something I don't understand. I saw you in my dreams. The cornfield."

Father's face twitched.

"I remember that place," he said.

"I was told you would go mad if you stayed there long enough. And yet here you are, right as rain. I'm happy, of course, but I don't know how that happened. Last time I saw you—in a dream, at least—you were talking to empty air."

"You're wrong," Father said. "You must not have been able to see her, but I was talking to your mother. It was her love and companionship that kept me from losing my mind."

"But Mother's dead," Taff said.

Kara remembered the moment just before she had lost consciousness in Kala Malta, the feeling that Mother had been right there beside her.

I wonder . . .

"What did you talk about?" Kara asked.

"All sorts of things," Father said, and in his sad eyes she saw that part of him regretted coming back at all. *Her absence is a hole that can never be filled.* "We talked of how we first met, our friends, the days we shared. But mostly we talked of you and Taff. She's so proud of the two of you. We both are."

He reached out to hug them again, his eyes brimming with tears, but pulled away the moment he heard footsteps in the distance. The guards were returning. Setting his face into a look of cold disdain, Father marched away to meet them.

The children sat in silence for a long time.

"It's not fair," Taff finally said. "We saved him. We should get to stay together."

"It's just for a little while," Kara said. "We'll be a family again when all this is over. I promise."

Taff smiled.

"What?"

"I've always believed that," he said. "But for the first time, I think you believe it too!"

Taff rested his head on Kara's shoulder. Together they waited for the sun to rise and wash away the stains of night—for the world, in all its resilient glory, to begin anew.